BURN

BROTHERS OF INK AND STEEL
BOOK TWO

AURORA WILDING

Published by Wilding Love Publishing, Inc.
Edited by Nicole Hewitt and Maria Vickers

Burn is a dark romance with intense and mature themes
including abuse, violence and sexual assault, for a full list please
refer to aurorawilding.com.
Burn is intended for readers +18.
This book may contain potential triggers.

CONTENTS

BURN CHAPTER PLAYLIST

"More Than a Feeling" Boston
"Hurricane" Theory of a Deadman
"Shatter Me" Lindsey Stirling ft. Lzzy Hale
"You Found Me" Kelly Clarkson
"Secrets" One Republic
"Fire and Rain" James Taylor
"Torn Apart" Bastille
"Can't Forget You" My Darkest Days
"Wish You Were Here" Pink Floyd
"Sugar" Maroon 5
"Dare You to Move" Switchfoot
"I Wonder" Kellie Pickler
"Fix Me" 10 Years
"If You Ever Come Back" The Script
"Say You Love Me" Jessie Ware
"Yours" Elle Henderson

"The Humbling River" Puscifer
"All of Me" John Legend
"Ho Hey" The Lumineers
"Burn" Elle Goulding
"Thinking Out Loud" Ed Sheeran

DEDICATION

For anyone who has ever spent the night outside on cold concrete—alone and terrified. Who has experienced the horror of being homeless, the pain of being betrayed, or the sting of abuse. If you have ever felt like there was no one in the world who loved you. With no one to love or protect you at your most vulnerable, And no place to call home.

BURN

PROLOGUE

**QUINN
AUGUST
(PAST)**

The heat of the night is oppressive.

With every step, sweat streams down my back, matting my hair to my forehead.

I pick up the filthy old payphone receiver and try not to hold it too close to my mouth. My hand is trembling—I'm in the worst part of the city after midnight.

Most of the street lamps in this section have had the bulbs shot out. It's dark, and there isn't a visible star in the sky. I peer around me cautiously, like a mouse that's attempting to move across a long stretch of field will watch for an owl, the harbinger of death from above.

The street is empty—void of cars driving by or even parked. A low-lit bulb flickers in staccato above my head, illuminating a tiny circle where I stand, shaking with nerves amidst the empty store-fronts with iron bars on the windows and doors.

I know better than to wander through here, but my mom lives on the edge of town, and there's still an old payphone in front of the rundown, out-of-business gas station. But it's dangerously close to the area we locals call Westhill. Bars, strip clubs and sex stores line the streets; junkies search the place with their hands out, hoping to find another hit, while the dealers stand watch in full force, looking for new customers—anyone they can tempt to get high on a free ride, knowing they'll have to come back for more.

Then there are the gangs—the most powerful and influential of them is the Westhill Cartel, led by the brutal warlord Vince Ortega. His ruthless gang manages all the drug vendors in this section of the city. Vince is also a pimp. He and his cronies scour the streets and well-known hangouts for homeless kids—especially girls, especially the newbies who have fear in their eyes and empty bellies—and promise them a safe place to sleep and food in exchange for their "services."

He test drives each one personally, and then she's passed around to his top lieutenants before she's tossed onto the street. After the girl turns over a certain number of tricks, she gets a meager fifteen percent of her earnings. And from what I've heard firsthand when supply and demand aren't in balance, these girls are usually kept like slaves by Vince, beaten and sometimes tortured, then discarded—often in the river or a nearby dumpster.

Last year, I met a girl who worked for him. He tried recruiting me, but I caught him off guard when I kneed him in the balls and ran like hell.

I shudder and remind myself he has so many girls that he certainly doesn't have time to think about me.

After pushing aside the trash and cigarette butts with my foot so I can stand closer to the phone, I turn my attention to the keypad and dial North House.

How could I have been stupid enough to think my mom would really want me? How can you love somebody so much, so deeply that it burns inside of you like a consuming flame … but they don't love you back? You hold onto that fire because you're so freaking sure that if you love them hard enough, they'll wake up one day and feel what you feel and want what you want.

That somehow, that happy ending would come true, and everything in the world would be alright.

"Operator."

"I need to make a collect call from Quinn."

But that isn't the truth or the reality, not in my

world. Not in Liam's world. Not in any of the worlds where the people I hold closest to my heart live in. Living in the group home for these past several months has taught me that life isn't only unfair, but most of the time, it's utterly and mercilessly cruel.

Is it horrible that I've taken comfort in the fact that I'm not the only kid in the world whose parents couldn't give a shit about them? Who couldn't care less if we lived … or died? How? How can you not care about your very own flesh and blood?

Anger is good. It's like a shield. Hope it lasts.

"Hello?" the sleepy man on the other end of the line says.

"I have a collect call from Quinn," the operator informs. "Will you accept the charges?"

"Yes, absolutely." Hearing Cade North's voice comforts me. It's easy to imagine him as the father I never had.

"Cade! It all went so wrong! She threw me out!"

"Okay, slow down. Where are you?"

"I begged my mom to let me use her phone, but she wouldn't let me!" I cry. "And by then, it was late and everything was closed. I had to walk to the payphone on State Street."

"Oh, Christ, Quinn! I'm on my way right now!" I can hear him shuffle out of bed.

"Cade, what's wrong?" his wife Debra asks in the background, and he explains.

4

Cade and Debra North are the house parents of North House, the group home for teens I live at with Liam—and twelve other kids whose parents love them about as much as mine loves me.

"What kind of mother doesn't let her child use her phone for a ride?" Debra exclaims angrily.

"Yeah, and the only payphone is the one left over by the old Town Pump." Cade curses, which he only does when he's seriously pissed off. "Didn't that goddamn social worker give you a safe phone, Quinn?"

"No, sir, he didn't. He just dropped me off at her house, but she wasn't there, so I waited. She didn't show up until after nine o'clock," I continue to explain. I feel self-blame wash over me. "I shouldn't have waited for her."

"You did what you felt you had to do. Don't get down on yourself for that."

"Didn't matter anyway. When she got there, we got into a huge fight, and now I'm here. And, Cade, I'm scared."

At that moment, I hear the engine of his Pontiac GTO turn over. "I'm en route right now. I'm twenty minutes out. And that's with running the red lights."

I breathe a sigh of relief. Knowing Cade's on his way makes me feel safe.

I tell him, "I'm not going to do it anymore. I

won't! I don't care what the social workers say; I never want to see her again!"

The social workers call it *reintegration*. You go home for a visitation period and try to reconcile with your family.

"No, sweetheart, you don't have to. And you can bet, after I get you, I'll be making some late-night wakeup calls to some seriously irresponsible people."

I nod, grateful he'll stand up for me.

"Don't hang up with me, Quinn," Cade instructs.

"I won't trust me." I feel like this cheap, beat-up piece of plastic is my only lifeline.

"You know," I begin, and here come the tears, stinging my eyes and blinding my vision, "I've tried going home and making her love me too many times. Fuck it, and fuck her! I don't need her! I don't want her anymore!" It hurts so bad; the agony is indescribable. "Will the pain ever go away?"

"You know the answer to that, Quinn," he reminds me softly.

The answer is no, it won't. But other love can fill and mend the hole.

I think of Liam. He's the bone that keeps me standing and the muscle that makes me strong. He loves me … like no one ever did, or has, or ever could. And I love him just as much. We've been together for almost a year. He's asked me to marry him. We're just waiting until we turn eighteen.

At sixteen years old, I've come to understand something about love.

Real love always burns.

In the case of my mom, the fire is threatening; it blisters, damages and destroys me every time I let my guard down. It ravages the relationship we should have as mother and daughter. The effects leave lifelong scars. Fire can be a wicked killer.

When it comes to Liam Knight, our love burns bright and brilliant, shining the way home like a white-hot star. But instead of scorching me, it warms my soul; it guards me and keeps me safe, feeds me and gives me light.

It's ironic to think of the great power of love as fire. It can burn destructively, leaving only pain, death and ash, or it can nourish and sustain the existence of life like the sun.

How it's used is dependent upon the hands that wield it.

My attention is taken by a pair of headlights from a lone vehicle as they crest over the hill. I can feel more than hear the deep thud of the bass cut through the stillness. As the black SUV with tinted windows passes me, it slows down.

"Cade." My breathing quickens.

"What's wrong?"

"It's a big SUV …" Panic drowns every clear

thought in my mind as the vehicle pulls to the curb and stops.

"Quinn!" Cade seems so far away now.

Every false sense of safety holding onto the phone has given me is yanked harshly from my psyche.

Vince Ortega, the gang leader of the Westhill Cartel, steps out from the passenger side of the vehicle.

I have to run! The thought screams through my head but doesn't shake me from the paralyzing effect of Vince's intentional gaze.

"QUINN!" Cade shouts.

"It's Vince," I whisper, watching as several of his friends follow him out of the vehicle, and all of them walk toward me.

"Can you run?" Cade's calm demeanor is betrayed by his own fear.

I know my surroundings. There's nowhere to run and no one to hear me cry for help.

"You're a smart girl! You talk them down, stall them. I'm coming," Cade says. "If you have to, fight them. You're strong. Whatever you do, do not get in that SUV!"

Cade sounds like he's talking underwater or through a dream.

My entire world is now focused on just two things—Vince's cold, ruthless eyes … and my death.

CHAPTER ONE

LIAM
OCTOBER
(PAST - ALMOST A YEAR EARLIER)

"**W**hat the hell is she doing?" I say, leaning up against some dead guy's headstone.

"Fuck if I know," Randy answers, popping the top of another can of Bud as we watch the girl across from us. "Maybe she's stoned."

At that moment, the sound of Boston's "More than a Feeling" reached our ears.

Randy's head spins around. "Hell yeah!" he shouts and slams against my shoulder. "Jamie and Scott are coming … and they brought girls!"

I turn and watch Randy as he jogs up the worn dirt path that leads down the steep hill into the old cemetery. Sure enough, it looks like half the senior class is coming down to meet us. Good fucking thing they're carrying coolers—Randy and I have already plowed through our six-pack since getting here. And although I can't see it, obviously someone has music! This has the potential to become a real fucking party.

School let out a couple of hours ago, and the Vine Street graveyard is where everybody comes to hang out. The freak warm autumn weather is giving us one more outdoor party before we'll have to go to someone's house. Best part is, cops never bother us down here since they figure we're out of the way. They don't give a shit about us unless we're fucking around where it bothers the community. Here, we're out of sight and out of mind. A lot of shit goes down in this cemetery. It's not a safe place.

My thoughts turn back to the girl over by the towering granite angel statue. She's climbing around the pedestal with a white plastic grocery bag, but I don't have a fucking clue as to what she's doing. Whatever it is, she's doing it meticulously. I squint my eyes to focus on her better.

I recognize this girl. I met her briefly at a group home where I had stayed overnight at the end of summer before I was transferred the next morning to a new foster home. I was a little surprised to see her at South Senior High a few weeks later in my same year. I've never talked to her. With her long blond curls and more than filled-out t-shirts, she's hard to forget, but fuck if I can remember her name. Come to think of it, I haven't seen her in school for a couple weeks.

I look back up the hill. The group's getting closer, and so is Gina. Gina's a junior—a year ahead of me. She let me know before school got out today that she'd meet me down here and made it quite obvious that was exactly why she was meeting me.

But that girl is gnawing at the edges of my mind … what the fuck is she doing over there? And why the fucking hell do I care?!

I steal another view of Gina getting closer, in her skintight jeans and formfitting jacket, before I push myself up out of the dried grass.

"Fuck it." My curiosity demands to be quenched.

My boots crush over the crisp, fallen brown, orange and yellow leaves as I trek my ass across the expanse of lawn to where the girl is.

As I approach, I can see she's picking up shards of broken glass from the pedestal around the statue. Shit must have been left over from parties past. Probably a bunch of partiers doing target practice with their booze bottles.

"What the *fuck* are you doing?" I ask, folding my arms over my chest, annoyed.

"Why the *fuck* do you want to know?" she stings back without bothering to look up at me.

Her tone almost makes me laugh out loud. She's a little thing, trying to sound all big and bad.

Gingerly, her fingertips work around a jagged piece of green glass. She picks it up and drops it in the bag.

"Why are you cleaning the glass?" I try impatiently.

I look back at the party forming behind us. All the coolers are opened, and they're digging in. I notice Gina smile my way, and I throw her a smile.

"Somebody has to," the girl says. "It's disrespectful to smash glass all over someone's tombstone!"

Is she fucking nuts? "Who gives a rat's ass? They're dead."

At that, she turns on me vehemently. Her blue eyes flash with indignation. "You don't even know who it is! She could have been someone's mom … or daughter. She was obviously loved to have been given such a beautiful angel to look over her." Her eyes follow the weathered concrete angel upward, almost adoringly. "And if she wasn't, and this was a mistake, someone should be loving her now." She looks back at me, her gaze still searing. "And you guys are assholes for vandalizing this place."

I lift my hands in front of me to halt her accusation. "Whoa … hold on there! I didn't break this shit."

"Maybe not—" she disregards me again to

continue her task, "but you'll all leave your cans, bottles, cigarette butts and shit down here, won't you?"

I'm incredulous. Fuck this. *Fuck her.*

I start to turn away, but for some reason, I wait and scan around to see who's here with her.

"Who are you here with? Where the hell are your friends … or parents?" I demand.

"Like you give a shit." She climbs off the pedestal. "Look, I know who you are, Liam Knight. You're a sophomore at South."

"You know that?"

"The school's not that big. Not to mention that last year you went to a dance with Alexis Nichols." She faces me as she straightens her red sweater and pulls on her black quilted jacket. She's wearing ripped-at-the-knees jeans and a pair of worn black Chucks.

I feel my ego puff at the idea that she'd learned who I was. But then she continues, "And she's still talking about what an asshole and user you are."

Nice.

She smirks and says, "Plus, we met at North House during the summer."

"LIAM!" a female voice rings out. I look over my shoulder to see Gina waving me over.

"Don't want to miss your party." The girl turns away.

"Hey!" I grab hold of her arm and spin her

13

around to make her pay attention. "It isn't safe down here by yourself."

She yanks her arm back. "Leave me alone," she growls defensively.

"All right, calm down," I say, backtracking. "Why haven't you been at school? Graduate already?"

"Something like that," she quips with a tilt of her head. Her bright blue eyes are the color of a perfect afternoon sky.

Trying to call a truce, I say, "You know my name, but I don't know yours."

"My name is Quinn," she says softly, then snaps, "Are you finished with your interrogation?"

"Okay … Quinn. That wasn't too hard, right?" I ask. "Why don't you come over and have a beer with us?"

She looks past me to the group. "I don't know."

There's something about her—it's like she's trying to act unaffected, but she can't mask the sadness.

"Come on, none of us will bite," I coax. I consider her. What kind of teenager comes down to the graveyard *alone* to clean up random acts of vandalism?

"Okay, one beer."

I smile.

She doesn't smile back.

At least she follows me over to the party.

I lean into the cooler for a couple beers when Randy comes over.

"What the fuck are you doing, man?"

"What the fuck does it look like?"

"Gina's waiting for you, and you come back with the fucking bag lady!" he exclaims. "Albeit, a hot bag lady."

"Shut the fuck up." I shove him. "And I can handle Gina."

Walking back over to Quinn, I hand her the cold can.

"Thanks," she says without meeting my eyes.

"I thought you'd never get back over here," Gina whines and slides her hand into the back pocket of my jeans, stroking my ass.

"I'm here now," I remind her and drape my arm around her shoulders.

I catch Quinn as she rolls her eyes at me and Gina. She's so blatant I almost laugh, but again, the gnawing won't be ignored. I went over there to quell my curiosity, but instead, it's become deeper. Why is she here alone? What was she doing at North House during the summer? Why hasn't she been at school? What's her story?

Gina's hand rubbing my ass is making my dick grow, but I'm staring at and thinking about Quinn. This is probably not the best combination.

I watch as she cracks open her beer and chugs it down for all she's worth. Liquid streams escape from between her lips and create channels running down the sides of her chin. She quickly lowers her head and eyes as she brings her sleeve to her mouth to catch the errant drink. She must have been really thirsty.

"Now that's the fucking way to drink!" Dylan Porter, who's a senior, comes over and casually snakes his arm around Quinn's waist. "First time getting drunk?"

She stiffens but doesn't look up at him or make an effort to move away. Meanwhile, Gina begins to run her lips up my neck. She whispers something, but I don't make out the words.

Dylan drops his hand to Quinn's ass. "I bet that's not your only first."

"Leave her the fuck alone," I tell him threateningly.

Dylan, who's a head taller than me and the varsity quarterback, gives me a once look-over. "Fuck off, Knight. You got your piece of ass."

Gina giggles beside me.

He waves his half-empty bottle of Jack in front of Quinn's face. "This will get the job done faster." When she doesn't take it, Dylan leans in closer. "I've never seen you at South High. Are you a freshman?"

"No. A sophomore. I just wasn't around last year," Quinn says, looking at the ground.

I can see why Dylan thinks she's a freshman.

There's something innocent about her. A *something* an asshole like Dylan would like to take. I'm one of the oldest kids in the sophomore class, so I know she's probably younger than me, but she *seems way* younger—like she could be fourteen, easily.

"I've got to go," she says, still staring at her shoes.

"Not yet, you don't, I just got here." Dylan licks his lips. "Have you ever been kissed before?"

She winces and tries to take a step away, but he holds her fast against his side.

"Oh, you like to play rough ..." Dylan smiles.

"Hey, *dick*, leave the girl alone," I say, making sure to emphasize *dick*.

"What the fuck did you call me, asshole?" Dylan looks surprised anyone would ever challenge him.

Our words are getting everyone else's attention, and people are starting to gather around us.

Quinn's deep blue eyes are tainted with fear when she lifts them to mine. It does something inside my gut I can't explain; like her eyes are a conduit to the electrical current that flows through my body, the voltage shoots through me. An extreme shot of adrenaline is injected into my muscles.

"I know I didn't stutter, fuckface," I warn, very seriously. "Move on."

Tina stops sucking at my neck and nervously steps away.

Dylan's eyes turn hard, and his smile turns wicked. Dramatically, he lets go of his grip on Quinn. It's apparent she has been trying to pull away from him as she stumbles under her own force. Douchebag doesn't even attempt to help her; he just holds his arm out straight.

"Knight, you should have minded your own fucking business," he says before he takes a pull from his bottle.

"Maybe," I retort. "But something about you holding a girl against her will just doesn't sit right with me."

"I'm going to kick your motherfucking ass."

"You only think you are, douchebag." I hate assholes like Dylan. He has an over-inflated sense of his own popularity and thinks he's entitled.

He hands his Jack bottle to a nearby friend and pulls his coat off unsteadily. I shake my head. Smug bastard is already half in the bag; I've only had a few beers, which means I'm going to sweep the fucking floor with him.

Out of the corner of my eye, I catch Quinn, who has been slowly and cautiously backing away from us, run through the dusk-covered graveyard.

Fuck! She ain't coming back.

Dylan's fist collides with my jaw, but the only thing I'm thinking is that Quinn's going to disappear into the night, and I'm not going to be able to find her again. Now, I don't know why I give a shit since I'm guaranteed to get laid with Gina, but ever since the girl entered my field of vision tonight, I obviously haven't been able to think of much else.

A fight would have been entertaining. Oh well.

I position my right foot behind my body to anchor myself, and then I hit him beneath the chin, just right, so he goes down.

He hits the ground hard and stays there. My friends start laughing, while his friends look like they expected it.

"I'll deal with you more thoroughly another time," I promise before I turn and start a quick stride after Quinn.

"Hey, man! Where are you going?" Randy calls out.

I wave him off. "There's something I have to take care of." I doubt he hears the entire sentence because I'm already halfway down the hill, weaving between the old granite headstones—and over the dead bodies with no voices to protest or encourage me. The only sounds I hear are my breath and my boots crushing the dried leaves underneath my feet.

"Quinn, wait up!" I shout when I get closer.

"Leave me alone!" She has zero intention of stopping. In fact, she picks up speed.

Two can play at this. I can run all night.

Quickly, she looks back, and the frustration is clear on her face. She's not happy I'm gaining ground.

"Come on, I just saved your ass back there! I only want to talk!"

"I've got nothing to say!" she counters.

We run like this until she shoots like a bullet from a gun out of the cemetery gates onto River Road—a dead-end street. This is the back area of the cemetery, where no one comes through. Plus, the river washed out the road last spring, and the city hasn't bothered to deal with it yet.

I stop and yell, "I give up!"

She doesn't answer me; she just keeps her pace as she tears through the trees. Carefully, I trail her, hoping to follow her more covertly.

Where the hell could she be going? There aren't any houses over here.

Soon enough, she's climbing down the bank to the river. I keep a good distance between us and duck into the brush to hide myself as she slows to a walk. She follows the bank until she stops under the overpass bridge.

I watch her settle in. A moment later, she lights a fire in a small circle of stones. In the illumination, I see a rolled-up blanket next to a black garbage bag.

I know this scene all too well.

My foot begins to slip on the rocky bank. As I move it for better footing, dirt and stones become dislodged and scatter down the hill.

Quinn jumps up, pulls a baseball bat out from behind the bag and is ready to strike.

Goddamnit!

"Who's there?"

"Hey! Chill. I'm not going to hurt you." I come out of the bushes with my hands up.

"What the fuck?!" She's still holding the bat in front of her. "You followed me anyway! What is wrong with you? Are you here to finish what Dylan started?"

"Of course not! I just …" Damn, I don't have an answer. *I decided to follow you to see where you'd go … for no reason other than … I've acquired the new talent of stalking?* No.

"Just what?" She's still on the defensive.

I try a different approach. "God damn, it's freezing out here! Do you mind if I share your fire?"

"Why should I trust you?" The blond strands of her hair are tossed around her head in a mess, and she's sweaty from running. She's stunningly gorgeous.

"Got nothing to recommend me, Quinn, except I've lived out on the streets since I was nine years old."

Still, she doesn't drop her guard.

"I know it's real hard to trust or make or *keep* friends." I point to the garbage bag that looks about half full. "I know what it feels like to have every-thing you own in the world fit in half a trash bag."

Her expression becomes pained, and her brow creases.

"Why aren't you at North House?" I ask.

She hesitates, then says, "Because … they'll find me."

"I get it. Foster homes suck."

"So does St. Anne's, I hear." Finally, she tosses the bat down on the ground.

"St Anne's? You must have done something pretty serious." Slowly, I walk toward her and her makeshift campsite. St. Anne's is a lock-down detention home for girls and has the reputation of being a really rough place. Quinn doesn't look like the kind of girl who'd survive in there.

"I didn't *do* anything. I'm being falsely accused, but my word won't count for shit in a juvie court." A mix of sadness and defiance settles firmly over her face.

"Adults control the system, and thus the system sucks ass." I hold my hands over the little fire that already threatens to extinguish. "What are you being accused of?"

"Doesn't matter. Just made me run from yet another place where I thought I'd be safe, and that turned out to be a nightmare." Wearily, she sits on a rounded stone close to the flame. "I'm sorry you've been homeless on and off since you were little. That's horrible."

"You get used to it," I lie. "I've been at my latest foster home for two entire months. It's a fucking record." I try to make it sound funny, but it doesn't. "When my foster parents are around, they're both real assholes. Fortunately, they're hardly ever around. They like to go down to the reservation to gamble and drink up their government money. At least they usually leave some groceries before they go."

Saying that makes me think about food. I look around at her meager supplies. I'm not seeing any food. There's not even a water bottle.

She runs her hands through her hair, rests her elbow on her knee and cradles her head in her palm.

"You don't have anything to eat, do you?"

She sighs and closes her eyes to avoid the question, or maybe because she's hoping I'll disappear.

"You know, it's only going to get colder out here," I say.

"Yeah, I know. You better go home."

"Yeah, okay." I start to turn, but it's only for performance's sake. "I have an idea."

"Of course you do," she mumbles. "Like the beer idea."

"Why don't you come with me? We could get something to eat," I suggest.

At that, she lifts her eyes to mine. "Where would we go?"

"Like I said, my foster parents are gone a lot. They're gone now and won't be back until Sunday night."

"What do you get out of it?" she comes back at me.

"Good karma."

She cracks a smile, a real one.

I turn the key and open the door to the rundown townhouse in a crappy neighborhood. I feel embarrassed having to even bring her in here, admitting this is where I now live, and that's pretty bad considering she's sleeping under a bridge.

"Help yourself," I say and turn on the lights.

But Quinn is skittish and shy suddenly. She's going to need coaxing. I lead her into the kitchen. It's a real mess in here. The Richardsons haven't been home in a week.

"Sorry, the cleaning lady quit," I joke.

She's staring at the fridge.

I open the door and wish there was more to offer her. In the past week, I've eaten almost every-thing they left for me—which wasn't much—I had to ration it carefully, too.

"Here." I reach in and grab an apple. "Start on this."

She looks up at me with such gratitude. "Thank

you," she breathes before she begins to devour the fruit. It reminds me of when she drank the beer.

Rummaging through the cabinets, my fingers gain purchase on a box of flavored oatmeal packets.

"Do you like apple cinnamon?"

She nods.

"Good. 'Cause I really know how to make this stuff. It's my specialty," I say extravagantly.

She just rolls her eyes playfully.

I grab a bowl and heat the water in the microwave. After the water's bubbling, I pour a packet of sweet smelling oatmeal into the bowl. Once it cools, she scarfs it down.

It'd be funny how fast she eats if it wasn't so pathetic.

"You know, I'm pretty sure I have a few Pop-Tarts left in my room. Want to come check it out?" I offer.

She nods uncomfortably, and I wish there was a way to make her feel better … safe.

"It ain't much," I murmur as we enter the cramped space. A twin bed and chest of drawers are set against the wall. Other than that, it's empty.

"Where's your stuff?" she asks.

I open the top drawer and take out the Pop-Tarts. I hand her a silver foiled packet and keep one myself.

"Fuck, no milk," I realize out loud. "How about some water?"

"I'd really love some water, thanks."

I go back to the kitchen for some glasses of water. "Do you like ice?"

"No, thanks. I'm just going to drink it quickly."

She's very polite.

When I get back to my room, she's sitting on the edge of the bed. She drinks down half the water and sets the glass on the hardwood floor as she tears the wrapper of the treat and nibbles the Pop-Tarts carefully, as if she's savoring them.

I wish that was a good thing, but I know it's because she's unsure of the next time she'll eat.

"Where's your mom and dad anyway?" I ask.

"Where's yours?" she volleys.

"Ahh … you want to play it that way." I nod, smiling.

"Yeah, I want to play that way. Anything you want to know about me, you answer about yourself first, and then I'll match your answer."

Why do I want to open up to this girl? I've had enough friends come and go. But the desire to get her to open up to me draws me like a piece of steel or a smashed car to a mega-sized electromagnet; I'm going to play her game.

I sit on the bed and rest my back against the wall so I can watch her face, expressions and body language when she answers my questions. I'm pretty good at detecting when someone lies … but if I'm truthful with myself, it's just because she's so damn pretty. I want an excuse to look at her.

"My mom is in Brookside Apartments," I say. "She likes to have the place all to herself, especially when she's entertaining guys, so I always get a free street pass on Friday after school. Sometimes she lets me back in on Mondays, but most of the time, she's in bitch mode and decides she never wants me around again. That's when I sleep where I can and usually get picked up by cops at some point and get reintroduced into the magical, wonderful world of social services."

She nods sympathetically.

"Your turn," I remind her.

She shrugs over her Pop-Tart. "My mom would rather live in the mansion she works at as a private nurse to an elderly woman she hardly knows than be home with her daughter. That's what she's been doing for as long as I can remember. When I turned ten, she didn't want to pay for sitters anymore, so I was on my own. Didn't matter to me; when she was home, she ignored me or told me what a miserable disappointment I was and how she never wanted me in the first place.

"When I was little, I used to think there must be something I could do to make her love me. I'd try to hug her or tickle her or *something* to make her talk or smile at me. She'd grab whatever was in reach and rap it across my knuckles, or my head or back. She got her point across and made sure that there'd be no marks to show later. She's big on show. She's happy as long as everything appears to be good on the outside, so her friends think she's Mother-of-the-Year," she says sarcastically.

Fuck! Quinn's so sweet; I couldn't imagine anyone doing that to her, let alone her mother.

She goes quiet. I wonder where her dad is.

I lie for this next one. "I don't know my father. Never met him."

Quinn sighs as if maybe she thinks the question-and-answer gig we have going on should be over, but she continues anyway. "My dad lives in Florida with his *new* family. His wife came with two kids. They're both well-to-do corporate execs. The courts placed me with them when my mom kicked me out —or when I ran away, both have happened so many times, I don't remember which it was—when I was fourteen.

"Anyway, I was with them for almost a year before his new wife presented me with an ultimatum; either I leave or she would, which I believe would have devastated my father. So I told him I wanted to go and live with a friend. I should have told him the truth … but I was already such a disappointment to my mother; I didn't want to be responsible for the breakup of my dad's marriage and be the same burden to him. Just more guilt I'd have to live with.

"I don't talk to either my dad or stepmother now. She's made sure of that." She pauses. "If I have to be honest, he hasn't done anything to try to get me back either. That's hard to admit to myself. Guess the truth is, my mom and dad both love me about the same—one would rather have a pretend rich life, and the other would rather have his shiny new family—either way, neither of them wants me."

Quinn looks at her silver wrapper. "Do you have a wastebasket in here?" she asks, breaking the spell her pain has cast over me.

"Yeah." I reach over, snatch her empty wrapper and toss it on the floor.

It makes her laugh. The sound makes me laugh, too.

"Are you still hungry?" I ask.

"No, I'm good. Thanks again."

"No problem."

"Have you been in many foster homes?" Her voice is soft and quiet as if she's trying to protect herself against the inevitable answer.

"Yeah, by the time I was twelve, I'd lost count." I fold my hands behind my head and lay back on the pillow. "You?"

"No. Like I said, my mom was all about show and too concerned about her reputation being tarnished to do anything to me outright. When I was younger, she sent me to school in nice clothes, and we pretended that she fed me and didn't leave me home alone night after night, week after week … month after month. That sucks after a while— not only does it suck 'cause you've got no one to talk to, but the isolation makes you start to hallucinate." She shakes her head, remembering, and her eyes go dark. "Whatever. She had the perfect set-up. She'd leave for work before I got home from school in the afternoon and wouldn't come home until after I left for school in the morning. She never had to see me except for the weekends. And when I turned four-teen, she cried to all her friends about what a rebel-lious, ungrateful kid I was. Soon, I had a new home on the pavement … until I was sent to live with my dad … and then sent to yet another hell."

It makes sense—the way she holds herself and speaks—she's smart, educated, but you can see the stain of street living spreading over her. I want to ask her why they're looking to put her in St. Anne's, but before I can, Quinn reaches down, finishes her glass of water and declares with finality, "I should probably go now." She's looks over at the digital clock on my dresser. It's close to eleven p.m.

"Go where?" I bark out incredulously. "Under the bridge?"

"That's my new place." She shrugs.

"Fuck that! Stay here."

"No way. I can't!"

"Of course you can. Then, in the morning, we

can have more oatmeal, and I'll hock an item I've acquired during my travels at the pawn shop, and we'll get some groceries and eat something good. What do you say?" Not the best-sounding date, but it's all I can offer.

"Where would I sleep?" she asks skeptically.

"You can take my bed; I'll sleep on the floor."

"I don't know. It's pretty cold in here and probably a hell of a lot colder on the floor," she deduces.

"I can handle a little cold." I scoff. "And it's a hell of a lot warmer than outside on the ground."

"Why is it so cold in here anyway?"

"Mr. and Mrs. Richardson—who I have affectionately given the official titles of Dick and Bitch—like to keep the heat so low it might as well be off. But if I touch the thermostat and the bill goes up a cent, Dick'll beat my ass."

"He … beats you?" she asks timidly.

"Nothing I can't handle … or haven't handled before."

She winces, and I regret telling her.

"I'll sleep on the floor. You're right; it'll be warmer than the ground outside." She stands.

"Wait a minute, that's not what I meant …" I think, then speak slowly. "You could lay up here with me. I promise to be good, and we'd stay a hell of a lot warmer together … you know—body heat."

"I'm not going to offer you any fringe benefits," she says squarely.

I laugh. Not that I wouldn't mind or accept if she offered, but I'm not looking for *that* at this moment. I'm not sure what I'm looking for.

"I don't need anything like that from you, Quinn."

"Oh, you don't? I'm not as cute as Gina, I guess."

I can't tell if she's got a great sarcastic sense of humor or if she's actually insulted. Because of that, the next thing I think just rolls out of my mouth before I can filter it. "Oh no, Quinn, you're a million times more beautiful than any girl I've ever known."

Her eyes drop to the floor, and I immediately wish I could take it back. What an asshole I am! But her response surprises me.

She wiggles up onto the bed… and attempts to curl up to the size of a snail by my feet.

"There's more space if we both just lay together. Plus, we can share the pillow," I say, wondering if it's going to get me smacked.

"Fine." Gingerly, she crawls up toward me, and as she does, my heartbeat gets erratic.

Her old gray sweatshirt is anything but sexy, so I'm not sure what my internal

organs or muscles or whatever are doing at the moment, but my dick is certainly responding.

I think about math class, hoping to settle *it* down.

She lies next to me, her back to my side as she's turned toward the wall. No part of her body is touching mine except a lock of her hair that has fallen over my arm. I can't *not* look at it. It's like an ember from a fallen star or a treasure of spun gold. I desperately want to touch it with my fingers.

I hear her yawn. It makes me wonder how long it's been since she had a safe and warm full night's sleep.

"What can we buy to eat tomorrow?" she asks softly.

"What do you want?"

"I'd love a cheeseburger, Snickers bar and Pepsi … or a chocolate milkshake." She almost giggles. "Is that too much money?"

"Not at all." I decide I just might rob a bank for her. "I just thought you'd choose something more … healthy."

"You mean like Pop-Tarts?" I can hear the smile in her voice.

"Yup."

At that moment, she shivers a little. I lean up and catch hold of the dark blue blanket at the foot of the bed and pull it up over the two of us. When I secure it over her shoulder, my arm reaches around her. I become very conscious that I'm touching her. I like it and don't want to pull away, but I know I have to. As I start to move, Quinn moves her body into mine so her back is fully pressed against my chest and front.

I can't move; I can't even breathe.

"Thanks for protecting me tonight against Dylan."

"Yeah, no problem."

"Are you sure your foster parents aren't going to come home early and freak out?"

"Positive," I manage.

"Thank you for letting me stay," she whispers, and soon, her breathing changes.

I let my arm rest where it is, over her shoulder and around her chest. I'm fifteen years old, and I've never held someone or been held except during sex. This is the most comforting, most soothing and most perfect gift I could have ever asked for. I shift in closer as Quinn's body radiates its peace and heat into me, into my brain, into my body.

No matter how close I get, I can't get close enough. She's burning her presence into my soul.

CHAPTER TWO

LIAM
PRESENT

F*ucking alarm clock!* Right jab, left jab.
   Fucking radio station! Uppercut, uppercut.
   Fucking Boston … "More than a Feeling!" Elbow strike.

"Fucking Quinn!" I kick the bag hard with the bottom of my foot before I step back to catch my breath.

I can't knock the sparring bag out, and that's a real fucking problem because the memories hit me like a fucking Mack truck this morning before I even had the chance to roll my ass out of bed.

It's usually worse in autumn when the cold weather creeps into the air as the memories creep into my mind. The sound of dry, brittle leaves under my feet. Hell, sometimes all it takes is the swoosh of a beer can tab—I've long since learned to drink from bottles. But today, I woke up to *"DJ Spinner spinning those rock classics to bring you back!"* Insert deep voice and over-the-top radio personality.

In an instant, I felt her all around me, like a bitter cold but sweet-smelling wind. I could see her beauty, catch the fragrance of her shampoo and feel the gentle touch of her soft skin as if it were only yesterday and not just memories from almost a decade ago.

I should have known when I ran after her in the graveyard that evening—that a girl like Quinn would burn into my soul, and I'd never be rid of her.

I feel the beads of sweat drip over my forehead and watch the droplets as they journey from the tip of my nose to the floor. My knuckles hurt, and my muscles are sore. But no amount of physical release —or blasting Tool and Chevelle through my earbuds—is going to help the emotional pressure that's raging through me. I'm going to have to go to the needle and ink for that.

I'll have Talon create a new mandala on my arm—something spiritual—something to focus my energy. Maybe a series of chakras down my spine. That's sure to be pretty fucking painful too. I love the high from a tattoo needle, that sweet agony reverberating through my skull and bones. After a while, everything numbs, and all that's left is the hum of the needle. When the artist is finished, you're wearing a piece of your soul on your skin.

The second best feeling is creating a tattoo on someone else. When I get the right client, it's like I'm tattooing myself—I have all the same sensations —and I leave having created a masterpiece on another human being.

For me, that kind of meditation is better than any fight in the octagon.

It's fucked up and twisted, but I know the only reason I fight is because she hated it. It gives me a sick satisfaction.

I might as well just accept it; nothing I do today is going to stop the pain. All I can do is wait until the emotion recedes again into the back of my psyche, where it'll lay there, ready to pounce over me again like a stalking mountain lion studying its prey for a flaw or weakness before it runs swiftly in for the kill.

She's a ghost that keeps me from moving on.

Would I have chased her down that night if I'd known what the future would hold for us? I think about that for only a moment before the corners of my mouth curl up into an undeniable smile. Yeah, I'd do it all over again—every minute of it— because she'd been the greatest love of my life.

"If you don't give it a rest, your fingers are

going to be so swollen that Ryder and I will have to take over your tat clients for the next three days," Talon says from behind me.

Talon is the most intuitive of all the brothers. The brothers of ink and steel—as named by our surrogate father, Cade North—are bonded together by a deeply shared history ... and we have an affinity for tats and piercings. We know each other all too well, and Talon doesn't let anything get past him, so I better sound nonchalant when I answer back. "I have a fight in a month. How else do you expect me to train?"

"Yeah, but it's against Milano, so you have it in the bag." He goes about readying the gym equipment for the North House kids, who'll be here soon with Cade. It's our day of the week to work with them. "Unless, of course, it's not about Milano."

Good Christ! Leave it alone, Talon.

"And there's only one person I know who can make you that crazy—"

"Say the name, and I'll kill you," I interrupt before he lets it fly off his tongue.

"I fucking knew it! It's a sign," he says decidedly.

"Fuck you, it's no sign."

"Yes, it is," he replies. "I had a dream last night."

"Of course, you did." I roll my eyes. "And I don't want to hear about it."

"Yeah, you do."

"The fuck I do."

"Tell me, then, what made you think about … it." He chooses the word carefully.

"You're not going to let this go, are you?"

"Not a fucking chance in hell."

I check the wall clock. The kids will be walking in at any minute. The kids mean the world to me.

I spent several years at North House—a group home and halfway house for teens in Minneapolis —when I was younger. Quinn was there with me for several months. It's probably the best place of its kind in the country. It's owned by Cade North and his wife, Debra, who are literally the greatest people I know. If it hadn't been for their commitment, love and devotion, I don't think I'd be alive.

And Quinn … the thought of the night Cade found her in the back of the convenience store parking lot reminds me of the smell of blood in my nostrils and the moment everything in our lives changed. Quickly, I shake my head to eject the image.

The kids. North House is a lot of things—a safe haven for teenagers who've experienced abuse and neglect, who've lived on the streets or in deplorable conditions. It's a place for kids who are intimate with pain. Most importantly, North House is a place to grow and become who you were meant to be before this life and circumstances stripped it away from you.

Cade is a martial arts expert and trainer. He designed The Core, the state-of-the-art gym I'm currently working out in, as a place where anyone can come to learn or train, but most importantly, it's where the kids come to release their pain and aggression, to learn new techniques to master their emotions and to regain control of their destinies. It's a goddamn amazing place, and I love living in this city that I can finally call home after so many fucked up years of nowhere to go. And I love paying it forward to the place and the man who changed my life.

"Liam …"

Talon won't stop. "The radio … 'More than a Feeling.' It was my alarm this morning."

"I fucking knew it was a sign."

"The DJ playing a popular classic rock song is a sign?" I won't fall into his everything-happens-for-a-reason and the-universe-is-trying-to-tell-you-something bullshit. I don't believe it.

"I dreamt she was talking to you," he says, now in my face, making me look at him.

I want to punch him.

"She and I talked a lot."

"No, it was you like you are now. Ten years older. So was she."

"Are you done?" I don't bother trying to hide

my severe frustration. "'Cause if you're not, I could take out the box of old photographs, and we could reminisce."

"Even if that's all it was, a memory to help you heal, accept it."

"Accept it. Let it be ... got it." Why try fighting all that?

At that moment, the buzzer that lets us know the door's opening goes off, and we watch as fourteen broken boys and girls come into The Core, with Cade walking behind them.

I'm not in the present; I'm in the past, by ten years.

"Talon?"

"Yeah, bro?"

"I'm going to need some new ink."

"Yeah, I figured."

SOMETIMES IT'S TOO MUCH—LISTENING TO THESE kids' stories, watching the way they withdraw, as if trying to disappear from existence, or act so tough, like they don't care about anything, hiding behind a protective shell of hate—it's all the same survival mechanism.

Survival.

No kid—no adult for that matter—should have to go through life barely *surviving*. How has our society come so far and still, we don't have enough love or regard for our fellow humans to ensure that each and every one of us gets to *live*?

The kids file in. Cade, Talon and I get to work. We divide the kids into two groups. We each take our turns instructing them how to hit the sparring bags, knee and kick the training dummies, lift progressively heavier weights; we push the limits of what they think they can accomplish.

They come in feeling like their trash, and we work to prove them wrong, changing their mindsets, reversing some of the psychological effects of the abuse they've suffered, and helping them discover a dream and a goal.

Our most daunting task is to get them to believe they were meant for more than what they've been dealt.

One boy, who's twelve, watched his own mother kill his four-year-old brother; she drowned him in a bathtub while his stepfather held him back, not allowing him to help. He was going to be next. By some miracle, he got away. He'll be deeply scarred for the rest of his life. He also blames himself because he couldn't stop it and save his brother.

It's that kind of shit that makes me seriously lose my faith in humanity.

One of the girls, a fourteen-year-old, was beaten by her stepfather for years. Her mother knew all about it and helped hide it. It makes me want to kill them both. I hope someone shivs the piece of shit while he serves his time.

I try not to have favorites, but she reminds me of Quinn. Quiet until someone pisses her off, gapingly wounded herself but ready to save the world around her.

And I'm back to Quinn. Truth is, even though she left me, I've never left her.

Some of the brothers say I'm stuck because I'm not moving on, while others know better than to open their fucking mouths. And Cade? He watches me. I don't know if he knows I realize it. The guy has new kids all the time—but there are seven of us who are like his flesh and blood. Quinn made us the brothers we are today. Even though she's been gone for ten years, she's still here, in me and around me in every possible way.

I'm a nearly satisfied man; I've overcome and conquered almost all of my demons—except for the one I keep caged and tied in ropes and chains, hidden in the deepest, darkest cage within me, the one no one—not even Cade or Quinn—knows about. I've tried to release it, but after she was gone, I didn't have the heart. Since then, it's become my biggest tormentor.

But I'm the head artist at my own tattoo shop. I have an incredible surrogate, a found family of people I love and trust and an incredibly rewarding volunteer position with the kids.

And it's here, in this place, that I feel closest to Quinn—call it carrying a torch, call it feeling connected to my soul mate, call it weakness—I don't give a flying fuck what anybody wants to call it. I tattoo 'cause I want to do it, because she encouraged me to follow my dreams and passions. She believed in my dreams before I ever could. She loved my artwork, and unless she's covered it, she still wears the first real tattoo I ever did—two small bluebirds flying free from a wire cage on the back of her shoulder. They represented the two of us.

So, I tattoo because she loved it, I fight because she hated it, and I work with the kids because, if she were here, she'd be doing it with me.

Okay, so I'm a fucked up mess. Aren't we all?

"COME ON, JONAH, YOU CAN DO THIS!" I CHEER him on.

He's a skinny kid, and he gets bullied and picked on all the time. Doesn't help he's autistic, and his mother tried to murder him by throwing him off a bridge. He doesn't talk much. He'll be moving on to what we all hope will be a good foster home next week. Cade has been working with social services to be part of the interviewing process for potential foster parents since God knows how many people interview just to get some extra money each month and then inflict further trauma on the child.

Jonah shakes his head and backs away from the bench weight set. Maybe it's too intimidating.

"I have an idea," I say excitedly and lead him to the weight machines. "These are fun." I set the weight to five pounds. "All you have to do is pull on the rope!"

I put the handle in his hand and position his fingers so he's gripping it properly.

He still looks unsure. I smile, flex my muscle to make it bulge, point to my muscle and then point to his arm. "It will help make these muscles stronger. Do it like this," I say and demonstrate again. His eyes and face light up with understanding. Jonah pulls on that cable for all he's worth. I nod to him in encouragement. Jonah lifts the weight a few more times before he lets it go and wraps his bony arms around my waist in a bear hug.

I have to quickly swipe away the forming tears.

He's such a fucking amazing kid.

"Thanks for that, Jonah. You give the best hugs."

I'M IN THE LOCKER ROOM, FINISHING GETTING dressed after showering. Pulling on my 10 Years concert t-shirt, I start to get nostalgic. They're still one of my favorite bands. They toured with Breaking Benjamin and Smile Empty Soul. That concert was particularly cathartic. That summer was when my enemies became my brothers, and my best friend left me forever. "Through the Iris" became my theme song for her. I wish she would have held on when we went through the eye of the storm like the song describes, but she couldn't.

Or she didn't.

"Let's get the fuck out of here and get some lunch," Ryder says as he walks in with Talon.

"Sounds good to me," I agree.

"Hey, how many clients are on the Ink and Steel roster tonight?" Ryder preens himself and his leather coat in front of the mirror. "'Cause I hooked up with a real hottie the other night, and she and her friends want to go out tonight. Connor and Reese are already in; what do you say?"

"Where's Chase?" Talon asks.

"Down on the White Earth Rez. Something about studying for some big exam … blah, blah," Ryder quips.

"Yeah, getting your degree, blah blah," I mock.

"I'm not saying he shouldn't get his degree; I'm just saying he should also be putting in the same amount of time getting his dick wet."

Talon and I bust up laughing.

"Hey!" Ryder continues to drive home his point. "Use it or lose it."

"I don't have anything that the other artists can't handle." I could use a night out with a pretty face.

"Hell, I'm in," Talon says as we walk out of the locker room.

We take the stairs to the back door. "Whose car are we taking?" Ryder asks. "I only have my bike."

Talon laughs. "It's the frigging Arctic out there! How the hell do you ride that thing in the middle of February?"

I try not to visibly shiver as we step out into the below-zero temps, but it's a useless effort. I love the changing seasons, but sometimes I think we must be fucking morons living up in Minnesota, where it's freezing half the year. If we weren't all so dedicated to Cade—and each other—we probably would have escaped a long time ago.

"We can take mine," I offer, reaching into my jacket pocket. "Fuck me."

"What's wrong?"

"I left my car keys in Cade's office. Be right back." I turn and jog back through the door.

I plow up the steel grid stairs two at a time and then take long strides through the hallway. Cade will be with the kids on the mats doing hand-to-hand combat class, so I just let myself in.

Every muscle in my body seizes and locks.

My boots hold me, frozen against the carpeted floor. I feel my jaw unhinge as my blood stops its flow through my veins. Maybe I died, and this is what it feels like? Maybe it's an out-of-body experience? Maybe I'm still in bed dreaming, and that fucking song is still playing?

I close my eyes and shake my head to rid myself of the hallucination. But when I open them again, nothing has changed. In my peripheral vision, I watch Cade's eyes drop to his shoes before he takes a step back.

"Quinn?" It comes out hoarse and strangled.

This can't be right.

But it's her. It's Quinn!

She wears an elegant, brown cloth coat that hugs her hips, black knee-high riding-style boots with low heels and matching black leather gloves. Her hair is so long; the golden curls flow to the middle of her back. She's no longer a pretty teenage girl of sixteen.

She's a woman. A stunningly beautiful woman.

Could she really be twenty-six years old? Somehow, she had stayed frozen in my memory the way she was when she left.

Her sky-blue eyes lock with mine.

"Liam …"

At the sound of her voice, the dagger that's been plunged through my heart twists …

Again.

CHAPTER THREE

QUINN
SEPTEMBER
(PAST)

I wake up to Monica's mother, Linda, yelling and kicking me in the ribs. I roll off the floor mat and get to my feet, trying to make sense of her accusations through my sleep-rattled mind.

"I don't *do* drugs. I've never done drugs!" I say. And I never had.

After my mom kicked me out—again—about a month ago, I started staying at my friend Monica's house. She and I go to the same high school.

Her mom and stepfather own a large Victorian house that's been divided into several apartments, which they rent out. Monica's oldest sister Marissa attends the nearby college and lives in the upstairs apartment by herself. Monica hates her stepfather and often stays at Marissa's to get away from him.

This was one of those nights.

But tonight went south really fast. Marissa had a bunch of her college friends over for a party— mainly guys—and even though Monica and I are only fifteen years old, a few of them kept hitting on us the drunker they got.

Monica and I decided after a couple beers to escape into Marissa's room when the hitting-on turned to hand-grabs, and it was obvious Marissa wasn't going to say anything to stop the douchebags. So we camped out on her bedroom floor. We had school in the morning anyway.

Which led to this moment …

LINDA SLAPPING MY FACE AND KICKING ME IN MY ribcage was one hell of a way to wake up.

Now, she grabs a fistful of my long hair and drags me into the main room. She shoves my face against the coffee table.

I see small, clear plastic sandwich baggies filled with pot. Rolling papers lay haphazardly close by. There are also small mirrors with white powder lines—meticulously straight—across them. A razor blade is covered in the stuff.

I'm not stupid. I know it's cocaine. I've seen it

before, but I've never tried it. The party must have switched from alcohol to drugs.

Linda presses my face into the table, and searing pain radiates over my cheekbone with the force. "If it isn't yours, whose is it?"

She's got to be joking, but the pain in my face and scalp says otherwise.

"I swear, none of it's mine!" *Why would she think it was mine? It's obviously Marissa's!*

Linda yanks my head up fast and flings me into the wall. "I knew you'd deny it!" she shouts.

I turn to face Marissa, who is obviously wide awake—and *obviously* stoned out of her mind! She looks at me with pleading eyes.

"I take the word of my own daughters over yours." Linda comes at me again and slaps me across the face. "And I opened my home to you!"

"I was sleeping!" I shout back, raising my arms in front of my body defensively. "How could I be doing drugs in my sleep?!"

None of this makes sense to me, but then I watch Monica step to her sister's side. And I get it; I'm the convenient scapegoat.

"I should have never taken you in," Linda says, seething.

At her words, my heart breaks. I've known Linda since Monica and I were in elementary school. Her daughters have always been like sisters to me. And when I had nowhere to go …

I'd been hoping she'd become the mother I didn't have.

My eyes veer to the clock, and I'm filled with the horror of being thrust back out on the city streets with no place to go. "It's three in the morning ... we have school tomorrow ... can I please just stay until—?"

"Get out!" she screams.

"Okay ... okay." I realize I'm crying as I scoop up my few belongings. I need something to put them in.

Marissa goes to the kitchen and comes back with a black trash bag. I mash them inside.

"I know where you belong, St. Anne's," Linda threatens me as she marches down the stairs back to her apartment.

I've heard of it—Saint Anne's, a prison for girls. It isn't a place I want to be. I'm soft, and I know it. I'd be killed.

Monica disappears behind her mother as Marissa grabs my coat and puts it around my shoulders. She slurs, "I'm so sorry, Quinn. My mom came up here and—"

"Yeah, I get it," I say bitterly. "You didn't want to get in trouble." As if on some mystical cue, thunder slams through the sky.

Perfect, even God has it out for me.

I zip the coat. Marissa shoves a twenty-dollar bill into my hand. The gesture is way too little, way too late! It's not even enough for a dive hotel room on the worst side of the city.

"You need to hurry. She's called the police." Monica's voice comes from behind me.

I turn on her. "I don't get it! I thought you were my best friend!"

She doesn't meet my eyes when she says, "Things changed. Guess she doesn't think you're so perfect after all."

And that's when I got it. Monica's been acting weird lately, making little jokes about how her mom and sister like me more than they do her. I can see it now in the look on her face—smug satisfaction mixed with guilt. She's *happy* that her mom thinks I'm a druggie screw-up; it just makes her look that much better in comparison.

I shake my head, dumbfounded. It's obvious from my life that I have bad judgment when it comes to trusting people.

I back away from them, take the steps down to the back door and run into the night.

The sky is black as pitch. The heavy rain pelts me until it's soaked through the layers of my coat and clothes. I run until I'm out of Monica's neighborhood.

I have to find a safe place to hide until morning. Truth is, there is no safe place at three o'clock in the morning for a fifteen-year-old girl.

The wind blows my rain-drenched hair into my

face. I've lived in Minnesota long enough to know when a storm is brewing into a tornado.

I turn down into a dark alley back behind an old abandoned-looking warehouse. The doorway is almost invisible in the shadows. I get under it and find at least a little protection from the storm.

I wonder … my fingers wrap around the cold door handle, but the door is locked up tight.

I'm suddenly aware of the silent tears spilling down my face.

I fold my body to make myself as small as possible in the narrow threshold and curl my knees up against my chest to protect myself from the storm.

Alone.

Unloved.

Unwanted.

THERE ARE PLACES I'M AFRAID OF. LIKE SWIMMING out toward the center of a lake. You can't see through the murky waters, and you can't touch the bottom. Your imagination takes over, and it's like someone hits the panic button. As much as you tell yourself there is nothing in the water that can hurt you, you feel it, the whispering hand against your ankle threatening to pull you under to join it, underneath, in the darkness forever.

I'm afraid of my basement. It's ridiculous, being terrorized by the black, empty space under the stairs, but hell if I can talk my rational mind into believing that, because every time I have to go down there, my hands tremble and my heart races, while a metallic taste forms in my mouth and I can't talk, like during a nightmare. I run my ass off to get back upstairs and hope slamming the door against the ghosts will keep them from getting me.

And although both *feel* real, I've never really been hurt in either place. I have that same feeling right now, like I'm descending into a hellish reality that I won't be able to escape from once I'm snatched and then surely killed. But here, in this place, I don't need an overly active imagination.

This is the place I'm most afraid of.

My ripped, scuffed black Converse slap against the pavement. I'm not paying attention and trip over the curb. I right myself and walk as quietly as I can while making myself as small as possible.

Brave.

Stupid.

Helpless.

Whatever. I have no options.

I think back to my first year in high school; I hated my science class when our teacher forced us to watch a film where a pride of lions stalked and took down a baby elephant.

"They need to eat," she said.

Didn't matter, I hated the lions for it. First, they separated the baby from her mother; then they got her turned around, confused and afraid; that's when they jumped on her back, each taking a turn biting and clawing until she fell.

And then they ripped out her throat.

"Hey, hey, sweet thang! I've got what you need." A tall, skinny guy comes out of the shadows, seemingly from nowhere.

I don't answer. I keep my head down and my eyes on the ground.

He reaches out his hand to me, and in it, I see a little white packet. He wants me to try his drugs—which I don't want. Things are bad enough, and I've seen kids fall into meth and coke or heroin. They don't last long, strung out and pleadingly desperate for the next hit or shot. The drugs make them do anything for more while they slowly eat them away from the inside out. You can see it happening—and the user loses all will to fight.

Don't make eye contact! my mind screams. I feel like, at any moment, a group of them will jump me and rip out my throat—just like the baby elephant.

Another block down, a silver sedan pulls up alongside me.

I hear the passenger side window open. "Girl, what's your price?"

My heart pounds. *Jesus! Just keep walking. Don't look.*

The car tears away from the curb.

This place—State Street after midnight and the area of the city called Westhill—is the place I'm most frightened of. And what scares me isn't in my imagination.

A cold wind wraps itself around me, and I pull my hoodie tighter around my face. Not like boys around here get a free pass, but I wish I could hide my breasts and appear tougher.

"About time! What took you so long?" Diamond croons as I get closer.

I shrug, not wanting to tell her the truth—that I was establishing a hiding place past the washed-out road down by the cemetery on the other side of town. I don't know her enough yet; we just met a few nights ago after I had been wandering for hours. Guess she knew the look—when you live on the street, you have nowhere to go, no destination, so you walk, sometimes for hours, moving from place to place, trying to stay safe and not loiter in one spot for too long while you're hungry and cold.

She started talking to me, then bought me a grilled cheese and Pepsi at the all night diner on State Street. I was pretty shocked when I saw all of her money! She noticed I noticed and laughed.

"I've been exactly where you are. But I know this guy who can give you a great job! You can make this"—she waved the handful of cash at me—"every night! The work is easy, too."

She's definitely older than me by a few years—and obviously has connections I don't.

So I agreed to meet her and her friends.

"You ready?" she asks.

"Yeah." I was hoping she'd offer another grilled cheese before we went, but she didn't.

"It's not far; just up the block," she says, and I follow her as we walk along the dirty sidewalk.

She's really beautiful, almost glamorous.

"Why do you hang out down here so much if you have a good job?"

"This is where I find the best clients," she says.

Clients. Clients …

"Here we are."

The sign over the bar and hotel reads, *The DuBois.* The windows are tinted dark, and I can't see through them, but I can see out once we're at the door. Men are standing around laughing and smoking with women hanging all over them. Other girls line the curb, beckoning to cars and passersby.

I freeze at the door.

"Come on, it's not as bad as it looks," Diamond encourages me.

"I don't … think so," I stammer fearfully.

"Look,"—she comes over and places a hand on my shoulder—"these girls are having fun. They were just like me and you once, but now they make good money and have a warm place to sleep."

I'm not budging. I get it. I didn't before, but I do

now, and all I want to do is run in the opposite direction.

"They'll have pizza and drinks upstairs."

Food. I haven't eaten for two days. It's frightening and pathetic what you'll consider doing when you're hungry and scared and have nothing.

"I don't … want to …"

"You don't have to do anything you don't want to do. Just come up and meet my friends, have something to eat, and then leave. Then you can think about it all on a full stomach," she coaxes.

"I can go if I want to, if I don't like it?" I ask, unsure.

"Absolutely. I promise."

"Okay." My stomach twists, and I'm not sure if it's from hunger or fear or the intuition to run like hell that I'm ignoring.

I follow her through the main door and up the stairs. It smells awful—like smoke and sweat and urine. Guys watch us as we make our way to the first floor, where she knocks on the door.

A large black man opens it, and along with the bad smells, I detect pizza.

"It's Diamond," he announces in a heavy bass voice.

She walks in like she owns the place while I try very hard to hide behind her.

"Hi, Vince," she purrs.

"You brought me a gift," he says to her.

"She's a shy one," Diamond responds. "She's hungry, too."

Vince's eyes scrutinize me from head to toe before they wander to a table on the far side of the room. "Help yourself," he tells me. "But when you get your plate, make sure you bring your pretty little self over here so I can get to know you better."

All reason leaves me when I see the table covered with food—pizza, soda, cake, candy—I rush to it and jam as much of a slice of pepperoni pizza into my mouth as I can. Two long days without food. I can't think of anything else, except how ridiculously good it tastes. I down it with some Coke and then stuff my mouth with the other half, up to the crust.

"She looks good ... and young," I hear Vince say behind me.

"Fourteen," Diamond tells him.

"Fifteen," I correct her, mumbling through my food-filled mouth. I've always looked younger than I am.

After I gain enough composure to wipe my mouth, I go back over to sit next to Diamond, but she's in an armchair all to herself. Vince pats the seat next to him on the L-shaped extended sofa. Nervously, I take stock of what's happening in the room.

Two big guys are now standing on each side of the door, looking in at us. One's black, and the other's white—both are probably four times bigger than me. Then there are other men sitting all around, many of them with hardly-dressed girls on their laps. The men eye me like I eyed the pizza, while the girls look less than friendly. A few look like they may want to start a fight with me.

"Come on, girl, I won't bite," Vince says.

I'm not comfortable at all as I walk over and sit carefully on the edge of the couch cushion.

"Look at her!" Vince laughs. "Baby, what do you have to be scared of? Nobody's gonna hurt a sweet little piece of ass like you. Now lean back and make yourself at home."

"Vince is the leader of the Westhill Cartel," Diamond offers.

A chill runs up my spine. I may not have been out on the streets long, but long enough to know that the Westhill Cartel is the roughest, most brutal gang this side of the city.

"I'm sorry." I stand up and set my plate on the coffee table in front of me. "I think I made a mistake."

"You're looking for a job, right?" Vince asks. He wears a pair of black dress pants with a blue button-up and a black vest. He could easily be mistaken for a fresh-out-of-work businessman.

My body feels numb. "I should go," I say.

Everyone laughs.

"You haven't even heard my proposition."

Vince's dark, wavy hair is combed back, and he sits with a relaxed demeanor. I think he's of several nationalities, but I can't tell what—may be a blend of Caucasian, Latino and African American. If I met him on the street, I don't know what I'd think —maybe that he just left his bank job—but here, in this atmosphere, now that I know who he is …

"I don't think I need to. I'd like to leave now … please," I respond, realizing my freedom may be denied.

"Fifteen years old. Young thang, you and I could make a lot of money together." He stands up and gets close to me. "Is this your natural hair color?" Vince runs the back of his hand through my hair. "Yeah, it is!" He laughs, and his friends laugh with him.

His hand slips from my hair to my arm, where he caresses a line down to my elbow.

His touch makes my skin crawl.

"You're a virgin, aren't you?" He cackles. "I haven't had me a virgin in over a year." Vince licks his lips. "Best meat ever."

At that, Diamond jumps up and approaches me, too. "Don't worry, like I said, it's easy. I'll help you through it. You get to keep fifteen percent of every-thing you earn."

"Oh yeah, baby, you're so fine; you'll make more money in a week than these bitches make all month."

Diamond winces at his words. "You're scaring her, Vince."

"Don't tell me how to run my business, cunt," he says in a threatening tone.

She swallows hard and steps back.

"You know how they make veal so tender, girl?" he asks me.

I think I shake my head no, but I'm not sure.

"They take that newborn cow, and it never sees daylight again. They chain it down in a dark little cubicle so it can't move—that way, its muscles atrophy and get nice and tender—while they feed it nothing but milk. It makes the veal so soft it just melts in your mouth."

I get it. I'm the veal. I want to scream, but I still can't make myself move.

Screaming won't help me now anyway.

I thought Diamond was going to help me. I'm sorry I ever met her.

Vince leans in and licks his tongue against the side of my neck.

My eyes shift to watch what he's doing. Up close, I can see the scars covering his face, as if he's been in a lot of fights. My breath becomes painful as my chest heaves in terror.

"Oh, she tastes just as fine as she looks," he says before grabbing one of my breasts in his hand. "Such full, round titties for a girl so young. You'll be just about perfect."

I feel the pizza start to come back up.

"Get my room prepared, Eric. And you know what to do with the whore waiting for me now," Vince orders, and the Caucasian guy at the door nods and leaves the room.

"Vince,"—one of the girls sitting in one of the guy's laps gets up and walks over to pet Vince's arm like a lover—"the girl in your room is my recruit. She's my cousin, too."

"Bitch, get back over there where you belong and blow his dick!" Vince shoves her hard to her knees and back into the man she walked away from.

"Please, Vince, she's only seventeen!" she pleads.

The guy she's with backhands her. "Do what he says, cunt."

The girl is in tears as she pulls down the man's zipper.

This is when my feet begin to move. I find myself taking a step back from Vince.

"Now, where do you think you're going?" He smiles ruthlessly.

"My mom will be looking for me," I say shakily.

He laughs, and so do his friends. "How many times I've heard that! And yet, you don't see no mamas."

"NO, PLEASE!" We all hear a female voice yell from the hall. "JENNY!"

The door busts open for a fraction of a second

64

before Eric gets his thick hand around the runaway girl's throat and lifts her off the ground. Her legs make short little kicks.

"Get her the fuck out of here!" Vince roars. And the two disappear from view. "Diamond, take our little girl here and get her ready for me.

"I'm leaving." *Was that my voice?*

"Only place you're going is my bed chamber, where I'm gonna fuck that tight little pussy till it bleeds."

From the corner of my eye, I see the other guard at the door step out, and I wonder if he's helping his friend with the girl. I hope she gets away.

No guards at the door. And they left the door open.

The guy getting his dick worked on by the young woman howls in pain. She jumps up and cries, "Please, Vince! You've already had her, and so have your lieutenants, so please, let her go!"

"Fucking bitch just bit me!" the man cries.

One of the other guys drops the girl on his lap to the floor, stalks over and punches the biter in the face. The momentum throws her against the wall.

"Looks like you're getting too lenient with your stock, Vince," one of the guys sitting in an over-stuffed armchair quips with a smile, relaxing as a girl rubs between his legs.

"We'll have to teach these two cousins here a lesson," Vince replies coldly.

That's when my knee goes up fast and hard into Vince's soft groin.

I don't wait to see what happens next; instead, I tear out through the unguarded door and run.

After literally sliding down the stairs and bursting free from the downstairs door, I use all of the adrenaline that's been pumping through my muscles to propel me faster, and I don't look back.

Afraid they'll get into their cars and catch me, I steal down the alley behind the diner and hide. When the cook comes out to empty a bag of trash, I sneak through the open door and into the large pantry behind some storage boxes.

I curl my knees up and hug them to my chest. I'm not sure how I'm going to get out of here—and every noise I hear makes me jump—I won't be sleeping.

I stay like this for hours until someone opens the pantry door and leaves it ajar. I grab what food I can and stuff it into my jacket before I shoot out the kitchen door. I hear someone swear from behind me, but I don't stop … until I physically run into a cop outside in the alley.

"What's your hurry?" he asks gruffly.

"School. I'm late for school." As I say it and my eyes adjust to the morning sunlight, I see that the alley has been sectioned off with yellow crime tape.

"Were you around here last night?"

"No, my dad just brought me to the diner for breakfast before he took off for work."

I can't tell if the cop believes me.

"Tell your dad that he shouldn't be bringing you anywhere around here. A lot of bad things happen on this side of town."

"Yes, sir."

At that moment, two other cops pull a woman's body out of the alley dumpster.

It's Diamond! She's naked and covered in blood and bruises.

"Do you know her?" the cop asks me when he catches me staring.

"No." I shake my head.

"Go on, get out of here, and don't let me see you on State Street—or anywhere around Westhill —again."

I nod obediently, duck under the crime tape and take off running.

FOR WEEKS, I STAY HIDDEN UNDER THE SAFETY OF the bridge and in the cemetery with the concrete angel. I'm scared to death to leave. I keep thinking Vince and his gang of thugs are going to find me and make me pay for kneeing him and running away—like they made Diamond pay. I shudder to think what happened to the two cousins.

The cemetery gives me solace. I can't explain why. Maybe because the people here are dead and can't hurt me like living people can and do.

Maybe it's the love that someone living had for someone who's now dead. I imagine I can feel that love every time I go to the angel. She's so beautiful; she has a soft smile on her lips as she looks down toward her charge. The engraving on the tombstone is so old it's impossible to read. Someone must have loved whoever is buried here very much to give them the angel. I imagine the person is a beloved mom or a daughter.

And the angel has become so much more to me than a statue or someone's headstone. I like to think of her as a guardian angel. Or a guide—maybe she led the soul of the body she stands over to heaven. I thought that maybe if I touched the hem of her concrete gown, she'd help me. Maybe somehow I could prove to her that I'm good—a good person— that I'm worthy of being loved.

She's become my only friend.

Today, I tell her, "I'm so thirsty, I'm desperate. I've started drinking dirty river water. Maybe if I could find a pot, I could boil it over the fires I've figured out how to make. I'm hungry too ... and cold. I don't know how much longer I can do this, and I don't know where else to go."

I swipe at the hot tears running down my cheeks when I hear footfalls approaching.

"Please protect me," I beg her. She's my only hope.

When I tuck my head over my shoulder to see who's coming, I realize I've begun to tremble. I breathe a sigh of relief when it's only Liam Knight, a kid from school. My heart is pounding in my chest.

Some hiding job, Quinn!

I figure I must look crazy—walking around a grave, cleaning glass and talking to myself—but instead of walking away, Liam apparently decides he's going to talk to me. When he invites me to have a beer, my stomach rumbles, reminding me how long it's been since I've had a meal.

I've been living off the food scraps I can find in the neighborhood garbage cans before the truck comes in the early morning. A couple of times, I've stolen some stuff from the nearby convenience store, but the owner and workers are starting to suspect me, so I haven't gone back in over a week. And between the threats of Vince and St. Anne's, I'm too freaked out to go any farther away from my hiding place. So, yeah, a beer sounds good—maybe someone will have a bag of chips, too.

I follow Liam back to where he and his friends are partying. He gives me the cold can right before his girlfriend starts pawing him all over the place. I'm about to ask him if he has some snacks when one of the older boys starts coming on to me and acting like an asshole. To my surprise, Liam protects me.

Maybe that's why, after he follows me—uninvited—to my hiding place under the bridge and asks me to go to his foster house with him, I feel like I can trust him enough to say yes.

We share our stories of how we've gotten into this mess of having no parents and no home, and after a couple of hours I get this feeling, like I've known him all my life. And when I get so tired I can barely keep my eyes open, he invites me to stay and sleep there.

I'm sure it's a ploy and a ruse to get me in his bed, but dear Angel, I hope not because I feel compelled.

Maybe it's because it's been so long since I've had companionship; maybe I just *want* to trust him; maybe it's his blue-green eyes that are so intense they make me think that they're what the stormy ocean must look like; maybe it's his messy short dark hair and his amazing smile that makes him seem genuine and keeps him approachable. But, now, here with Liam, I feel almost safe for the first time in a very long time—maybe ever.

His black jeans and work boots make him look tough—and he obviously is, the way he had no fear defending me against Dylan—but the way he's acting with me doesn't make him seem so fierce. In fact, it makes him seem willing to be … vulnerable.

He's offering trust for trust …

When he tells me we can share his pillow, I come up and lay beside him. Facing the wall, I snuggle my back close to his front so we fit together in the small twin bed. The old mattress springs creak with my every move. I feel shy and brave and scared and safe all at the same time.

He pulls his blanket over us. It's a ragged, tattered thing, barely big enough to cover him. He's confessed that his foster parents keep the heat down in the house and if he touches it he'd get beaten. When I feel his arm come around my shoulders I feel like I know him well enough from this short time to realize that he'd go cold to make sure I was warm, even though I don't know why.

So I decide he doesn't have to; I take the risk and press my body against his. The sensation makes my face grow hot. He becomes utterly still.

"Thanks for protecting me tonight against Dylan."

"Yeah, no problem."

"Are you sure your foster parents aren't going to come home early and freak out?"

"Positive."

I reach my hands up and hold his arm over me, hoping he won't take it back. Tears well in my eyes. The feel of his arm … everything he's done … I wonder how I'm ever going to let go.

But right now, I don't have to.

"Thank you for letting me stay."

WHEN I WAKE UP THE NEXT MORNING, LIAM'S ARM is still around me. We hadn't changed positions all through the night. Normally, when I wake up in a strange place—which is all of the time—I get this uneasy, frightened feeling. My heart pumps with adrenaline to remind me I'm not safe and I may have to run at any second. But I don't feel that way at all right now. I feel perfectly content … maybe even happy. Okay, definitely happy. The smile that I feel spread over my face is proof of that.

A funny breath escapes my chest, sort of like a laugh of disbelief and a sigh of relief all mixed up together.

"Hey, you awake?"

Is it possible that Liam's voice is more amazing when he's sleepy? It's deep and rough and gives me tingles deep in my stomach.

"Did you get a good night's sleep?" he asks me.

"Yeah, actually, I did." Surprisingly. "What time is it?"

He laughs and sits up. "One in the afternoon."

"No way." I run my fingers through my hair.

"Yup, but I'm happy you got a good sleep—maybe we'll get rid of those dark circles under your eyes. Now, let's get some food like I promised."

The thought of dark circles makes me reach up and gingerly trace my fingertips under my eyes. But food … "Yeah, I could totally go for food."

"Snickers and a cheeseburger coming up." He goes to his closet and pulls down a black camo backpack, sets it on the bed and starts digging through it.

He pulls out a couple of outfits, a change of shoes and some other stuff, until he gets to a small metal box with a padlock on it.

Once he sets it out, he goes through a smaller, zippered pouch and pulls out a steel key ring with four keys on it. He unlocks the box, and inside are various trinkets, pieces of jewelry, a small wad of cash secured with an old rubber band and some folded papers and envelopes.

"This is my life bag. When my mom tosses me, or I run, or a foster family gets ugly, or I'm sleeping in a doorway someplace, it's always packed and ready to grab in a second," he explains.

"Do you run away a lot?" I ask quietly.

"You have no idea." He shakes his head as he stuffs the money in his pocket. "For a while, I stayed with my grandmother, but she died when I was nine."

"I'm sorry."

He studies me for a moment and keeps talking. "I was forced to stay with my mom, but that's like sitting on a rowboat on top of an active volcano—

BOOM!" Liam brings his closed fists together, opens them, and then throws them up in the air so I can visualize the explosion.

"How did you get caught up in foster care?"

"Got nabbed in an alley fight." He shrugs. "Made fifty bucks that night—it helps you win when you bet on yourself. But now, my name and face are in their system. No big deal, I just have to be smarter than the cops, which isn't too difficult."

He relocks the box and puts the pack back in its safe place. Liam turns and pats his pocket of money. "This'll be plenty for cheeseburgers, candy bars and milkshakes. Oh, I have an idea for some fun too. You'll need these."

Liam passes me a black, hooded, zip-up sweat-shirt. It smells of musk and earth and *him*.

"I require your sweatshirt?" I quip to hide how much I like being enveloped in it.

"And this." He pulls a purple and yellow Minnesota Vikings baseball cap over my head and helps me tuck my hair inside it. After lifting the hood, he steps back and studies his handiwork. "No one will recognize you now."

"Okay then, what do you have in mind?"

He answers with a smile.

FIRST THING WE DO IS HOP A BUS. I FOLLOW HIM TO the very back seats, where he puts me on the inside, close to the window, and sits on my other side.

"Where are we going?" I ask.

"You'll see."

I make a face at his cryptic answer, but I can't quell the growing excitement.

When the bus stops at the Mall of America, he says, "This is our stop."

"Shopping? I didn't take you for one who does a lot of that," I say.

"Ha. Ha."

We go through the heavy glass doors and walk into the wonder that is the biggest shopping center in the United States, maybe the world, for all I know. Liam has a plan because he makes a beeline to the amusement park.

"Um ..." My gaze travels up the tallest, most frightening and puke-inducing rollercoaster ever. "Not doing it."

"Sure you are." He laughs as he pays for two tickets.

"It'll make me sick for sure." Vomiting is not attractive.

"That's why we'll do lunch *afterward*."

That's faulty reasoning, I think as he begins to walk up the ramp to the line.

I grab his arm in desperation. "I'm serious ... I'm scared."

"Have you ever ridden one?"

"No," I admit.

"Trust me, by the middle of the ride, you'll be screaming in excitement." He looks at me with this —I don't know—this *look* … like everything is going to be okay.

I walk with him into the line. "I appreciate your confidence … sort of." The damn machine stands all the way to the ceiling.

"Are you afraid of the height or the motion?"

"Yes." I nod solidly.

He laughs. "Good … maybe you'll need to hold my hand."

Hold his hand? He *wants* me to hold his hand?? I turn my face to the side as I feel the blood rise and paint my cheeks with a rosy flush.

We climb into the rollercoaster, and the bar comes down over our shoulders and between our legs.

"You should see your face!" he cackles. "You look terrified!"

"If I don't die, I'm going to kill you!"

As the ride begins, I feel Liam's fingers prompting my hand to open. I open my fist, and his fingers twine through mine.

The rollercoaster throws us and spins us; it lifts us and drops us. The force and gravity tries to pull our hands apart, but we hold on for all we're worth. It is the most frightening, exhilarating feeling ever!

We finally stop. I'm still alive, shockingly.

The security harness lifts. I take a tentative step forward, but I am totally unsteady.

"Sick?" Liam asks.

"Not sure what I am," I say, struggling with my balance. "Walking might take a minute."

He laughs before he pulls me up onto his back and carries me piggyback through the mall.

When the vertigo does recede, I don't tell him. I like the feel of my legs wrapped around his waist and my arms draped over his shoulders, which are broad and strong. I breathe in his shampoo and soap.

"Did you like it?" he whispers to the side where my head rests.

"Yes." *I really like being so close to you.*

"Want to do it again?"

"Absolutely not," I answer and am met with his happy laughter.

He marches us to the elevator. There's a crowd waiting to get on. We wait with them.

"You can put me down now," I whisper, a little embarrassed over all the stares we're attracting.

"Nope," he says. "I like you just like this."

"Liam …" I hiss.

The elevator doors open, and in we go.

"She got sick on the rollercoaster, but don't worry, folks, she'll be alright," he tells the people boarding with us.

"Oh my God! Are you crazy?" I whisper.

"Probably."

We're quiet until we stop at the food court.

"You have to be tired. You really can put me down."

"I know," he says. "I just keep thinking of yesterday when I was dealing with Dylan, and you ran off, and I wondered what would happen if I couldn't find you."

"You wondered that?" I feel those tingles in my belly again.

"Yup."

All of a sudden, he steals the rationality from my mind. It's all I can do to halt the giggle before it comes out.

We make it to Burger King and he orders two Whoppers with cheese and chocolate shakes. He also gets onion rings and French fries. He sits me on the hard plastic table, goes back to grab the tray of food and sits across from me.

"Dig in," he says without formality.

We do.

Starving, I lift the lid to my shake and dip a fry into the thick, creamy chocolate.

"Really?" he asks, seemingly entertained and perhaps disgusted.

"It's good," I say, tempting him with the milk-shake fry.

"No thanks, I'll stick to normal things like ketchup."

"You made me ride a rollercoaster, and you won't taste an ice cream fry?" I'm incredulous.

He shakes his head no, but I'm not about to let him off that easy. I'm overwhelmed by the urge to mess with him.

"You leave me no choice," I warn.

"Oh yeah?" He grins.

I swipe the fry across his face so a line of chocolate goes from one cheek across his lips to the other cheek. It's like I've given him a giant chocolate smile.

He smirks and nods slowly, and I feel a little nervous. He's definitely up to something. "Oh, you asked for it."

Five fingers covered in ketchup latch onto my face.

"NO!!!" I howl.

He laughs and smears the ketchup down my nose.

I move quickly, lift the lid to his shake and throw my entire hand into it! Liam and I both start laughing uncontrollably. I jump into the seat next to his. When he tries to duck and dodge my cold, chocolaty hand, I miss his face, but I get to rub it into his hair. Oh, it's satisfying!

"Truce! Truce!" Liam calls.

I have a feeling it's a fragile truce. "What are the terms?"

"No more shake or ketchup war," he declares, "and I agree to taste your disgusting chocolate fucking French fry."

"Thank you."

We grab a handful of napkins and mop the ketchup and chocolate off ourselves as best we can. When Liam helps me wipe a bit off the side of my face, I just about melt at the sensation of his fingers on my skin. I'm fairly certain I still have ketchup in my ear canal, but I really don't care at this point. I don't even care that people are staring at us. This moment is worth it. I can't remember the last time I had so much fun!

Once we're both cleaned off, I dip a fry and give Liam a pointed stare. He opens his mouth, and I shove the fry in. First, he starts to gag and holds his throat like he's choking to death, then he falls to the floor.

"Stop it! You're drawing even more attention to us!" I'm laughing so hard, and so much that I can't catch my breath.

He acts normal again, looks around at the people near us and announces real loud, "I'm okay, folks, nothing to worry about. Enjoy your meals."

I slap his arm before I move back to my own seat. "You're crazy." I smile.

He smiles back. "You haven't seen nothing yet."

We get back down to the business of eating. He wolfs his burger down so fast it makes my head spin and then gets back up and orders another.

A few girls at a nearby table watch him stride over, then put their heads together and giggle. Can't say I blame them, he really is that gorgeous.

When we're finished, he grabs our trash and drops it in the garbage pail.

"I've got an idea," he says brightly.

"Another one? If you think you're getting me on another ride after I just ate ..." I shake my head, showing him he'll be disappointed. "Worst idea ever."

"That isn't it." He starts walking away.

I catch up. "Okay then, where are we going?"

"Do I need to carry you again?" he asks in a playfully warning tone.

Yes. "No."

"Quinn, duck into the clothing store right now," he says, his tone suddenly totally serious.

I don't have to be told twice. As I turn into the store, I can see the two police officers walking toward us. My heart thuds powerfully as I run/walk between the racks of clothes.

"Can I help you find something?" a helpful sales clerk asks.

I snatch up something on a hanger. "Dressing room?"

She points to the back of the store, and I move

my ass to hide behind the closed door. I have a mixed sense of security from the fragile hook locking the door, which seems to be my only defense. It makes me feel like a pheasant hiding in a scant bush with the hunter and his rifle inching closer.

Sitting silently, I try to think of anything but the possible fate about to befall me. I try not to think of St. Anne's and how I should have never come out with Liam.

A few minutes later, I hear, "Damn, you know how to hide."

It's him.

"I think I'm having a heart attack."

"I don't blame you. Coast is clear now."

"No, I can't stay here, I have to go …" The word *home* hovers pathetically on the tip of my tongue.

"Don't freak. You're going to like what's next," he assures me.

"I don't think so, Liam." It's like the protective bubble I've been feeling has burst. I need to go back to my hiding place.

"Whatever happens, you can't stay in the dressing room. The lady is definitely starting to look over suspiciously."

"Shit." I come out while making sure I hold the shirt I grabbed away from me so she can see I didn't try to stuff it in my jacket. That's all I need is to have her *call* the cops or mall security because I lingered too long.

"Do you like that shirt?" Liam asks me.

"I don't know." I never really looked at it.

I do now as I hang it back on the rack. "It's pretty." It is. Light blue, a low v-neck and a midriff cut—it would show my belly button. I'd have nowhere to wear it. "Not much use for it under a bridge."

"Would you wear it if you owned it? It's sexy. Is it your style?"

"Yes, I'd wear it." I punch his arm. "Shut up!"

We take off and walk quickly to the end of the mall toward the exit. But instead of turning toward the door, Liam grabs my arm.

"Detour," he says and pulls me through the double doors of the mall's cinema.

"What are you doing?"

"I still have money to burn, and I want to burn it on you."

I look behind us. "Liam, the police could come back."

"They're not going to be looking for you, or anyone for that matter, in a dark theater," he reasons. "Anyway, after the movie, we can go out the theater exits, which lead directly outside, and it'll be dusk."

"You have a point," I concede.

"Of course I do," he states smugly. "And this movie is supposed to rock!"

A second later, he speaks to the guy behind the glass ticket partition. "Two for *Cellular*."

I look toward the marquee to check out the signage. The movie stars Chris Evans and Kim Basinger—and has something to do with a cell phone. It's been a long time since I've been to a movie.

Liam buys a vat of buttered popcorn, a Coke and a jumbo sized Snickers bar for us to share. *Perfect.*

We find seats near the front of the theater. When it goes dark, Liam's hand finds mine again. The movie is great—scary and thrilling—but the biggest thrill by far is Liam holding my hand. Again.

QUINN
PRESENT

I DID IT ON PURPOSE, COMING HERE TO THE CORE. I hoped so hard I'd see him; maybe he'd be working out with the kids or by himself. Then I'd be able to get a glimpse of him, remember what he felt like, resurrect the memory of his love and pretend it was still alive.

But I hadn't expected to be trapped inside this little office, where I couldn't escape the heat of his anger and the burning pain in his eyes.

I'm sorry. I'm so sorry. I swallow it. He doesn't want to hear it; it'll just sound like another lie, another betrayal from someone who told him they loved him and then left.

It's all too much too fast.

My mom is dead. She made her choices, and now, for us, the past is completely unredeemable.

And here's Liam. I made my own choices— choices that didn't include him—and now, for us … the past is …

I turn away from him as the tears come hot and fast. The word *unredeemable* sticks in my throat, cutting off my oxygen.

Oh God, what he must think of me … how much he must hate me.

"I'm sorry for your loss." He speaks, but it's soulless.

"I appreciate that," I respond, just above a whisper.

Two men crash through the doorway, and I can't help but look. It's Ryder and Talon.

Do they hate me too?

"QUINN!" Ryder scoops me into a suffocating

bear hug. "Look at you, girl! Damn, you grew up beautiful."

"There wasn't any doubt that you would." Talon smiles, and I'm so grateful for the peace I feel in him and in his expression. He pulls me away from Ryder and into a welcome-home kind of embrace. Talon could always sense people's moods and somehow make things better—it was like his superpower.

"Quinn's mom passed away this week," Cade tells them. "She's here for the funeral."

"Damn, Quinny, I'm sorry." Ryder takes my hand and holds it.

I smile in spite of the pain. "No one's called me Quinny for a long time."

He smiles back and I'm grateful for the friendliness in it. God knows I could use a friend right about now.

"Ten years," Liam states coldly.

I can't help but look up at him. His eyes are hard and unforgiving.

Talon says, "Quinn, do you need someone to accompany you to the funeral? I'd be glad to."

A shaky breath escapes my lungs. "I did come alone. You guys were my only friends here."

"We still are," Ryder says with finality.

Talon nods in agreement.

Liam looks away.

I've longed for him … but I expected nothing else after what I did to him.

Liam Knight *was* my home … once, but I lost it. I haven't been home since.

"Quinn, when is the funeral?" Cade asks, breaking the awkward silence that hangs in the air.

"Monday."

"Today is only Friday," Cade continues. "Where are you staying?"

"Motel 6," I reply. "Student budget. I figured it was on the bus route too, so I could get from place to place."

"Bullshit," Ryder breaks in. "I'll be your personal chauffeur while you're here."

"I don't know …"

"I do," he says. "There is no reason for you to have to do this alone."

"Thanks." I know I'm going to cry again. *Shit! Here it comes.* My voice shudders. "My friend Shellie wanted to come with me, but final exams are looming … and I don't know how long it will take to deal with my mom's stuff."

Cade steps forward and wraps me into his chest as the sobs break through me. "I'm sorry," I whimper, feeling like the weak little girl I used to be—with no light in the darkness.

"Nonsense, you have nothing to be sorry about. And you are not staying at any motel. Ryder will take you to get your stuff and then bring you back to the house. It's always there as a home for you."

Home. I manage a nod. My *home* is the person standing within arm's reach of me, yet we're separated by a thousand miles.

"Well, it looks like you guys have this all taken care of," Liam says, looking completely dumbstruck. "I'm late getting to work. I'm sorry again for your loss …"—he hesitates before he says my name—"Quinn."

He turns and strides out of Cade's office as if the building were on fire.

"He's going through male PMS," Ryder quips. "It happens sometimes to guys his age."

"Come on, let's get you settled into North House. We'll take my car," Talon says. "Ryder is a robot and rides his bike even in February."

They start their banter, and I'm caught in the turbulence of the man Liam has become—and the memories of the boy I knew and loved …

CHAPTER FOUR

LIAM
PRESENT

The pain that clouds over her countenance because of my reaction is horribly apparent, yet I can't stop the forward tumble I'm taking.

I let my eyes cut away from her—despite the fact that the act of doing so feels like a thousand tiny jagged splinters going through my iris.

Goddamnit, I'm crumbling ... right here in front of her ... I can't. I can't let myself be that vulnerable. Not again.

I watch as her pretty little mouth moves. Her thin, petal-colored lips work, but no words take form as tears fall from her eyes.

I need a wall! I need a concrete and steel-fucking-reinforced wall.

Oh my God, I would rather die than stand here. I don't think dying would hurt as much as this moment does. I want to grab her into my arms and hold her so tightly that our hearts would have no choice but to beat together. What kind of man am I that I can't look at the best friend I ever had? How can I simultaneously hate someone so strongly and love them so fiercely?

I loved her with everything I was, and she left me. She promised—*we promised*—we'd never leave each other. No matter what happened! I want to hate her, to loathe her.

I don't want her to know that when she stole away that fateful night, she took, right along with her, my breath and my heart. My very soul.

When Talon and Ryder come through the door, I know I have to get the fuck out of here!

I can't get into my car fast enough. I tear out of the parking lot in a daze, the wheels of my Nissan Skyline GT-R creating smoke on the blacktop.

What the fuck? "WHAT THE FUCK?!" I shout at the windshield.

For seven years, I couldn't move on with my life. I waited for her, watched the phone, checked emails, begged Cade to tell me if he had heard from her. Nothing, not one fucking word!

"I waited for you, Quinn!" I rage into the empty car. "I believed in you so much that I *knew* you'd come back, was *sure* you'd come back, but you didn't! You obliterated me!"

It's been just over the past few years that I've been able to piece my life together. A future without her was never part of the plan. And it still hurts like hell, but I moved forward. I got my business up and running, started fighting professionally, got laid when I wanted to …

But everything I've done, everything I've accomplished, I've done as half of a whole.

With just one look from her, I feel like my fucking vital organs were just ripped open.

I've never gotten over her, not in the slightest.

LIAM
OCTOBER
(PAST)

"THAT MOVIE WAS FRIGGING AWESOME!" QUINN crows happily.

"Yeah, it was," I agree.

We talk about our favorite scenes as we walk out into the safety of dusk and hop the bus back to my foster home.

We're almost there when she says. "I don't know, Liam. I shouldn't get too used to sleeping at your house … or being with you." Quinn stares down as she picks at the frayed material of her jeans, exposing her knee. "I should go back … to where I belong."

"You don't belong on the street, and you know it. Give me a little time to figure out what to do."

She eyes me skeptically. "No one belongs on the street," she says.

I stand my ground. Quinn, considering what she's been through, should be a hardened, street-tough girl, but she isn't. Far from it. She's sweet, soft and sensitive.

It's not hard to talk her into coming with me. We pick up some Subway sandwiches and cookies for dinner and take them back to my room. All the cash I'd accumulated is gone, and I don't mind at all. Money is liquid; I'll get more.

We're sitting on my bed when I take an intimate leap.

"I have something I want to show you if you promise you won't laugh." My tone is a lot more serious than I meant for it to be.

She takes in my countenance. "I won't laugh."

"I've never shown anyone before, not a soul," I confess.

The nervousness that began deep within my stomach when I suggested it spread through my entire body. I can't believe I'm about to do this.

I take out my backpack, unzip the back

compartment and pull out my most prized possession.

Reaching toward her, I pass her my art portfolio. "I used to travel with my sketch pad only, but after a while, I had done so many drawings that I felt something about, I put them into a binder to protect them."

I need a distraction. I can't watch as she looks through it, so I plug my MP3 player into a mini speaker and put on Linkin Park's *Meteora* album. Somehow, they say everything in their lyrics that I feel. I start it at "Somewhere I Belong."

Peering back over at Quinn, I think maybe I shouldn't have shown my deepest shit to her. What the fuck was I thinking?

I'm so fucking nervous that I decide that the best thing to do—instead of watching her reactions —is draw. I sit beside her against the wall at the head of the bed, prop my pad on my knees and work a pencil against the paper.

"These are amazing!" Quinn exclaims.

"You think so?" Is she lying? Being polite?

She catches my eye. "I know so."

I take a deep breath.

She flips through the pages of dragons and knights, swords and fancy script. There are skulls, trees and flowers, old time ships, animals, sexy pin-up girls, fiery phoenixes, eyes dripping with tears or blood …

"I draw what I feel at the moment. Some of them are gruesome," I say when she reaches a particularly dark drawing of a monster crushing a boy's skull.

"Yeah, and some of them are beautiful. All of them are incredible. You're so talented."

"Thanks." I almost want to tell her that if she studies the pictures, she might be able to discern which are from my real life—like the boy and monster—and which are simply just for the hell of it, for the fun of drawing. "I think if I can get really good, I want to be a tattoo artist."

"I think you already are *really* good. You could totally be a professional tattoo artist if you wanted to be." She says this matter-of-factly, but the weight of her words and compliment impacts me like a meteorite striking a planet. "Do you have any tattoos?" she asks.

"One. I made a homemade machine last place I was at."

"You tattooed *yourself?*" She's incredulous.

"Yeah." I laugh.

"Didn't it hurt?" Her eyes are so wide. "I hear they hurt wickedly!"

"Yeah, it hurt." I'm lost inside her blue oceans as they look back at me. I have the strongest urge to grab her face and kiss her.

"Can I see it?"

Can I kiss you? "No."

"What do you mean, no? Let me see it!"

After an exaggerated eye roll, I lift the left sleeve of my t-shirt.

As she studies the messy script above my bicep, her fingers reach up and gently trace the lettering I etched into my flesh. Her brow creases, and her expression is pained.

"*Damned?*" she reads aloud with a questioning inflection.

"Everyone wanted to brand me, so I decided to brand myself."

"You're not damned," she argues.

"Yeah, yeah, I am," I insist. "I have enough fuck-ups to fill a lifetime."

"What have you done that's so bad?" She's still touching my shoulder, and I don't want her to stop.

"Enough, trust me." I decide to rework the direction of our conversation. "Anyway, I want to get some really cool tats with someone who's willing to do my artwork on me."

"Do you have a specific one in mind?" Quinn looks back at the portfolio, studying it carefully.

"I want to do something great someday and have the horse and knight tatted on my arm or maybe my back," I explain. "You know, as a play on my last name."

"I love that idea, Liam Knight. And you know, you've already done something great," she says.

"Oh yeah? What's that?" I fire back.

"You became my friend and helped me when I needed it. That was pretty brave."

I can't answer her. I never thought that making friends with Quinn would make her look at me or think of me that way.

I find my voice. "So you don't loathe me like you did when you first looked at me when I bothered you down by the angel."

Gently, she shakes her head. "I was only trying to protect myself."

Of course, she was.

"What tattoo would you put on me?" she asks.

"You'd get a tattoo?" I don't believe her.

"If you did it, I might."

"I'll think about it." But I wouldn't ink anything into that China-teacup-perfect porcelain skin of hers—I wouldn't want to fuck it up!

"How do you become a tattoo artist?" she asks, passing me back my binder.

"I don't have a fucking clue." I shrug, putting it away again, into hiding. "Maybe an apprenticeship under another artist … I certainly don't see an art degree at a university in my future. What about you, Quinn? What do you want to do? What do you dream about?"

"My dreams are stupid."

"No dream is stupid."

"Okay, then it's unrealistic," she retorts.

"Hey, I just shared mine with you …"

"Fine. I want a family," she says firmly. "When I was living with my dad and his new family, I felt like an outsider the entire time. My stepmother wouldn't even let me sit next to my dad, like during family time. She'd tell me she was going to sit next to him, then she'd have one of her kids sit there instead. He never seemed to notice. After a while, I stopped trying." She leans her head against the wall. "She made sure we had no time together, ever. And like my mom, he worked all the time. I felt like he didn't care if I was there or not, and my stepmother was usually criticizing me—telling me how fat I was, how ugly my nose was, or how stupid I was—I soon learned it was better to stay alone in my room and read books. On the rare occasion I actually got my dad to hug me, he'd do it for the quickest second before pushing me away, saying, 'That's enough.' But it was never enough.

"My mom didn't want me, my dad didn't want me, my stepmother didn't want me … but to anyone looking in, it looked like I had a perfect life. Nice furniture, designer clothes, new cars and upper-middle-class money. Abuse isn't always bruises and cuts; sometimes, it's selfish, materialistic, cold, unloving people who learn to inflict pain in ways others can't see. Being smacked around with a ping pong paddle, being refused physical affection and food, being told that no one would ever love you—how could they if your own mother doesn't?"

Quinn wipes a tear. "I want a family and a home of my own. That's my dream."

She's right. That's not a dream; it's a *need*, a necessity for existence.

"You know when you go to someone's house and see a family picture with all of them together in it? I've never been in one of those. I want to be." She shrugs. "My dad, stepmom and her two kids have one—I wasn't invited."

"That sucks, Quinn, I'm sorry." It feels natural to put my arm around her shoulder.

"I don't belong anywhere, Liam." I feel her tears against my arm.

"I get it," I say. "My grandparents loved me; at least, I thought they did when I was little, but my mom hated them." I did, too, now. "My grandmother's the one who really raised me. My mom couldn't stand looking at me and refused to take care of me. She took off completely when I was still a baby. My grandfather died when I was eight, and my gran died about a year later. The court found my mom and gave me back to her." I go quiet as the buried memories threaten to crawl up out of their graves. "And that obviously hasn't gone well."

"So, you want a family too," Quinn says decidedly.

"I guess maybe I do, probably. I don't know. I gave up on the notion a long fucking time ago," I snap. "Plus, a family isn't a dream."

"It's my dream," she whispers.

It bothers me terribly, like the gnawing when I saw her in the cemetery; I want to smash that stupid idea of a dream! She needs to know that homes aren't real for kids like us. She needs to toughen up if she's going to survive out here! But part of me hates myself for even thinking that. I like her tenderness ... too much.

I don't know what to say, so I move my arm and lay down. "Tomorrow is Sunday, and I need to think."

"What do you need to think about?"

"You, and how to get you somewhere better than under a fucking bridge."

She lies next to me but doesn't turn and face the wall this time. Instead, she curls against me and lays her head on my chest.

God, the feel of her against me is amazing.

And just like that, she's my place where I belong.

I'M STIRRED AWAKE AS I HEAR ANGRY VOICES shouting in the other room. I look over at the clock. Two a.m.

"I told you not to fucking bet all the money!" Mrs. Richardson screams. "You gambled away our fucking rent!"

"Shut up, bitch! I don't need your shit anymore; I heard your grating voice all the way fucking home!" Mr. Richardson shoots back.

Goddamnit! They're back. And he sounds drunk!

I shake Quinn awake. "Wake up; you have to get under the bed."

"What's wrong?"

It only takes a moment before she hears them fighting. She presses her lips together and bravely nods.

Once she slips underneath, I pull the blanket so it drapes over the edge of the bed to hide her.

"You don't *need* my shit?!" Mrs. Richardson yells. "Good! I don't *need* to look at your ugly, worthless face anymore!"

Fuck! If they keep this volume the neighbors will call the cops!

"Bitch, shut up!"

I hear him smash against something. I squeeze my eyes closed against the inevitable.

"You can't even hit me, you're such a pussy!" she taunts him.

I've been here long enough to know exactly what's going to happen, she's going to go to her room or go to the kitchen for something to eat, and he's going to come in here and start shit with me.

I tune out for a second and wonder if two people like Quinn and I ever got together, would we be miserably dysfunctional like these two asshole excuses for human beings? I could never imagine Quinn like that—and I'd rather cut off my own fucking arms than ever hurt her or a kid.

My door blasts open so fast it makes me jump, even though I was expecting it.

"The little douchebag *is* awake." Mr. Richardson staggers in. "This room is a fucking pigpen!" he rages as he looks at the food wrappers on the floor. He grabs a fistful of my hair, pulling me up off the bed and throwing me to the floor. "PICK THEM UP, PIG!"

I quickly snatch up the two Subway wrappers and smash them together in my hands.

"Two sandwiches, you fat fuck? Where did you get the money for those?" His foot kicks into my ribcage.

I steal a glance under the bed at Quinn, who looks terrified.

I'd like to reassure her. I can take the asshole easily—I have before. I've stopped fighting back, though, since the weather turned colder. I usually let him hit me a few times until he gets tired and goes off to bed. My biggest concern right now is that I don't want him to discover her.

I pull myself to my feet.

"Where you hiding your money, boy?" he seethes. "This is my house! Anything you bring in here is mine!"

He gets his hand around my neck and pushes

me against the wall. In that movement, my eyes catch mine and Quinn's shoes together near the wall.

Fuck, fuck, fuck!

He sees them, too, and understanding dawns on his face. "*Two* Subway wrappers and *two* pairs of shoes? Who have you let into my house, prick?"

"No one. I was hungry, and I found the pair of shoes by a dumpster," I lie.

He spins me around and forces my head toward Quinn's sneakers. He presses my face into them.

"They're way too small to be yours, bigfoot!" He considers them and then smiles. "You got a girl in here? Got your ass laid, didn't you?"

I shove him off of me. "I told you, I fucking found them. I'm bringing them to school on Monday."

"You think I'm buying that?" He backhands me across the face so hard I hit the far wall. The cheap wall material reverberates with the force.

I touch my hand to my lips and catch the blood in my fingers. "Goddamnit!"

"What did you say, asshole?" He leans his ear at me.

One of his fists pummels my gut, and the other cracks against my jaw.

The next two blows I block, which infuriates him! The question is, do I let him beat the shit out of me or fight back? We've done it both ways before. He might throw me out on my ass either way—we've done that both ways, too—and I can't leave Quinn in here alone.

"Hey, guy, you're drunk as shit! Just go the fuck to bed and makeup with your old lady," I say, exasperated.

"You good-for-nothing bastard!" He maneuvers me into a headlock and starts dragging me out of the room.

I'm not entirely unhappy with this; it keeps Quinn safe under my bed. For now.

If I can tire him out, he might forget all about the conversation and simply pass the fuck out.

"Did you say that piece of shit brought somebody into my house?" Mrs. Richardson squawks. "Is there someone in *my house*, boy?"

She must have been in the kitchen because I can smell something cooking, and she's brandishing a large serrated kitchen knife.

"Jesus Christ! So, I got laid and threw her out when I was finished. She was carrying her goddamn shoes with her cause she was wearing her boots outside. This is not a big fucking deal!" I've never seen the woman with a knife before; in fact, she's never been involved with her husband's rages, but it sinks in that I could be in serious danger.

"Did you let the slut in my room? Did she take anything?" She breathes into my face; her breath is rancid, and I can only wish that they'd been picked up by cops for driving drunk.

"No, ma'am." I use respect, hoping it helps.

But it looks like they're enjoying what's transpiring.

"Let's make him really sorry," she says.

Mr. Richardson—Dick—throws me to the couch and pins me with his knee in my kidney. I feel the cool of the knife blade slide under the collar of my shirt, and Bitch cuts it in half down my back.

What the fuck! This is an entirely new MO for them, and I'm definitely freaking the fuck out! I hate men being so close to me … on top of me … behind me … so much so that I lose my sense of perspective and my self-control.

I struggle and try to kick up, but Dick laughs and puts all of his weight on top of me, pinning my legs and torso, with his knee driven deeper into my kidney, causing terrible pain.

"Captain of the high school wrestling team," he crows proudly.

Why do people take in kids if they hate them? The government doesn't hand out that much fucking money.

I can't take in a good breath. As Bitch is holding my head down and the knife against the back of my neck, I'm smothered within the filthy cloth of the cushion.

The most frightening part is that, as I'm sucking through the fabric for air and feeling the weight of

Dick on my back, my mind begins to dredge up the darkest waters of my soul.

I start to thrash. I know I'm in trouble.

"That's not going to help," Bitch says. "You need to learn a lesson."

The next sensation I feel is a thick, hard rubber tubing being lashed with terrible force across my exposed back. At the end of it is a piece of metal or something, and it feels like it's flaying my flesh open.

It hurts like nothing I know, and my scream is caught in the cushion.

I jerk my body up, more calculated this time. I almost throw Dick off when the whip comes down again, three times, fast and violent.

My body crumples against the couch in agony.

"Stay down! You piece of shit! We'd be doing the world a favor, snuffing out your pitiful existence."

I hear a crash above me.

"What the fuck!?" Dick shouts.

I realize I don't feel the knife on my neck anymore. I use the moment of surprise and lift up with every ounce of strength I've got and manage to throw Dick off of my back. He goes over but takes me with him. We crash down against the coffee table, which snaps under our combined weight.

Dick's breath is pushed out of his lungs as he cushions my fall.

"LIAM!" Quinn is yanking me to my feet. "Are you okay? Please tell me you're okay!" She's crying.

Between my oxygen-deprived brain, the resurrected monster in my thoughts and the stinging fury of my back, my mind is too addled to think coherently. I stumble back a few steps, but catch myself.

What's the damage?

Bitch is lying on the floor, motionless. "Did you kill her?"

"I don't fucking know!" Quinn yells, a frying pan dangling from her hand. "They were beating you with a piece of hose! They were going to kill you!"

Her eyes trail to the floor, where in the melee, a cut piece of thick green garden hose about twelve inches long lays like a dead snake. The metal screw-like connector is still attached.

"LIAM!" Quinn screams and points behind me.

Dick is back on his feet.

But so am I. And I'm hungry for blood.

My first blow cracks over his jaw, and I can hear the pop as it dislocates. As he tries to catch himself from falling, I pull him across me, knee him hard in the gut and push him away. He falls forward and sprawls across the floor.

"Make sure they stay down! We've got to get the fuck out of here, now!" I race back to the room and pick up our shoes and coats and my backpack.

Running through the living room, I tell Quinn to follow me.

"You'll pay for this," the Bitch hisses.

Guess she's not dead. Pity.

I lead us out the side door and down the alley so we stay out of the streetlights.

We run full-on until we're far enough from the townhouse that I feel safe enough for us to take a minute to get on our shoes and coats.

"Are you okay?" I check Quinn over.

She shoves my hands away. "Of course I'm okay! Are *you* okay?"

Her soft fingers pad the swell of my lip and eye. She's trembling. I take both her hands in mine to calm her down.

"They were going to kill you!" Tears spill down her face.

"It's not the first time, Quinn." If she only knew how many times the adults in my world had threatened my life.

She wriggles out of my hands and throws her arms around my neck, pressing against me in a full-body hug.

What if they'd succeeded?

I shudder and wrap my arms around Quinn's waist. Then, I lift a hand and sink it into her beautiful, comforting, golden hair.

"Maybe you saved my life."

LIAM
PRESENT

"You make no sense." Talon chastises me as I aim a dart into the red center of the target. "You've been pining away for a decade. Here she is, and you're going to be a douche?"

"Leave me the fuck alone, Tal." I throw the dart, but I'm off, and it hits the wall. The tip sinks into the plaster. *Goddamnit!*

"Jesus Christ, man, *she's here!*" he implores. "Don't bite the hand of fate."

"Fate doesn't give you anything but agony and heartache. It makes you believe in something good, or even great, and then it rips it away and watches while you bleed."

"You don't believe that shit you're shoveling, and you know it."

"It doesn't matter what I believe now or what I believed then; that's just reality," I say finally and fist my jacket off the chair. "I've got to let Bailey out before he destroys the house. We also have blind dates to get ready for."

"About that ..." Talon says. "Ryder canceled it."

"Why the hell did he do that?" I growl.

He just answers me with a stare like I'm an idiot.

"You know she has a life we know nothing about. Nada! She could be fucking *married*, for all we know. She could have kids!" I shake my head. "I don't know who that Quinn is."

"Bullshit! You know exactly who that Quinn is. Her life may have changed and her circumstances altered, but she's still Quinn. Beautiful, amazing, intelligent, demanding—"

"I KNOW!" I hurl the words at him. "Do you think I don't know? What am I, fucking blind?! I saw her! I saw the pain she's going through because of her mom and the pain *I* instantly caused her by my mere presence. And don't tell me you know what you'd do if you were me—you have no fucking clue!"

"Dude, you're a smart guy, always have been a born leader. You're closer to me than any brother could be. And when it's about Quinn, you always think with your heart first. When it comes to her, you've always had a sixth sense or some kind of direct line to her psychic energy. I don't care what people believe in—God, the Universe, themselves— you have a connection to her that's unexplainable. You're soul mates, you and Quinn."

I hate Talon.

"Right now, asshole, you're thinking with your brain—the injured, sore, unforgiving part. It won't tell you the truth. It will nurture your pain by feeding it pity."

Now I hate him more.

"Self-pity certainly tastes good, doesn't it? Mmm …" He makes a face like he's eating dessert or maybe pussy.

"Shut. Up," I say.

Then he throws a spoon at me. I dodge it.

"WAKE UP! You knew she was coming. You felt her."

"Goddamnit!" I find the spoon and chuck it across the room hard. It skips across the floor. "This is my place, Talon. You can leave if you don't like the company!"

"HA! I've put just as much sweat and heart into The House of Ink and Steel as you have. A name on a piece of paper is only ink on burnable tree pulp," he challenges.

"Fine, I'll leave you to yourself then." I stride toward the back door of *my* tattoo and piercing shop.

"Even this place is full of her," Talon says just before I get out the door.

I halt in my tracks.

He continues, "The House of Ink and Steel— the brothers of ink and steel—these …"

I turn to see as he lifts the hem of his t-shirt to reveal the *"I am my brother's keeper"* tattoo across his left rib.

Seven of us have it—me, Talon, Ryder, Josh, Chase, Connor and Reese. We were troubled kids who hated each other, forced under Cade's roof at North House. Quinn was always trying to make us get along, but it was her near-death plight that brought us together that fateful night.

Fucking-ass fate—I'd give up every one of my friendships with the brothers to have her back. I don't give a rat's ass if the idea is selfish, it's the fucking truth. And I would certainly give them all up in a fucking heartbeat if it meant she didn't have to suffer the way she did that horrible fucking night-mare night.

I feel the sting of tears pool in my eyes and blind me for a moment before they fall. Yeah, Talon is one hundred percent correct; Quinn is and always will be everywhere. And wasn't that the argument I'd been having with myself all day?

"I don't … I can't …" I stammer and squeeze my hands into fists. "How do I do it—with all of this rage and hurt and unreciprocated love inside of me—without breaking?"

"No one said you wouldn't have to break," Talon replies in all seriousness. "Might be the only thing that'll put the two of you back together again."

"Two halves of a whole, she used to say," I think out loud.

I take a quick glance at the wall clock. It'll be

dinner time at North House in a couple hours. She'll be there. Could I handle it?

"I've got to run Bailey and think."

"Remember to use your heart."

"Yes, oh spiritual master," I throw back over my shoulder.

"Don't forget it," he gets out before the door closes.

An icy wind rides up my shirt and swirls around me before I can get my coat zipped. I slide into my car and tear out of the shop's back lot.

I drive too fast to my house near Lake Nokomis.

Thinking straight is obviously out. Every thought, every word, every memory, proves to be alive and well in my psyche. It feels like a fucking hurricane of torment with Quinn as the eye of the storm.

Can I really handle going to dinner? At North House? And have every bit of the destroyed part of me thrown in my face—like a Technicolor replay?

I pull into my driveway and stalk like an angry, frustrated animal up to the house. I'm greeted immediately by Bailey, my all-black Newfoundland puppy, who, under a year old, weighs almost one hundred pounds. And try as I may, I can't stay mad when one hundred pounds of fluff and love comes to playfully maul me.

"BAILEY!" I open my arms, and he leaps up,

places his huge paws over my shoulders and licks my face in our I'm-home ritual.

"Come on, boy, I bet you want to go for a run!" I grab his leash off the hook, and we head off to the greenspace by the lake.

I know *what* to do; it's the what to *say* and *how to say it* that's stumping my pre-psychology play-through. It's a trick all professional athletes use—you visualize the fight—the opponent, how calm and confident you feel in his presence; you imagine yourself punching and kicking; you visualize each strike hitting its mark.

This is not the same psychology at all. I really want to speed dial my brother, Josh North—the Light Heavyweight champion of the UFC—and get into the ring with him. He'd give me the satisfying challenge I could really use right now to release these feelings and this pent-up self-fucking-pity … he wouldn't let any of that shit slide. But he's too busy right now to bother.

I'm on the UFC fight card against Milano a month from now.

First, you're on the fight card with Quinn Kelley in about half an hour.

CHAPTER FIVE

QUINN
OCTOBER
(PAST)

"Fucking snow! Not tonight." Liam curses the sky once we get away from his foster house and tries to figure out the new and almost as bad situation we've been thrown into.

It feels worse than if we'd been dealing with the cold all through the night; instead, we were warm and asleep just a couple hours ago.

The wind is blowing badly, too.

"If I was alone, I'd go to Randy's," Liam says. "Crawl through his basement window. But if his mom found me there with a girl … not good."

"Then, go on. I know where the bridge is!" I snap back, hurt.

"I didn't mean it like that. I was just thinking out loud—"

"That you'd be better off without me. Trust me, I've heard that one, Liam." All of a sudden, the cold doesn't bother me anymore. "You know what? Fuck this and fuck you."

Abruptly, I turn and walk the opposite way.

"Quinn!" Liam catches hold of my arm.

I scream, "Let go of my fucking arm!"

"What the fuck is your problem?" He shoves my arm down.

"You! You're my problem!" I get in his face. "I didn't ask you to take care of me!"

"I didn't say you did!" he yells.

"Yeah, well, you're acting like it!" It's not right, and I try to stop myself—he just had his asshole foster parents try to snuff out his life, and I'm going to be a bitch? "I'm not stopping you from going your own way. Go to Randy's! Maybe you can call Gina, and it can be like you've never met me!"

Fuck! I'm going to cry. I run away from him. I'm acting like a baby, but I can't seem to control my freaking thoughts or mouth!

"Gina?" Liam shouts at my back. "What the fuck are you talking about? And get back here!"

"None of that would have happened with your foster parents if I hadn't been there. You'd be sleeping in your safe, warm bed."

"That's ridiculous; he's been pulling me out of

that bed since I've been there—it was never warm or safe."

"Look, I'm really not trying to be an immature bitch. I'm serious. You're better off without me. You don't owe me anything."

"Would you just shut up? Stop talking like that! Jesus Christ! You're a real pain in the ass, you know that?"

"An even better reason to go our separate ways."

"Quinn, I don't want to go my own way. Friends don't do that."

"I haven't had many friends who *haven't* done that. Could be I'm just a loser."

"You're a pain in the ass, but you are definitely not a loser! You're anything but a loser."

"I don't want to be weak. This world isn't kind to weaklings."

"You just feel weak 'cause you're tired and have been fucked over so many times," he says. "You're not weak; you're not a loser. And what I said before about wanting a home and a family not being a dream … I was acting like a dick. They're perfectly real dreams … and maybe I want to help you get them."

I take a deep breath as Liam pulls me into his arms and holds me.

"Christ, you're freezing. Now stop fucking fighting with me, I have a good idea." He takes my bare hand in his and stuffs them both in his coat pocket.

I like it—the warmth of our skin together creates a thawing heat inside his pocket. We walk on the outskirts of the city for a while until Liam stops in front of a 24-hour laundromat.

We go in. It's so wonderfully warm.

As my eyes adjust to the bright fluorescent overhead lights, Liam leads us to the back of the place, next to the cement wall.

We carefully step past a homeless guy who is lying on the floor, bundled up in a blanket.

That makes me seriously nervous. Liam catches me eyeing the guy.

"I'm here; you don't have to worry."

I nod, then think of his back. We need to do something about those wounds before they get infected. Plus, I know he has to be in a lot of pain, even if he doesn't want to show it.

Looking around, I see a sink.

"Take off your coat," I tell him. "And turn around."

He does. The blood from his wounds has soaked through his t-shirt.

"We need to clean your back." I go to the sink and find soap and paper towels.

When I walk back over, Liam has removed his shirt and sits on the floor with his head cradled in his hands.

"It didn't hurt until we stopped running," he admits.

I move around him to examine his back. My heart lurches in my throat. He has horrible, swelling welts crisscrossing his back from the hose and jagged rips from the metal end. Gently, I clean the blood and sweat. I can feel Liam flinch, but other than that, he stays incredibly, eerily, still and quiet.

Silent tears spill from my eyes. At this moment, I hate the human race.

In the wake of such evil, it's hard to believe in anything or anyone good.

But then I think about how Liam and I protected each other and wonder, even if everyone else in the world is evil, maybe we can be good together.

"Thank you, Quinn." Liam's voice is soft and unsure.

I can't think of a moment since I met him when he sounded *unsure*. I want to comfort him, but I don't know the best way.

"It's good that you had your emergency back-pack ready." I open it and pull out a fresh t-shirt for him. "You should try to get some sleep."

"I've slept enough," he says with a far-off look in his eyes. "Here," he balls up his coat and sets it in his lap. "Rest your head. By the time you wake up, I'll have figured out another arrangement."

I think of something I want to do to comfort

him, but when I play it out in my head, it feels … clumsy and silly.

Forget it, I tell myself and lay down.

I feel the weight of his arm as he lays it protectively over me.

I can't not do it. I feel compelled. Sitting on my knees, I get face to face with him and lay my palm on his cheek. My body shakes with the action.

"I'm so sorry they did that to you. You didn't deserve it. And if I could take the pain from you, I would." I slide my hand away and replace it with a soft kiss before I pull back and lie down again.

I STARTLE AWAKE.

"You're okay, Quinn," Liam's voice reassures me. My head is still on his lap. "I'm sorry to wake you, but we need to get someplace safer before the sun comes up. The Richardsons probably called the cops."

"Okay." I climb to my feet, not very enthusiastic about having to go out into the cold. "How is your back?"

"Sucks, but I'll get through it," he says. "I found some gear in the lost and found crate."

After I get my coat on, Liam starts shoving mismatched mittens over my hands.

"It's too cold to go back under the bridge now, isn't it?" I ask.

"Yeah,"—he positions a black knit hat on my head—"but there's an old abandoned house we can get into a few miles from here."

"We don't have to go near …?" I ask cautiously.

"Vince's stomping grounds? Not a chance. I'm not taking you anywhere near that fucking place!" he guarantees, remembering what I told him about my encounter with the pimp and gang leader. "We'll lay low for the day, and when school gets out, I'll call Randy and see if he can let us stay at his place. His mom works a lot of double shifts at the all-night diner on 3rd Street. She usually brings home good leftovers."

I nod, and we step out into the cold.

We get a mile into our walk, when a police car goes by on the other side of the road.

Liam carefully looks behind us once it's past. "If we get separated, Quinn, get yourself to 411 Huron Street. No one has been living in it for the past year. Get into one of the upstairs bedrooms—stay out of sight and away from the windows. I'll meet you when it's safe."

"You think they're going to turn around."

"I think we need to be prepared if they do."

Adrenaline is rising through me. A moment later, we both see the blue lights reflected in the windows around us.

Liam says, "Run through Park Alley and then double back. Cut in between the houses and stay off the roads. Do you hear me?"

I nod. I don't trust my voice.

He uses his hand to tilt my head toward him. "I promise I'll come back for you." I feel the pressure of his lips press over the hat as he kisses my forehead. "Run now."

The second after I bolt, the cruiser's sirens howl, slicing and echoing through the early morning quiet.

I run as fast as I can and as long as I can without slowing down and pray to the angel that neither of us will get caught.

I follow Liam's instructions until I can't hear the sirens anymore. My lungs are burning, my side is hurting, and my muscles are aching when I finally have no choice but to slow my pace.

A yellow school bus picks up a group of kids waiting at a stop. I hide behind an old car and watch, burning with jealousy—jealousy that I'm not one of those kids, that I won't be going to school today or meeting Liam in the hallway for a stolen kiss next to my locker. I'm jealous that they came from their warm beds and protective parents who kissed them goodbye and told them to have a good day.

I sink into my hiding place and wait.

It's an hour later when I turn down the alley behind Huron.

I hang out for a while, watching the house. I don't see anything going on in it or around it, and there are no cars in the surrounding homes' driveways. Maybe—hopefully—everyone went to work.

Holding my breath, I move through the backyard and get to the doorway. The window on the door is shielded by a curtain, and I can't see inside. I work the knob carefully.

"Shit!" *It's locked!* "Now what?"

I'm at the back of the house—moving around to the side or front doesn't seem smart. I press my eyes closed and do the only thing I can think of. I knock on the door.

I practice what I'm going to say if someone answers. "Hey, I'm wondering if you saw a black kitten? We lost her last night." I whisper it over and over while I coax my heart to calm down.

No one comes.

"Okay, now what do I do?" I worry the inside of my cheek. I hope to God Liam is right, and the house is empty."

I find a rock and use it to break through the glass. Then, I reach in and turn the lock. Opening the door slowly, I put my head in first. This door goes to the kitchen, and I can see all the way through the dining room into the living room.

A big sigh of relief blows out of me.

There's no furniture. It's empty.

Carefully, I let myself in and close the door behind me. My heart doesn't stop pounding for some time, and I don't go any further, just in case someone does respond to the breaking and entering I've now gotten myself into.

Once I feel more secure, I walk soft-footed through the lower level. It's cold; I watch my breath steam in front of my mouth.

I'm confident no one is here.

Luckily, the water is still on in the house. First thing I do is use the bathroom; second thing I do is stick my head in the sink and drink from the faucet until my stomach hurts. There are no towels and the water is like ice, which means it tastes good, but there is no way I can wash up.

I tip-toe up the stairs. Honestly, I'm terrified. Just because the downstairs was clear doesn't mean the upper floor is. If Liam knows about this place, who else does?

The floor creaks, and panic races up my spine, but the sound is only from my own footfalls.

The quiet is eerie, and after checking through the barren bedrooms, I curl up like a ball in the closet in case someone else comes in from the cold.

I have nothing here to do or to entertain me. Since my mind isn't occupied, it starts wandering to crazy shit—like when my mom was gone for days on end. How I'd be afraid and do exactly what I'm doing now. I'd pretend that she came home, what she'd say—if she'd been a good mom—how we'd bake chocolate chip cookies, and she'd give me a handful of chocolate on the side. She'd hug me and kiss me on top of my head.

Liam kissed me on the top of my head. I don't think anyone ever has before. I don't remember it if they did.

Did he mean anything by it? Why would he have done it if he hadn't? What if he doesn't come back? What if he decides that I'm not really worth it and that it would be easier for him to go to his friend's without me? Maybe he was hoping we'd get separated all along.

"Oh God, what if he got caught?" I whisper into the dark of the closet. Would they hurt him? Would he be in trouble for defending himself against his foster parents? Would they even believe him?

I hug my knees to my chest. The idea of Liam in cuffs at the station, or even behind bars, could be a reality! He'd be gone. They'd send him to a boys' home, and I'd never know.

"Don't think like that, Quinn; it'll make you crazy," I chastise myself.

Oh, shit! What if he tells them where I am? That's what they do—they pressure and scare people into giving up information. That could totally happen.

I'm cold and afraid and tired—such a sucky combination. I stink, too. I want a shower. I want to change my clothes. I want to have something to eat because my stomach is growling angrily.

I want someone to tell me they love me and prove it.

Staying as tightly rolled as I can, I lie on the icy closet floor and rest my head on my arm. I imagine this house is filled with beautiful furniture and heat and delicious smells. I pretend I'm Liam's wife, and I just got home from work. I'm a school teacher, and he'll be home from work soon. He's a tattoo artist and even owns his own art gallery in the city.

I wake up abruptly. I hate that. I didn't realize I'd even fallen asleep. There is zero concept of time since it's pitch dark in here and the closet door is flush with the floor. But it feels like I've been here forever. I have to go to the bathroom. I'm about to move when I hear the familiar creaking of the stairs.

My heart pounds. *Liam!*

But then, fear injects into my veins. What if it isn't?

Footsteps come closer, and I hold my breath.

If it is Liam, why won't he call out my name?

Whoever it is, they're coming toward the closet. I can hear them getting closer.

If that door opens, I'm rushing out to knock whoever it is over. Maybe I can get away.

I hear the knob wriggling. I cover my mouth with my hands and fight the urge to scream.

When the door opens, a pinpoint of illumination from a flashlight shines in. I throw myself out of the closet and crash into a hard body. The light jerks and scatters, and I hear something fall and see a large pizza box slide across the floor.

"Quinn!"

"LIAM!?"

"It's only me!" Liam puts a hand over his stomach where my head hit. "Jesus, that fucking hurt!"

"Why didn't you *call my name?* WHY DID YOU SNEAK UP HERE LIKE THAT?" I shove him with both hands.

"Because I didn't even know if you made it or if you would've stayed this long," he says, checking to make sure the pizza stayed in the box. "It's bad enough I'm in here with a flashlight, I didn't need to be yelling."

"Yeah, well, next time, at least whisper, 'cause if I'd had a weapon, I'd have *used it!*"

He laughs, then gets serious. "You waited for me."

"Yeah, well, I started thinking you weren't coming back," I say. "Why did you?"

"Why did you wait?" he counters.

"I asked first."

"I promised I would." He reaches out and strokes the locks of my hair that hang out from the hat. "I always keep my promises."

I take that in. He really came. *But* … "What took you so long? Did you get caught? Are you hurt? And, oh my God, that pizza smells amazing!"

"Come on and eat, I'm sure you're starving."

I am!

Liam makes sure the curtains are pulled tight across the windows as we sit on the floor, the light between us only shining across the floor. Our faces are bathed in shadows as the two of us scarf down the pizza.

"I didn't get caught but came close to it. When you ran, I stayed so I'd be a distraction. Once I figured you were far enough out of the way, I made them chase me." He smiles like he's *all that*. He deserves to. He shoves half a piece of pizza into his mouth and says with a full mouth and a smile, "Now we're both wanted."

He looks totally proud of us.

Wanted by the law, on the streets of the twin cities in October. That's not a good scenario.

"Oh! I went back and got you this." He gets up, grabs my trash bag of stuff and sets it next to me.

"Oh my God! Thanks!!" I open the bag, shine the light inside of it and check the contents. "How?"

"Your hiding spot was a really good place to lay low until dusk when I felt confident about getting here."

"What time is it? And what happened with Randy?"

"Randy's mom is home tonight. He gave me a key to get in tomorrow when she's gone. We just need to be careful and keep you hidden. It won't be too hard—I've hidden there an entire month before." Liam dangles the key so I can see it.

"Too bad we couldn't go to California or Florida or somewhere warm. It would be so much easier," I muse.

"That could be arranged," he says confidently.

"How?" I don't believe him.

"Remember the treasure box I showed you— where I kept the money?"

"Yeah."

"I also have a lot of … hot items I can pawn."

"You're a thief?"

"Small time. Each foster home I'm in—if they suck—I take something of value I can get money for. If they're real assholes, like the Richardsons, I take extra and don't even feel guilty."

"That's how you got the pizza?"

"Yup. I have another way to earn fast cash, too. And a lot of it. Last year I tried getting a legit job, but no one would hire me. I am too young, had no address, and had no license or birth certificate. So I found a fight club downtown."

I shudder. Downtown is Vince's domain. "A fight club?"

"I'm tough and quick, so the gamblers like putting money on me. I made almost two thousand dollars this summer for only five fights!"

"Doesn't it hurt?"

"Yeah, but it's a pain I'm in control over." He eyes me intently. "Would you really want to go somewhere else? Somewhere warm?"

"I didn't think about it seriously." I stare into my pizza slice. "This is the first winter I've been out without a place to stay."

All of a sudden, my pizza is ripped from my hand, and Liam has me pinned to the floor.

"Stop being so serious!" He holds both my wrists in one of his hands above my head while his fingers press mercilessly into my ribs, making me laugh uncontrollably.

But there's another sensation besides the tickling. His thighs straddle my hips as he squeezes me. It sets fire to other areas of my body and causes me to ache for his touch in another way.

As if he senses this, he stops his tickle assault as our gazes pierce into each other. We're both out of breath and feeling a new, deeper tension.

He breaks it first. "There." Liam pushes up and

away from me. "Now … if we want to run away to Florida, there's nothing stopping us.

I remember him close to Gina, and a rush of jealousy makes my face hot.

"I can set up a few fights while we stay at Randy's. By next month, we'll have enough money to get the fuck out of here."

I grab my pizza, shove it in my mouth and mumble, "Sure you want to take me with you?"

He rolls his eyes. "Dumbest question ever."

QUINN
PRESENT

My fingers trace the grooves of the carving Liam knifed into the back of the headboard of what used to be his bed at North House years ago.

Liam and Quinn FAA

Forever and Always.

Who knows how many kids have slept in this very bed over the years? But it's still here.

"I never could replace it," Cade says from behind me as if reading my thoughts.

A bittersweet smile stretches the corners of my mouth. I remember Liam's love. I remember it every day.

Cade muses, "The two of you are like my own kids."

I know that's true. He gave us more love than anyone ever had.

"He hates me."

"He doesn't hate you, sweetheart, he's hurt."

The wood feels rough and splintered against my skin. That's what we've become toward each other —rough and splintered. I betrayed him.

"I can't make it better, Cade. He'll never forgive me." I let my hand fall to my side. "At least he's moved on."

Cade snorts behind me. "Girl, he has not *moved* anywhere."

I shove the bed back against the wall. "Yes, he has. He has an incredibly successful business with his art, is fighting professionally now, and has a string of women waiting in line."

I won't admit to watching every episode of *Ink Master* whenever he's been a guest judge or *Tattoo Nightmare,* where he's fixed botched tats. I won't admit to sitting two feet away from my flat screen during MMA matches, cringing when he's hit. And I *definitely won't* admit to actually attending his fights live when they've been in my region.

"It was so awkward, so icy." I think of our first encounter in Cade's office after all this time.

How could these emotions still be so strong, so acute? How haven't they faded?

The dinner bell rings.

I smile with the reminiscence it brings. "It's been a long time since I've heard that sound."

"Some things don't ever change."

Why do I feel like he's talking about something deeper? Something more than Debra's dinner bell?

Cade and his wife have been together forever, so it seems. I always looked up to her.

I always thought that Liam and I would be just like them.

Cade grips my hand. "Let's go. We don't want to make her mad."

THE DINNER TABLE IS EXACTLY THE WAY IT WAS TEN years ago. The ultra-long wooden picnic table stands in the middle of the large dining room. Six teenagers of varying ages sit around it. It's already set and prepared for the evening meal, with two baskets of fresh warm rolls and butter, two braised beef pot roasts, mashed potatoes and enough green beans to stretch across one hundred miles.

"I thought we'd have to eat without you." Debra smiles at us. "You're just in time to give thanks."

Cade and I sit. Debra starts us off. "I'm grateful for all of the beautiful people around this table and that each of them is here with us tonight, safe and strong and healthy."

Each kid says something—even if it's biting and

sarcastic. You can always tell who the new ones are. They're so full, they're dripping with unresolved feelings and gaping, painful wounds—emotionally and physically.

As they speak, I remember the "Core Eight." We were here at North House the longest, and except for me bailing, they've stayed friends. Right before I left, Liam even called them brothers.

I feel a nudge in my side. It's Ryder who stayed here with us for dinner. He's reminding me it's my turn for gratefulness.

I'm alive, doesn't sound particularly uplifting. And at the moment I'm not exactly sure I'm grateful for it either.

"I'm grateful for this good meal, shared by friends I've missed and new friends I'm just meeting." *How is that for thinking on my feet?*

Everyone digs in.

Between bites, I recall the memories of sitting at this table with Liam, Josh North, Ryder Axton, Talon Ward, Connor Callahan, Reese Colburn and Chase Diaz Wolf—and their antics. None of them got along—*ever!*

"Dude, give me the food," one of the kids snaps at another, waking me up.

Cade fires him a warning look.

The boy rolls his eyes but complies, albeit sarcastically. "Dude, *please* pass the food."

The giggle bubbles up through me, pushing

aside all the tension of the day. I can't stop it, as it becomes a full-fledged laugh attack.

The kids look at me like I'm crazy, but soon enough, it becomes contagious.

"Remember that night Chase and Connor reached out for the last roll?" I ask.

Ryder laughs. "Each of them swore they touched it first."

"And while they were arguing over who had, Reese swooped in and snatched it!" I throw my head back, cackling.

"Chase and Connor were like, *what the …?*"

Cade laughs, too. "And they both tackled Reese to the floor to fight for it."

"Don't get any bright ideas," Debra cautions the kids, who are now smiling and listening intently. "It's all fun and games until someone dents my silver tray over someone else's head."

"Oh my God, that was during the macaroni and cheese fight!" Ryder launches into the story. "We'd all been so edgy that morning. Cade and Debra were doing an intake for a new inmate … no offense," he adds quickly to Cade before he goes on. "We were sitting at this very table. Two huge mixing bowls of macaroni and cheese were on either side, along with a monster platter of hot dogs—"

"*Homemade* mac and cheese, from scratch, that Debra and I had spent close to an hour making," I remind him. "And don't forget the condiments; those were a big part of it. Squeeze bottles of ketchup, mustard and a basket of mayo packets."

Ryder laughs. "So at first, everything's cool, then some stupid asshole makes a lewd gesture toward Quinn with a hotdog—"

"Language, Ryder," Debra scolds.

"Sorry," he says.

The kids are enthralled.

"Liam burst up from his seat and threatened him."

"But then the idiot did it again," I put in, giggling.

"So Liam vaults his body over the table like a freaking torpedo at the guy." Ryder stands and does the hand motions.

I look around at the kids, grinning ear to ear. "The two of them went rolling across the floor and slammed into Debra's nice wood hutch.

All eyes go to the polished wood hutch, which is now on the far side of the dining room.

"Yes, we've rearranged since then." Cade takes a bite of potato.

"I don't know whose bright idea it was, but while those two were fighting, the rest of the kids started slinging handfuls of mac and cheese at each other." Ryder laughs. "Of course, it didn't stay just a food fight. Connor grabbed the ketchup bottle and tried dousing me before I hit him with it."

Ryder points accusatorily at me. "And you ran out of the room."

"To get Cade!" I cry in my defense. "Liam was going to kill the idiot."

"Always such a kiss-ass." He smiles affectionately and rolls his eyes. "So Josh must have started feeling jealous that Liam had found a new sparring partner because his new mission was to get Liam's attention. He started yanking on his shirt, but when that didn't work—"

"He hit him over the head with my silver tray." Debra, who hadn't been in the room at the time, looks like she's remembering the damage.

Everybody's laughing now.

And I find what I'm grateful for: childhood memories that are good, warm, and funny—even if they do involve people bashing each other over the head with dinnerware. We can look back on those times now and smile, knowing that those crazy incidents are where it all started—our love for each other—even if we didn't know it at the time. And I'm grateful for the people who gave me those memories.

"Then what happened?" one of the girls asks.

"Liam turned his wrath on Josh. And no one else has ever fought with the unmatched rivalry of Liam Knight and Josh North!" Cade smiles with exasperation, but there's love and pride in his eyes.

"WHOA!" the kids all chatter together.

Then a boy exclaims, starry-eyed, "Josh 'The Jackhammer' North and Liam 'The Legend' Knight fought together, right here, when they were our age?"

"Yeah, they did." Ryder smiles.

"And by the time I got back into the dining room with Cade—"

"They were all knocking the holy living hell out of each other," Cade joins in. "The floor and walls were covered with food."

"Oh God, you were furious." Ryder's gaze floats to Cade, and for a moment, he looks like the young teenager he was back then.

"I gave them all buckets and sponges and made them clean everything spotless while I took Debra out shopping so she didn't have to see it," explains Cade. "Also made them work off the money to buy her a new silver tray."

"Man, we all lost every privilege we'd *ever* had for two weeks," Ryder explains. "No phone, no TV, no Xbox, no nothing!"

"Did it keep you guys from fighting again?" one of the kids asks.

"No. Not at all." Liam's voice from the doorway makes me freeze in my seat.

"Hey, man, I was hoping you'd show up!" Ryder gets up and embraces Liam with one arm.

"Am I in time for dinner?" he asks.

CHAPTER SIX

LIAM
PRESENT

The butterflies in my gut are in full force as I take the seat across from Ryder. He's sitting next to Quinn, and his proximity to her makes my blood pressure rise. How can I still feel that way after all this time, like she's still my girl? Like she's still mine to protect?

"So glad you could join us, Liam," Debra says kindly and hands me a full plate.

"Thank you, ma'am." It looks delicious, and eating here at North House usually feels like the closest thing to home I've got, but tonight, with Quinn right there, I know the meal will be tasteless.

"They were just telling stories of when you lived here," one of the teens begins.

I eat here once a week, and most of the kids know me. Of course, new ones are always coming in.

"Yeah!" another breaks in. "Is it true that you and Josh 'The Jackhammer' North used to fight right here when you were kids?"

Ryder looks proud of himself.

"Let's change the subject," Debra interrupts.

The kids groan.

She moves the conversation from kid to kid, allowing them to tell the group what he or she did today. I start out listening and responding, but all too soon, I'm preoccupied with the way the light is caressing Quinn's hair.

I'm envious of the light and want to sink my fingers into her yellow locks, pull her into me and cover her lips with my mouth so I can swallow every moan I tease from her body.

She's still so perfect after all these years—tender and vulnerable with a double shot of toughness around the edges. She's exquisitely beautiful, sweet and polite. Quinn listens to each kid, genuinely caring, and I know she's still trying to save the world.

For a moment, her eyes meet mine; the flash of blue lasts for only a couple seconds before she lowers them back to her plate, but she blushes.

She blushed! My heart sings. I can't help but grin.

A strong hand squeezes my knee. It's Cade. He

doesn't look at me, but I know what he's saying. Lay off.

Before I realize it, the kids are clearing off the table and getting ready for the evening group.

"Hey, Quinn, have you got anything going on tonight?" Ryder asks.

She makes a pained face. "I have to go to my mother's house to go through her things before the estate company comes in the morning to take everything."

"We were going to go with her, but two new kids are coming in about an hour," Debra tells us. "They are an emergency case."

Cade says, "It's good timing that you boys are here. You two can take her. Make sure she gets back safe."

QUINN SITS NEXT TO ME AS A PASSENGER IN MY CAR. Never imagined that would happen in a million fucking years. My brain is acting like an old pinball game on tilt—full of chaos—everything going every which way. Her proximity both infuriates and intoxicates me at the same time.

And then there's Ryder, who sits in the back seat, spouting off about his bounty-hunting business and motorcycle gang and inflating his holy self to new heights. Usually, I don't give a shit when he does this—with other girls—but with Quinn, it's bothering me like bamboo being shoved underneath my fingernails. If he doesn't shut the fuck up, we're going to have a serious problem.

I want him to start thinking with his *other head* and ask her questions so I can know what's happening in her life without having to ask her myself. I know nothing, and I feel like if I try talking to her, it's going to sound like the Spanish Inquisition.

I can't imagine what's going on in her mind right now. She hated her mother. Why—*fucking why* —would she have come back for her funeral? And why, in all of hell's fury, would she want to go to the woman's house? It makes no sense to me.

Be sensitive, Talon's voice seems to say … *Give her space*, Cade tried to say …

I feel anything but sensitive or understanding. I'm furious and jealous and scared as fuck to find out that she's happy and married and has that family with the white picket-fucking-fence. I'm pissed, and the mercury is rising.

SHUT THE FUCK UP AND ASK HER ALREADY, RYDER! I want to shout.

But nope, we've gone over fifteen miles, and he still hasn't stopped.

Do I really want to know? I could just give the ride and walk away. Right?

Right?

Quinn laughs at something Ryder says, and I'm ripped inside out.

I know that laugh. I know all of her laughs, all of her facial expressions, all of her body language and signals. She hasn't changed a bit, not one fucking bit.

The laugh was her I'm-letting-you-think-I'm-listening-but-really-I'm-thinking-of-something-completely-other-than-you laugh.

Is she thinking of me? Is my presence having any effect on her, like hers is on me?

Here, in the tight enclosed space of the car, she fills my senses: her sweet scent, her soft breath, her heat.

"Dude! You just blew through that red light." Ryder laughs heartily at my blatant error.

Ha, ha. I want to step on the brake and watch him slam his face against the back of my seat.

"Yeah, I wasn't paying attention." *Motherfucker!*

"Remember you teaching me to drive?" Her voice cuts through my F7 inner storm of a tornado and drifts over me like a sudden spring breeze.

I remember and smile in spite of myself. "Of course, I do."

LIAM

NOVEMBER
(PAST)

"No, asshole, I did *NOT* say I wanted *YOU* to teach her how to drive. I asked to borrow your fucking car!" I seethe at my cousin Frank.

He's got the coolest car on mother fucking earth —a sleek, muscled-up, classic Ford Mustang—and Quinn loves it.

"My ride, cuz. Take it or leave it."

"Take it," I grumble.

Quinn is gorgeous, and every guy in a one-hundred-mile radius who gets even a glimpse of her knows it.

She, on the other hand, doesn't.

She doesn't understand the power she wields— beauty, innocence, kindness—she radiates it, and it's like a freaking magnet. She's not a stuck-up bitch; she doesn't use her prettiness as a weapon to get what she wants—not intentionally, anyway—but all the guys I know would bend themselves into a pretzel just to make her smile. Her problem is that, deep down, she still believes people can be nice. Naivety is one of the reasons she needs to be protected.

Especially from guys like Frank.

We're having a mid-November bonfire party at my cousin's house. It also just happens to be my sixteenth birthday, November 17th, but the douchebag doesn't care. I thought he'd let me use his car for an hour, but instead, he's going to push himself at Quinn—as if he stands a chance.

I took driver's ed at school last year . It sucks Quinn won't get that opportunity. Frank took me for my driver's test so I could get my license earlier today, so I guess I should be thankful, but right now, I'm just fucking irritated with him.

"He's being a dick," I tell Quinn once I make it back through the crowd.

"It was a good idea, Liam." She shrugs.

It's my idea to teach her to drive. She needs to know how to use a car; she lives on the streets, for Christ's sake! If she's ever in danger or in an emergency situation …

"I didn't say he said no …" I smile.

"Really? I get to drive?" she squeals like I knew she would.

"Happy half-birthday!" I tell her, and she hugs me, full of excitement.

I love that Quinn was born exactly six months after me, on May 17th.

"Come on."

I take her hand and lead her away from the crowd to Frank and his friends. They're a few years older than me, so we don't hang out much. Frank earned the tit car working at a restoration shop in the city. The lead mechanic took a shine to him and gave him an apprenticeship, and now

Frank works there full-time. I have to hand it to him; he's the one who made this car as kick-ass as it is.

"Hey there, Quinn," Frank says. "Liam says you want to learn to drive. So let's start."

This sucks. I'm holding her hand now, but I'm going to have to relinquish her to Frank. We stop at his car, and he tosses the keys to Quinn, who catches them quick. Understanding dawns on her face.

"No way." She laughs nervously. "I can't *drive* the Mustang. I don't know how to drive at all!"

"Yeah, I get it. Liam explained it all."

"I thought he talked to you about one of the junk cars at your shop," she argues.

"No way. A girl like you should learn on a car like this," he says, stroking the smooth finish.

I can't help but agree. "Just get behind the wheel. You'll get the hang of it fast."

Quinn looks to me and I nod my approval. She slides in behind the wheel. I walk over to the passenger seat, pull it forward and climb into the back. Frank slithers into the passenger side.

If he even thinks of touching her, I'm going to punch him so hard he'll have a free lobotomy.

Quinn sees the seating arrangement. "Liam, I don't want to do this without you up front with me."

"It's Frank's car. I don't like it any more than

you do, but I told you that you have to learn, and this is the best car to learn in."

"Thanks, Frank," she says, but the joy has deflated from her tone.

It probably doesn't help that she can see me brooding in the rearview mirror.

Frank switches on the XM radio, and Quinn backs out of the parking spot, tearing up the lawn. I have to laugh. It is Frank's dad's house, after all. But Frank doesn't seem too fazed as he begins doling out instructions.

We head down a couple dirt roads; Quinn is getting frustrated with how Frank's telling her how to go about it. He's no teacher, and she really is no driver. She still stalls the car and grinds the gears too much. Soon, she exhausts Frank's patience—not only is she not paying him any extra attention, but he's also probably starting to freak out over his drivetrain.

Pretty soon, we're back at the party.

"Sorry," Quinn says. "I told you I wasn't any good."

"You'll get it another time," he tells her, now distracted and looking into the crowd—probably for a piece of ass he can be sure of—it is getting late.

Douchebag. He would have stayed with it all night if she'd been flirting with him or if he thought he had a chance of scoring with her.

"Don't drink too much, I have an idea," I tell

her. She doesn't drink much at all in the first place, but I have to say it anyway.

"You always have an idea." She gives me a playful shove. "Sorry, I was an awful driver."

"You weren't awful," I semi-lie. "You had a lousy instructor."

"Doesn't matter anyway, it's your birthday after all. And *this* is for you." She reaches into her coat pocket and pulls out a small black box with a gold bow. "Happy sixteenth birthday."

I stare at it … dumbfounded. "You got me a gift?"

"Of course! It's your birthday," she says with a glowing smile. "Open it!"

Carefully, I take it from her sweet hand, but I know I could stay suspended in this moment with her forever and not care one bit about the box's content.

My mother and grandparents never once gave me a birthday present. In fact, my birthday had never been celebrated at my house.

"You have to untie the bow," she says, all sassy.

I untie it and lift the lid to find a rugged wrist-band made with a black braided leather cord strung through a series of black and silver beads and knots.

"Quinn." I'm fighting all the powerful emotions that are crashing over me, like when the plates of the earth move and crash together deep under the darkest parts of the ocean, causing a tsunami to be unleashed.

"Do you like it?"

"Yeah, I love it." I've been trying to toe the line with her; I don't want to blow this friendship we have. But I know beyond every doubt that I have crashed into her hard.

"Awesome! Let me put it on you?"

"Alright." I'm all about her as I hold out my arm, and she happily fastens it around my wrist.

"It lies just right! I was worried it might not fit," she confesses. "I was also worried you wouldn't like it. And I can't quite tell by your expression." She squints up at me dramatically.

We can see each other just fine in the golden glow of the bonfire.

"The band is awesome," I reassure her while admiring it.

It's a simple gift ... Oh, but it isn't. It's so much more to me.

"You look serious. You're wondering how I got it, aren't you?" she says. "I didn't steal it."

"I wouldn't care if you had," I answer truthfully.

"When you were off doing stuff with Randy, I collected bottles and cans. Made thirty-two bucks!" She sounds proud of her endeavor. "And ..." She goes into her backpack and lifts out a small to-go style food container.

"Hold that. But don't peek!" She presses it into my hands. "Don't sniff either," Quinn warns while she looks in her pack.

"Whew! Here they are." She snatches back the container. "Did you peek … even a little?"

"And incur your wrath? Not a chance. No, ma'am." I wonder if she can even begin to understand what I feel right now.

Like she's the real gift.

Softly, she begins to sing the song "Happy Birthday to You," and as she turns, she reveals a massive gourmet cupcake with blue frosting—my favorite color—with M&M's candy, which is laid out in the number sixteen. She lit a long blue candle and is protecting the flame from the air at all costs.

She finishes and says, "Make a wish."

Can I wish that my birthday could be this incredible every year?

"Hurry before the wind blows it out!" She laughs. "You must have a wish in your mind."

I do.

I blow it out.

She squeals joyfully, and I'm so happy we're doing this away from the party. It's just the two of us.

"What did you wish for?" she asks, removing the candle from the cupcake.

"I thought you were the birthday expert … you know you're not supposed to tell."

She crinkles up her nose. She doesn't like that answer.

"Fine. Bite." Quinn has unwrapped the paper cup from around the cake and is holding it up for me to try it.

"Is it chocolate?"

"Yeah, it's chocolate."

"Are you going to smash it in my face?"

"I thought about it, but no. That'd be a waste of the deliciousness," she tells me. "So, come on and bite."

I don't close my eyes. I keep them locked with hers. She blushes, and it makes her even more beautiful.

As I sink my teeth into the moist, sweet cake, thrilled over the glow of her soft, blood-rushed cheeks, all I can think about is how I'm a sixteen-year-old boy who is totally in love with the girl in front of me.

"Good?" she asks.

"The best," I reply with my mouth full. "Your turn."

I take the cake from her and feed her a bite. Before long, we're laughing and trying to get blue frosting on each other's noses.

"Thanks Quinn … for all of this."

She nibbles thoughtfully at her bottom lip. "You're welcome."

Frank's parents are gone for the week on a

cruise somewhere tropical, which means a weeklong party and a place to stay to give Randy's a break. It's never good to stay in one place too long. People get tired of doling out hospitality after a while. So we hang out for another hour, and I watch Frank win a shots game against a friend, where they polish off almost an entire fifth of tequila. That's when my brilliant idea goes into effect.

I decide I'm going to "borrow" Frank's car without telling him. He'll get over it.

"Congrats on the win, man!" I slap his back hard.

Frank catches himself, his drunken gait unsteady. He slurs, "Oh yeah!"

Oh yeah! I think.

He never feels my fingers hook the keys inside his thick coat pocket. I give him twenty minutes before he passes out. He'll never know his car was even gone.

I go get Quinn. "Oh, Quinn," I jingle the keys. "Look."

She considers me skeptically. "How did you get him to relinquish those?"

I lie very convincingly. "He said you'd be better off learning it from me after all."

"Cool!" she crows happily.

We settle into the supple black leather seats. Her hands grip the steering wheel excitedly before she turns over the ignition.

"You focus on the feel of the clutch and gas pedal. I'll keep one hand on your knee." Innocently, I rest my hand on her leg, but it sends tingles firing through my nerves, up my fingers and into the veins of my arm.

Having been together for over a month now, we almost always have our hands linked, and we hold each other while we sleep, but we've never taken it any further than that. *I've* never tried to take it any farther. We have a good thing, and I don't want to fuck it up. For me, *I* feel this indescribable power *every* single time I touch her, but at this moment— maybe because of her gifts, or the extra dose of adrenaline from me knowing I'm stealing Frank's car or the combination of the two—it's even more intimate, more electrifying.

"Liam?"

"Right!" I snap to. "When it's time to shift, I'll press on your leg; that's your signal to engage the clutch. My other hand will stay on your shift hand." I place my hand over hers, spreading my fingers around her fingers until I feel the gear shift.

What the fuck is wrong with me tonight? Now I'm shaking.

Literally shaking!

And it's not from the cold.

"I'll work the shifter with you until you *feel* the way the car moves and *works* underneath you. Nice and easy. It's just like sex." It slides out of my mouth so fast I can't take it back. And dear Christ, I can't think of any way to soften the meaning.

"Like *sex*," Quinn repeats slowly and deliberately. "It seems like a great metaphor, but it's somewhat lost on me since I have *nothing* to compare it to."

Holy fuck! What is she saying? Her words and tone are full of something. How am I supposed to read into that?

Before I can figure it out, she jacks us into reverse, and then, with a few jerky pulls that make us lurch back and forth, she gets us out of the driveway.

I can't fucking believe I said that. *It's just like sex.*

We get some distance down the rural dirt road, and I realize neither of us has said a word since the "sex" screw-up.

I turn and check behind us for traffic, even though it's like one in the morning, and we're in the sticks. "Okay, you want to slow down and stop so we can practice sliding into gear."

She does.

"Now, just push the clutch all the way to the floor until you get the hang of it because if you don't have the clutch right, the gear can't get into place."

"Right, to get it into gear, you have to ready the clutch," she repeats the instructions.

She shoves the gear stick forward. The grinding metal whines in protest.

"No. Too hard and too fast," I say. "We're not in a hurry."

"Sorry." She tries again, and I wonder how loud the screaming metal is *outside* of the car. "I can't do it!" she cries out in frustration.

"Yes, you can. Try again," I reassure, but I'm pretty sure my ears are bleeding.

She grinds the gears a few more times, until I don't think I can take it anymore, then all of sudden she engages it smoothly. She beams the proudest smile ever.

"That's right," I praise.

"Oh my God! I did it! I did it!!"

"Yeah, you did!" Her happiness is catchy.

She drives a few miles up the road. Her steering is impressive for someone who has never driven. "You're a natural."

"Thanks."

"Try turning up here to the left," I tell her.

"Okay, clutch, shift, brake to slow down …" she says to herself.

"Good turn." I nod.

That's when she tries to put it back in first gear too fast. Her clutch-to-gas ratio suffers so badly that the car jerks forward, throwing the two of us up into the dashboard.

"What is wrong with you? I didn't tell you to do *that!*"

"Don't shout at me!"

"I didn't shout at you!" I shout.

She lands a look at me like she's going to shove me.

"Pull the fuck over," I say.

She does and lets the car idle, folding her arms over her chest. And even though she's angry, her bottom lip juts out into the sexiest pout.

I blew it. "What did you expect?" I try.

"I expect you not to shout at me!" she yells.

"Okay, fine. I was an ass."

"Yes, you were," she agrees. The anger dissipates a bit, but the pout doesn't change.

Keeping the engine on, I pull the emergency brake up and take the car out of gear. "We're going to try this another way."

I turn my whole body toward her, anchoring my right foot to the floor while kneeling with my left on the seat. "I'll keep one hand on your gas leg and the other on your clutch leg. I'll put pressure on or pull up in proportion to how much you need press down. Practice. Ready?"

Like working a puppet, I pull up and push down on Quinn's soft, denim-covered legs. When I'm satisfied, I look up from watching her Chucks working each pedal.

I'm right in her face—nose to nose.

I can feel her warm breath over the tender skin of my lips.

She's staring right at me.

I'm lost, swimming somewhere inside her blue eyes. Involuntarily, my fingers squeeze the flesh of her legs. My dick grows behind my jeans without permission, and my heart races hard.

Just like sex.

Her sweet mouth falls open as her lips part. She's holding me with her eyes, and I can't move. I can't think. I'm frozen.

The shaking that subsided while I concentrated on her driving is back.

"Don't you even *want* to kiss me?" she asks.

The tone of her voice is timid and shy … but it's something else, too. *Don't you even* want *to kiss me?*

It's the inflection on the *want* that has my brain grasping. "What do you mean, don't I even *want* to?"

Her eyes drop for a second, but mine don't. I watch her desperately.

"You've had over a month of chances to kiss me," she says. "And you never have." Now she meets my eyes again, and this time, they're filled with a million questions. "I know you *like* kissing. I know you've *had* sex. Aren't I … pretty enough to want to … try with?"

She doesn't think I think she's *pretty enough*? She doesn't think *I want to*?

Don't you even want to kiss me?

After so many all-night talks, I know she's never been kissed; she's never been *touched*. But she *doesn't* know about me, how dirty I am, how used up. I want to think differently of myself, I do, even if it's only for her, but she's this pure white, loving creature, and I'm a filthy, soiled beast.

I don't want to contaminate her. I can't.

I close my eyes. "Quinn, there is nothing and no one as beautiful as you."

That's when I feel her hands grip around both my wrists. We're wearing nothing but t-shirts since we took off our jackets once the car heated up. Her hands travel up each of my arms, leaving a trail of unquenchable, needy fire.

The air struggles through my lungs, and I can't look at her. The darkness of my past—that starless night—threatens to crush me.

"I love you, Liam." She says it so softly that I may have missed it had I not been paying attention.

I love you, Liam.

Of the three people I have ever loved, two of them—my mother and grandmother—never said it to me.

And Quinn … I love her more than my own life.

Her soft, unsure hands smooth over my shoulders, simultaneously releasing and building tension with each muscle she glides over, until she reaches my neck and places her hands up under my hairline, drawing me closer.

How is it that I believe she can fix what has broken me?

I don't believe in God.

I don't believe in the love of a mother or father or of grandparents.

I do believe in Quinn.

"Please, open your eyes, Liam."

Her request is so small, but I'm afraid of it shattering me, of it shattering her.

Damn it, damn it! But even though the war rages inside of me—the past, the present, the future —I'll do what Quinn wants and asks of me—every time.

Slowly, carefully, I let my eyes open.

Oh God! She's so close I can taste her. I taste her desire and need; I taste her fear and trepidation, and I sample both our pain and salvation mixed together as if our redemption could only be found in each other.

My fucking blood is boiling, my dick is throbbing, my heart is pounding.

As I take her mouth with mine, it's so unbelievably good that it hurts.

Her lips are so soft and warm; her hands are loving and gentle.

Soon, I remember myself and rest my forehead

against hers. I'm so overwhelmed. I can't open my eyes, can't look at her or face her.

"Quinn …" I sigh. "I can't keep kissing you like this."

"Why not?" She's out of breath, and I like the way it sounds.

"Because," I say, my lips just hovering over hers, "I'll want more. I'll want you to be my girlfriend."

Neither of us pulls away.

"I've never been a girlfriend."

That makes me smile. "I've never had a girlfriend."

"You've had plenty of girlfriends."

"I've had plenty of girls," I assure her, "but never a girlfriend."

"Liam …"

"Quinn …" My eyes are still closed.

"Kiss me again."

"I can't."

"Did I do it wrong?"

"No, you did it *too* right."

"Then let's do it again," she insists.

"I told you I'd have to make you my girlfriend."

"Then make me your girlfriend."

My eyes open fast. "You want to be my girlfriend?"

"Yes. Especially if it means you'll keep kissing me."

"Quinn, this is serious."

"I *am* serious," she says. "Remember when this started, I was the one who said I loved you."

I'll never forget. It's etched into my memory forever.

"Being girlfriend and boyfriend means commitment. It means we belong to each other—no other guys, no other girls—nothing, and no one can come between us. It means we love ,and we fight, and we love again. We fix it, whatever it takes."

"I like that. And it sounds like what we're already doing."

"I guess it does … it also means we don't leave each other, either. We can't, 'cause we're all we've got."

"I promise I'll never leave you, Liam," Quinn vows, our eyes burning into each other's. "I promise nothing … and no one … will ever come between us. I promise to love you forever. We're two halves of one whole."

I put my hands on either side of her perfect face. Her eyes reflect everything I feel.

My emotions are everywhere at once, but as I close my eyes, lean into her body and press my lips against hers, everything I feel—everything I've *ever felt*—culminates at this one point, releasing all of my energy, all of my darkness and all of my light into this moment—where Quinn and I become one perfect star as our souls fuse together.

CHAPTER SEVEN

QUINN
PRESENT

I shouldn't be here.

I shouldn't be in this house.

I shouldn't be here with Liam.

So what am I doing here?

What am I looking for?

I don't know. I thought maybe I'd feel it and know it when I touched it. Now that I'm here, the thing I was most afraid of—that dark, endless abyss that threatens me every morning when I wake up and every night before I close my eyes to sleep—is all around me.

For a decade, I've tried to outrun it. I've done the psychotherapy to vanquish it until it's nothing but a memory. Truth is, it created who I am, who I was. It's the chiseling force that has dug a crevice so deep inside my soul I can't climb back out into the light.

The boys are behind me. They stand uncomfortably inside the doorway. I know they'd pull me up if they could—maybe if they could find the rope, but there isn't one. I cut my safety line ten years ago.

As I walk down the hall to the kitchen, I hold out my hand and let my fingers trail along the wall. The old paper feels tacky from age and cigarette smoke. The ceilings are stained yellow. But the real stains this place holds are only visible to me. Maybe they're painted in my eyes.

Quinn, what are you doing here?

Trying to find the piece of me I lost.

You don't restore those things by going back, only forward.

It's a lie. It's a lie I tell myself to comfort myself so I don't really have to face my pain or my demons … the monsters that swallow me during the darkest nights.

I can't go forward until I … I don't know.

It's all the same inside this house. Exactly the same as the last night I was ever here … and the months before that.

I try to conjure a good memory, something happy, something I can take with me, but I can't remember clearly; I can only feel. And what I feel is fear and hurt.

The dining room table still sits stately in the middle of the room. Six chairs of smooth dark wood and velvet cloth stare at each other, empty and wordless. The matching wood hutch with glass cabinets is still filled with my mother's favorite displays—the things that made her feel wealthy and affluent. That's all she ever really cared about—things. If she ever cared about a person, I never saw it.

She never loved me.

And isn't that the hardest and heaviest memory you have, Quinn?

"Did she have a will?" Ryder asks.

"If she did, I wasn't in it," I reply.

Truth is, I don't even know if me being in her house is legal.

What do I have to lose? I've already lost everything.

I walk through to the living room. Two large, white leather sofas flank each wall; glamorous photographs of my mom line the mantle over the fireplace, her ice-blue eyes staring back at me coldly. Beside them are a cuckoo clock and crystal knickknacks. A hanging lamp with three women standing back-to-back in a garden is suspended in the doorway. There are thin cable lines that run down around it, and when it's turned on, oil drips down the cables to mimic rain. It's sort of pretty, really, but I hate it. I get a sick feeling in the pit of my stomach every time I see one.

I wonder if other people do that—see some benign object from their haunted pasts and associate it with an unwell, malaise feeling that's too hard to describe.

My eyes spy the bookshelf.

The old photo album is still there. I stare at it as if it were alive, like maybe it was being guarded by a demon that I'd have to battle and kill just so I could touch it.

"Fuck this," I hear Liam curse. He says it softly as if he doesn't want me to hear.

A moment later, he's beside me.

"You want that book." It's not a question.

My throat constricts, and I fight the tears that rush to my eyes.

How well he knows me.

I nod.

Liam leans forward and grabs the album. He tucks it up under his arm.

I feel him watching me.

"Is this all you want downstairs?" he asks softly.

I nod again.

The tears spill over my face, but I'm not sure if they fall because of my mom or because of Liam.

"You want to go up to your old room?" Liam places his hand tenderly on the small of my back.

The hurt and loss bubble up through me and make me cry. I try to do it as silently as possible, swallowing each sob.

"Come on, I'll go with you."

Why is he being so nice to me?

He's become yet another person to whom I'm a massive disappointment.

I nod anyway, and together, we silently walk toward the staircase. We begin climbing each stair slowly, following the blue carpet up to the landing. But I freeze. I'm only a few steps away from my room.

"I don't think I can do it," I whisper.

"You can do anything, Quinn." His tone is infused with admiration.

He holds his hand out to me.

But I can't move. I just stand there, looking at it, remembering its strength, the love that used to be attached to it, and the incredible rush of feelings I'd get every time I touched it.

I think of how badly I really need it right now.

How badly I need *him* right now. But I might crumble if I take it. I might turn to dust and blow away. Or maybe a miracle will happen, and I'll wake up, and the past ten years will have all been a dream, a terrible nightmare. And I'll be able to avoid the series of events that further destroyed me and sent me reeling so deep inside of myself that I couldn't even let Liam in.

I hold my breath and, like a child, wish beyond all probability that the latter might actually happen.

"You don't have to do this alone." He takes my hand and laces our fingers together.

Oh, the feel of his hand, the firmness of his grip, the security.

I can't stop the tears. He smiles down reassuringly at me before he leads the way up the stairs, promising to take on the waiting monsters.

I want to kiss each of his fingers and then lay his palm over my cheek to catch every cold and bitter tear I've cried without him.

Before I know it, we're standing at the threshold of my room. The one she told people she kept for me in case I ever came home. As long as she looked good for the people outside looking in, what really happened didn't matter. She didn't take any responsibility, hadn't even worried about me, and never said she was sorry—she never thought she did anything wrong. She had no sin to atone for.

"You want to go in?" he asks.

I shrug. Not a thing has changed since I left here at fourteen years old. The antique-looking brown and white flowered lace bedspread still lays over the twin-sized canopy bed as if it had been freshly made this morning. The white desk and bookshelf still sit against the wall. A paint-by-numbers picture I did when I was ten is still displayed exactly where

I set it, next to my pink and white Hello Kitty pencil sharpener.

"They don't seem real," I say. "I thought maybe I'd remember one good thing, something—a bedtime story, a kiss goodnight—but I don't. I thought coming and looking would make a difference."

The sorrow is momentarily pushed to the side by a blistering anger. "I know what it was … what I was looking for … some shred of evidence that maybe, in the end, she loved me or that, at the very least, she was sorry."

I walk over to my desk and open the drawer, rummaging through it. The contents have been untouched for years. I push aside erasers and cartoon-covered pencils; I finger through pink paperclips and old magazine cuttings. I come to my own folded notes, the ones I had written to her. Letters from a little girl and, later, a teenager who declared how much I loved her and missed her when she was away at work. Me asking her to spend time with me as well as my ideas for things I thought we could do together.

I used to leave them all around the house for her. But she never answered them or even moved them, so I'd fold them back up and bury them in my drawer—like the bones of skeletons I couldn't let go of.

I fish them out now. They're all folded into tight

squares and have *MOM* scrawled in my very neatest handwriting.

I gather them into my open hands, which I've shaped like a bowl, and offer them to Liam. He gives me a sympathetic look and takes them from me.

They're paper that weighs a ton.

All of a sudden, I've had enough of this room that's frozen in time.

I stalk out of my room and into *her* room.

I *hate* being inside this house, but I *loathe* being in her bedroom.

Chills run down my spine, and it takes every bit of courage I have not to run out.

I won't leave here until I'm satisfied, either way.

When I received the call from her co-worker Louise, whom I had never met, telling me that my mom had died, my first response was, *How did you find me?*

Not exactly proper etiquette.

Behind me, Liam clears his throat. He's not rushing me; it looks like he's dealing with his own emotions.

"She died of Leukemia," I say out loud. "I found out after the fact. She was buried in Grove Cemetery, you know, the one closest to the city's mansions. That old woman she worked for left her a nice inheritance when she passed away."

I dig through her desk drawers, her chest of

drawers, her jewelry box, under her bed, between the mattresses, everyplace intimate I can think of, but see nothing with my name on it, no personal notes, no diary or journal, nothing that said she loved me.

That she ever loved me.

I'm sure I'm missing it. I'm not going deep enough.

"It has to be here," I say stubbornly.

"What are you looking for, Quinn? I can help you look," Liam offers.

"Something … something important." I'm starting to paw through her clothes. To make sure I'm thorough, I start pulling clothes and shit by the fistfuls from her drawers and drop them onto the floor. "You know, a letter. Something that she would have written when she knew she was dying …" *To make amends, to say she was sorry. To say she loved me.*

I chance a quick glimpse over at Liam, who wears a worried expression.

"You know, you can wait downstairs if you want. I'm sure this is a real inconvenience, standing around watching me." I swing open the double doors to her walk-in closet. "Sorry, Cade forced you into babysitting duty."

Her closet is smashed full of gorgeous, designer and name-brand clothing and shoes. The things she took care of meticulously for years, so now, not a thread is left out of place.

I sink my hands into the deep pockets of the full-length mink coat she loved.

"Nothing here." I rip it from the hanger so it falls, crumpled, to the floor.

"I wonder if these silk blouses have pockets?" Violently, I wring each shirt, dress and pair of pants, feeling the pockets and then ripping the piece of clothing from its hanger and throwing it onto the floor.

"Quinn …"

"She had to have written something. She had to have left a note or a fucking code, a signal, *something*!"

When I'm done with the clothing, I move to the hat boxes and other boxes that line the upper shelf. I yank one down, knock off the lid, look through it, and then drop it and move on.

"Her friend, or co-worker, whatever, when she called me, I asked her how she found me," I explain like a lunatic, throwing anything in arm's reach to the floor. "I asked her if maybe my mom had talked about me or expressed a desire to make contact … especially while she was so sick." I laugh, and it sounds frightening to me. "She got real quiet. You know, that uncomfortable silence that happens when you don't know what to say? She finally told me that their mutual employer had called her and told her she remembered me being claimed on my mom's old income tax forms and health insurance at one time. They found the files with my name and hired a private investigator to find me."

I've finished in her closet, so I start again by her bed.

I pull the paintings from the wall, letting them fall to the floor. "They found … my name … on some decade-old tax file! They didn't even realize she *had* a daughter." I rip the bedsheets away from the mattress and then shove them off, away from the box spring.

"She *NEVER* even mentioned me—at all! She effectively made me *DISAPPEAR* from her very existence! How very convenient for her!"

I'm screaming and sobbing and trashing everything.

"Quinn …" I feel Liam's hands grip my shoulders.

I pull away. "It's here!"

"It's not here, Quinn." It sounds like he's crying, or maybe I'm just hearing myself. "Please, let me take you out of here."

"I CAN'T GO UNTIL I FIND IT!"

He wraps both his arms around my shoulders and chest from behind. "You have to stop."

"She didn't even leave anything for me … nothing … because I was nothing!" I break down in his arms.

He holds my weight. "Quinn, you were everything … you *are* everything. She was just too blind to see it."

I fold in against him, and we collapse to the floor in the middle of the mess I created.

"HOW? I only wanted a letter! I only wanted her to talk to me!" I lurch forward and shout a guttural, wild cry, consumed by the agony I've held inside of me all of my life.

"I'm so sorry." He holds me tighter, but he's crying because of my pain.

"How can I be all grown up and still crave her love so fucking much? Still want her to want me?" I rock back and forth in the safety of his embrace. I know Liam; he won't let go. "I haven't grown up at all … not really. I'm still that unwanted, unloved little girl, begging for her mommy to make it all better."

"Just because she doesn't love you," he tries to whisper calmly in my ear between his own sobs, "doesn't mean you're not loved. You are irreplaceable."

QUINN
JANUARY
(PAST)

"Where's Liam?" I ask Randy as I shuffle into the kitchen.

"He ran to the store," he tells me. "Something about the fight tonight and needing protein."

"That's right, it's Saturday," I say, wiping the sleep from my eyes.

Liam and I have been hiding out in Randy's basement off and on for the last couple of months. Liam has tried to find work all over the city and was able to pick up some temporary, odd jobs that paid under the table, but most people won't hire underage kids without proper identification or school permission papers. It's almost February, and the money he's made hasn't been enough to get us somewhere warmer, so now he's going to resort to the illegal street fights to earn funds.

I don't like the idea at all, but he thinks it's the fastest way. Two bus tickets and money for food and lodging, and when we get there, we can figure out the rest—that's what he says.

I pour myself a cup of coffee and sit down at the table, grateful Randy's mom is at work.

"Have you been to one? Of the fights, I mean?" I sheepishly ask Randy, who I don't think will tell me anything. He doesn't like me much; I think he's mad that I talk Liam out of fighting as much as I do and because he spends so much time with me.

"Every one Liam's been to." He's typing on his laptop and keeps his eyes on his task.

"What are they like?" I peer up over my cup.

Liam is more than vague when I ask him what goes on, and he's made it clear I'm *not* accompanying him there.

"Imagine the city's rival gangs and mafia underlings in one seedy place, pushing monster-sized wads of cash back and forth between them and raising their angry fists, yelling at the opponents like their life depends on how they fight," he says, undistracted.

"Does it?"

Now, Randy's gaze lifts over the laptop screen. "Fuck yeah, it does. But I don't think Liam wants you to know everything that goes on there."

"I won't tell him."

He pushes the laptop out of the way so it's not between us.

"Most of the time, they hold the fights in the old warehouses near the river, down by the railroad tracks. I've seen as many as five hundred spectators show up at one time. They tape a circle in the center of the floor to suffice as a ring. Some guy stands in the middle and introduces the first set of fighters—there are usually six sets. After the first six sets are finished, the winners then fight each other —a best of the best," Randy explains.

My heart rests a bit in my chest. "That's not *so* bad."

He laughs. "The spectators are on the ground

floor where the fighters are and make a nearly impenetrable human wall. If a fighter tries to get out of the ring, they push him back in, and not without getting a few of their own hits in on the unfortunate bastard. Oh, yeah, and there's no tapping out. You're either left standing, which means you won the set, or you're knocked out, which means you lose, and you're dragged out of the ring and left to the mercy of the crowd."

I'm horrified.

He continues, "These guys aren't big on mercy, plus they're all pumped the fuck up on adrenaline and drugs, and they'd just as soon stab you as push you off to the side." He shrugs. "Not to mention, if they had money on you and you lost? They're pissed."

"Have … people died?" I stammer.

"What the fuck do you think?"

I nod.

"That's why I go. If Liam gets knocked out, I make sure my ass is right there, ready to grab him," he says. "He's been lucky—he wins a lot—so when he does get the shit pounded out of him, the guys are more lenient. Not that he hasn't been knife slashed or had his ribs broken by a few angry assholes who put in their shots while I was dragging him."

Randy studies my expression. "You're going to tell him, aren't you?"

I shake my head but wonder if Liam might have a death wish. Is there really no other way to survive and get out of here? We could hitchhike. Hell, we could walk!

"You know, Quinn, I like you," Randy begins, but the nasty glint in his eyes betrays him. "You're a nice girl. But Liam is seriously bad news. He's almost gotten you arrested because of the fight at his foster home, and the truth is, he runs in dangerous circles. These guys he fights for are heavy fucking hitters. Liam told me about Vince and how he tried recruiting you."

At the sound of Vince's name, my blood chills.

"Liam's never fought for him or any of the other local gangs. He's good enough to get to fight for the mafia guys."

"Mafia in Minneapolis?"

"Don't be so naïve, Quinn. They come from Chicago and Detroit to show off their best street fighters—usually recruited from their local gangs." He scrapes his chair back, and the sound makes me jump. Randy walks over to the fridge and grabs the carton of juice.

I watch him guzzle it down as I sit, dumbly silent.

He wipes his mouth on his sleeve. "Liam's only been fighting for the past year and likes to think of himself as an independent, but the mafia guys like him, so they 'contract him' for their teams. But the way loyalty runs in these circles, he'll have to choose a side and color sooner or later. He keeps saying no, but tensions are only getting higher, so it's really just a matter of time."

"That doesn't bother you?" I shriek. "Aren't you worried about them killing him? Haven't you tried talking him out of it?"

"Fuck no! Liam loves fighting." He laughs. "And he's great at it!"

Then I understand; Randy must win a nice purse with each fight. So maybe he's not really Liam's friend. Maybe Liam is just a cash cow, and it gives Randy status.

An overwhelming terror crawls up my skin. *I really am … all alone.*

Liam's words have been nice and all, but the reality is he lives a life with one foot in with the gangs and city thugs. That's why he wouldn't tell me about fighting.

The omission feels like a lie. A lie that could destroy him … and destroy me too.

What did he get himself into?

What the fuck have I gotten myself into? Months of barely surviving, at the mercy of other people for food or a place to sleep or a warm pair of boots. Now I'm hiding in a basement. Until what? Until Liam can get the money for us to go down south to Florida? I don't want him to get money this way! I don't want him to fight ever again!

They could easily kill him tonight!

I'm so fucking confused!

The thoughts that claw and rip through my mind are unsettling and more than disturbing. I'm so afraid for him, and I feel sick to my stomach, like I'm going to puke up the coffee I just drank.

On top of that, I feel like Liam's betrayed me. How can I trust him?

And Liam going to that fight doesn't help us. He could die. He knows he could die! Or he could decide to go with a gang or mob from another city … they could even force him to!

I WOULDN'T EVEN KNOW!

What the hell would I do without him?

At this moment, I think I could die. It feels like I'll die—my insides are squeezing and churning—and for the first time since finding Liam, I feel lost again. Maybe more lost than I've ever felt.

I want to go home.

I want to go home so badly! That's all I want. To feel secure, to feel my mother's arms around my shoulders, to hear her tell me everything's going to be alright. I'd do anything for that right now. *Anything.*

"Randy, can I use your phone?"

He says he doesn't care and goes back to the world of his laptop.

I'm not here anymore. I don't understand the way my body feels. It feels empty—like I'm floating.

In the hallway is an old wall phone. I hold the receiver in my hand and stand close so I don't stretch the cord too far as I dial my mother's phone number.

My teeth grind together as I anticipate the sound of her voice. I can't make my heart calm down. I haven't spoken with her for months, and I'm freaking out!

I try to rehearse my words ... if I can say the *right thing* ... *maybe* she'll let me come home.

I miss her. I miss my mom; I miss the smell of her shampoo, the sound of her voice ... I miss the way it would feel if she would hug me.

"Hello."

I freeze at the sound of her voice.

What if she just hangs up? What do I say to keep her on the line?

"Hello!" I'm making her annoyed by not answering back, but I have this pit in my stomach, and I'm so scared.

"It's ... it's me ... Mom."

Silence.

My eyes squeeze shut. I hate silence.

"Why are you calling me, Quinn?" She sounds put out.

"I ... um ... wanted to talk ... to you," I stammer fearfully. She's not happy to hear from me, not at all.

"Talk then, I haven't got all day," she snaps.

"Yeah, okay. Um, I was thinking that … um, maybe I could um …"

"For Christ's sake, what do you want?"

I push each word out of my mouth. "I miss you."

More silence. Blistering, frenetic silence.

As it echoes and reverberates, it is swallowed into the darkness of my mind.

"Can I … come home … please?"

I had wanted to hear her voice so badly. I had wanted her to say, *Quinn, I love you so much, please come home.* But now I know it was a terrible mistake.

My very life is nothing but one mistake after another.

I'm a mistake. I know she's going to say it. She always says it.

"Why would I want you here?" my mother says, her voice low and harsh and serious. "This isn't your home, Quinn. It's mine. I should have had an abortion when I found out I was pregnant with you. You're the worst mistake of my life."

The darkness grows hungry, hungry for my blood and soul, hungry for every thought, good or evil, like a black hole sucking all of my matter and energy into itself—turning me darker and blacker and making me unreachable. I feel myself being pulled toward the lightless, lifeless cavern of nothing.

My heart pounds, desperate.

How can anyone love me if my very own mother doesn't love me?

The truth is miserable and simple: no one can.

The phone receiver slips from my hand and dangles lifelessly from the gray cord it's attached to, like a dead body hanging from a noose.

I know what the black hole is now; it's my death.

I'm gone. The essence that is Quinn is gone, forced away from the furthest reaches of my physical form.

It spirals into the black hole. That hole is hell. Real hell, not the biblical hell that tortures an eternal soul but a palpable hell, where the flames lick at your sanity and promise to obliterate your very existence so that there is nothing left … not even ash.

I streak from the hallway, through the kitchen and out the front door.

My feet pound the unforgiving pavement of the road. Hazily, I register the sensations jarring my legs. My physical form moves on its own … fueled by the deepest culmination of pain, rejection and heartache … there is nothing left for me here in this world.

I turn the corner.

The darkness knows exactly where it's taking me.

My fingers grip the woven steel mesh of the

highway's overpass safety fence. I jam the toe of my sneaker into the metal hole as far as it will go and hoist myself up.

My other foot finds purchase.

My body is more than halfway up the fence. The vehicles speed down the highway below me.

I make a final plea—that when my body hits the ground or a car, no one else gets hurt.

"I never wanted you. You're the worst mistake of my life."

My right leg curls up and around the barbed wire fence. The barbs pierce through the denim fabric of my blue jeans. It hurts, but I know it won't hurt much longer.

I think I hear my name, but I'm probably imagining it. I'm not turning back now, anyway. I've come so far.

I feel strong hands with long fingers grip painfully around my waist and heave me downward.

I try to hold on, but it's too much force. My fingers are torn away from the cold steel.

I land hard on the frozen ground, tangled around another body.

"WHAT THE FUCK ARE YOU DOING!?" Liam screams into my face. "WHAT THE FUCK ARE YOU THINKING!?"

The jolt of the ground wakes me up. The trance is broken. But now I can't answer him. I can't even look at him. I'm so ashamed of myself in so many ways …

"GOD-FUCKING-DAMN IT, QUINN!" he shouts. "ANSWER ME!"

I writhe on the ground. I'm ashamed that I would kill myself, disgusted that I failed, and sick because all the emotions I was trying to escape are crashing in on me with an unstoppable force.

Liam grasps my upper arms, forcing my face up, and shakes me violently. "FUCKING ANSWER ME!"

"I CALLED MY MOTHER! I DON'T WANT TO DIE!" I yell. "I DON'T WANT YOU TO DIE! I JUST DON'T WANT TO FEEL ANYMORE! I just want the pain to stop. And it's never going to stop! I'm going to feel like this forever!"

"Why did you call her, Quinn?!" he implores.

My lip quivers, and I begin to shake and cry uncontrollably. "I just want to go home! I need to go home! I want my mom! But she doesn't even *want* me. She hates me." I can't stop the flurry of thoughts as I bring my knees up to my chest and wrap my arms around them. "She reminded me, in no uncertain terms, that I'm her worst mistake, that she should have aborted me when she had the chance. I've heard it all before, but somehow … I guess I thought maybe since I've been away from home as long as I have been, she'd change her mind. She'd miss me. I knew I shouldn't have called her … I don't want to feel this." I rock myself back and forth.

"Quinn." Liam pulls me into his arms and holds me tightly. "Quinn, look at me."

I try to gather the courage to look into his face, but I feel embarrassed. I want to run away and hide, but there's nowhere left to run.

He sets his hands behind my ears and around my head and forces me to face him. "Open your eyes." His voice is different; it's choked.

I do what he asks. Tears are falling from his eyes.

"Just because your mother doesn't love you doesn't mean nobody else does!"

"What does that mean, Liam?"

"Exactly what it sounds like."

"Who? Who loves me? No one loves me."

"I love you, Quinn! I love you." His thumbs stroke my cheeks as he searches my eyes. "You are irreplaceable."

He's so beautiful and strong and sincere, and he makes me want to believe there can be something good in this world. He crushes me against him, hugging me so hard I can barely breathe.

"Promise me you won't *ever* do that again!" he shouts and cries at the same time. "You *promised* you wouldn't leave me, and killing yourself is most definitely *leaving me*!"

"And what about you fighting? Isn't that the same thing?" I whisper, afraid to make the only person who may love me angry at me and, at the same time, not able to stop myself. "I know what it is. I know the danger you're in."

Liam lets out a long, deep sigh. "Yeah, I suppose it is just like that."

"If you love me, please don't go through with it. We don't need the money. We could hitchhike or something," I try. "As long as we're together, we can do anything, right?"

He leans back away from me, and I know this is the part where he tells me to go fuck off and walks away.

"I already booked the fight, Quinn," he says, stroking my hair. "They'll come and find me if I don't show up."

My brain races for a cure. "There are six fights, right? I'm sure fighters have to cancel for … something."

"The only way you get out of it is if you're in the hospital or in jail," Liam explains, wrapping strands of my hair around his fingers.

Those aren't good options.

"Hospital or jail means police, and police mean I could get charged with assaulting the Richardsons."

"Even though they attacked you? And you were defending yourself?"

"Who is going to believe that? It'll be my word against theirs."

"Unless I speak up."

"Then they throw you into St. Anne's. I don't want you in a place like that," he says. "I'd have a better chance of doing my time and then finding you once I get out."

"We could run," I say. "Right now. Turn south and just keep going."

He considers me. "Is that what you really want to do? We'll be hand-to-mouth, with no help and no money."

"I'm positive," I assure him. "I can't stay here anymore." I need to be as far away from her as possible.

"We'd have to leave now, today before they come for me," he says.

I nod. "I understand."

Liam helps me back onto my feet. "Okay then. We'll get our stuff and go."

We're both freezing, neither of us have a coat on. He takes my hand in his, puts it to his mouth and blows warm air over it.

"Do you mean it?" I ask.

"Whatever I say, I mean."

"So, you love me?"

"I definitely love you."

I lay my head on his shoulder as we walk back to Randy's.

"Remember, if anything goes wrong inside of you like that or your emotions are fucking with you and you're scared, talk to me—about whatever it is. Don't ever run from me, and never, never give up your life. That would kill me."

I tearfully nod and hold on even tighter.

We get up on the sidewalk, closer to the house, when I see a brown paper bag of groceries that looks like it was haphazardly dropped to the ground. A carton of eggs is busted open, and they're oozing onto the concrete. Liam stoops over and carefully salvages what he can.

I know it's my fault. That was money and food wasted.

I swallow. "Liam, I'm—"

"Don't say it," he interrupts me. "You've got nothing to be sorry for."

I stand quietly, biting on the inside of my cheek —a bad habit I have when I feel nervous.

He picks up the bag, and we step into the house. Randy's still sitting at the kitchen table with his face buried in his laptop.

"What have you guys been doing?" he asks impatiently.

"Nothing. Hey, Randy, I've got to talk to you," Liam says.

"Yeah, what's up?"

"Quinn and I are going to take off."

"You have to leave for the city by nine o'clock," Randy reminds him.

"That's what I'm talking about. Her and me, we're going to blow town, get someplace warm, start over."

"What the fuck, man? You can't just fucking leave. This is a big fucking fight tonight." He stands from his chair, confused.

"Yeah, that's why it's better I'm taking off right now," Liam states with confidence. "Don't worry, man, we'll be out of town hours before the fight. They'll never know I'm gone until it's too late. I'm going downstairs to get our stuff. Thanks again, man, for letting us crash here."

"No problem." Randy looks unenthusiastic.

Liam and I go to the basement and start stuffing our belongings into our packs.

"It would have been nice to make something hot to eat before we took off." He shrugs. "But fuck it, we'll bring what we can and stop for cheese-burgers along the way." He smiles at me. "And don't worry, we still have some cash left."

I manage a weak smile back. Truthfully, I'm physically and emotionally drained. I'd like nothing more than to lay here under our blankets and let him hold me and kiss me in the warm safety of our pretend house. I dig deep for some reserve strength; I know I'm going to need it tonight.

We wash up our hands and faces, getting rid of

the tear streaks and grass stains, and change out of the wet clothes we rolled around on the ground in, putting on warm layers of fresh clothes to keep us going through the night.

Once we're packed and ready, we head back upstairs. Liam says goodbye to Randy. I thank him, too, and he walks us to the door.

The moment we step outside, we notice the disturbingly out-of-place black Cadillac parked across the street.

Liam eyes it cautiously.

The front passenger door opens. A big guy gets out and opens the back door.

"Keep walking, Quinn," Liam tells me.

But it's too late.

"Liam," I whisper. "That's Vince, leader of the Westhill Cartel!"

"Randy, what the fuck did you do?" Liam seethes.

"Man, I have five hundred dollars riding on you tonight," Randy admits.

"You sold out your friend for *five hundred dollars?*" I spit.

"Why the fuck would you call Vince?" Liam's hands keep pressing into fists as we watch Vince and his two thug cronies follow him into the middle of the vacant street toward us.

"It's easy. You're supposed to be fighting tonight *for* Tommy Bonito from Chicago *against*

Vince Ortega's guy. I don't have Bonito's number …"

"So you called Vince 'cause he'd be losing money," Liam finishes.

"Looks like you're going on a vacation, Knight." Vince's words ooze out like slime.

"Just checking out of this douchebag's hotel."

"Weren't going to skip town on fight night, were you?" Vince's fake nice guy tone is frightening.

"Why the fuck would I do that?" Liam stiffens his back. "You shouldn't get your information from an asshole; all you get is shit."

Vince laughs, but it sounds sinister.

That's when he turns his attention to me. "Hey, pretty little bitch. I haven't forgotten you still owe me."

"I don't owe you anything!" My voice shakes.

"You know, Knight," Vince begins. "I just came up with a plan that might allow you to live. I'll keep the girl with me as collateral, and once you show up tonight at the fight, I'll give her back to you." Vince licks his lips as he looks me up and down. "She'll be more—or less—intact."

His words and intent send chills shooting down my spine.

Vince's two goons come forward, closing in on me as if I'm simply an object to take.

Liam steps directly in front of me. "Call them the fuck off, or I'll light you up right here."

"Now that's the fighter I want to see," Vince states with a lift of his chin. "It'll be great entertainment to watch my guy kick the living fuck out of you tonight. Unless, of course, you're already dead because these guys kill you first," Vince says. "Get the girl."

Liam doesn't wait for them to get any closer. He runs at the bigger of the two and slams his fist into the guy's face.

The second guy closes in on him and sends a right hook into Liam's ribs.

Liam recovers, turns and elbow jabs the guy in the throat, which makes him back up and gasp for air.

I start screaming, praying someone will hear us, see what's going on out here and call the cops.

That's when Randy grabs my arms. "Shut up!"

I knee him hard in the balls.

"Fuck!" The single word squeezes from his lungs as he turns pale and buckles to his knees on the blacktop.

"Asshole!" I punch him in the face.

When I turn back around, Liam has Vince's guy on the ground and is pounding his face in, but the other guy is recovering from the throat hit and is moving back in.

"LIAM, WATCH OUT!" I cry.

Vince is leaning against his car with a wide grin

on his face. He looks at me and mouths the words, *You. Are. Mine.*

Liam bounces up and off his opponent.

"We don't want any trouble, Vince." Liam points his finger at him.

"I think you do." Vince is still smiling.

"I'll come with you now and fight tonight," Liam says. "But you don't *ever* bother the girl again."

"You're giving *me* a stipulation?" Vince laughs.

That's when the guy who'd been socked in the throat comes up and lunges at Liam with a long switchblade. Liam moves quickly to evade it, but the knife still catches his upper arm and slices a deep gash. Almost immediately, crimson spreads down the arm of his shirt.

"NO!" I shout and run forward to him.

"Quinn, stay back!" Liam yells at me, holding his good arm out like a barrier.

I halt in my tracks.

At that moment, the guy brings his knife hand up again, this time in a high arc. When it comes down, Liam spins out and away from him, pivots back up close and pummels the guy in the gut.

Then, just as Liam begins to pull back out of reach, the second guy bursts over and grabs him from behind, securing his arms in a hold so he can't punch or hardly even move!

"NO! STOP IT!" I scream.

I watch as the knife guy jerks up his arm and slits Liam wide across the belly.

Liam uses the guy holding him from behind as leverage, jumps up and kicks the knife guy in the gut with his boot. Then, he smashes his foot hard behind him on the thug's instep. He turns and punches the guy so forcefully across the chin that the momentum throws him to the ground.

But then I see it. While Liam is still turning away from the guy on the ground, the guy with the knife comes up behind him fast. I can barely form the words of warning before the knife plunges into his side.

Liam howls in pain.

"LIAM!" I scream.

I think he's going to drop, but he doesn't. He just looks angrier, spins around and punches the guy in the crook of his elbow, causing him to drop the knife.

When Liam lifts his knee to slam it into the guy's stomach, blood spurts from his wounds. He grips the guy's hair, shoving his head down, and rams his knee into his face. The guy flies backward and crumples to the street.

Both of Vince's assholes are on the ground, Randy is run-crawling back to his house, and I can hear sirens approaching.

"This isn't over," Vince promises as he walks over to the driver's side of the Cadillac and tears away, leaving his gang members broken in the road.

Liam stumbles toward me. I catch him, but he's so heavy I can barely hold him up.

"Help me to the stairs." He indicates the neighbor's front step. Once we're there, he half sits, half falls. "You have to get out of here."

"I'm not leaving you!" I cry. He's bleeding horribly! I drop my pack and pull out a t-shirt.

I press it to the worst of the wounds—the puncture where I think the knife could have gone all the way in!

He grabs my hands. "Yes, you are."

I shake my head and ignore him, focusing instead on the blood, his blood, soaking the balled-up t-shirt and now spilling over onto my hands.

I hear myself crying. I don't know if the knife hit any major organs! *He could die from this!*

His hands grip mine with urgency. "If you don't run, Quinn …"

"Maybe St. Anne's won't be so bad," I lie.

"Quinn—"

"Shut up! Just shut the hell up! I'm not leaving you!!"

"Look at me," he says gently.

I won't.

"Look at me, goddamnit!"

I force my eyes up to his. And I'm so fucking

frightened that I'll never see those ocean-colored eyes again.

"Run. I will find you."

I'm sobbing. I can't leave him! How can I leave him? What if they don't get him the help he needs?

"I can't leave you like this," I whisper.

"I can't get to you if they put you in St. Anne's. I'll be okay. I always am. Lay low for a little while, and I promise I will find you."

The sirens are so close. But there's so much blood. All of his blood!

"Go!" he begs me.

I shake my head.

"NOW!" He shoves me.

I run over to where we dropped our packs when this all started and throw mine over my shoulder.

I look at him one more time, knowing it could be the last.

"Go. Hurry," he tells me and looks so sad and stern at the same time, as if he's trying to talk himself into staying resolute.

I know he's right. But I hate it. We have no options.

I turn away and run, wondering if I'll ever see him again.

CHAPTER EIGHT

LIAM
PRESENT

As I pull the car up to my house, I see Josh's car taking up half my driveway. I wish this was a coincidence, but I know the almighty hand of Cade must have moved. That saying, *Be careful what you wish for*, comes to mind. I wanted to fight with him. He's going to want to talk.

After I park and turn off the engine, I sit quietly, listening to the sound of my own breathing and remembering how she was sitting here next to me just a little while ago.

Confused as fuck, I'd been torn between my own selfish wants and desires. I wanted to hurt her, to break her like she did me, wanted her to know the damage she'd done. But, then, there was the girl—no, woman—standing before me like a dream, and all I could think about was holding onto her and never letting her go again.

Of course, there's the miserable reality that she's dealing with, causing like ten different levels of premium agony.

I wonder if I fit in there at all.

I know her being so near to me with so much unresolved is like … fucked up, unfathomable cruelty.

I can't believe I said that to her … the same words I did when we were kids.

After she was satisfied with going through her mother's things, I dropped her back off at Cade and Debra's. I watched as she walked up the steps, stopped and looked back once before going through the door.

That look … it was all I could do to stay in the car. My body, my mind, and my heart still react to her like they always have.

"Want to go out for a few drinks? I know you could use one," Ryder offered right after I dropped Quinn off.

"I just want to go to my house and try to get some sleep. I still have a fight to prepare for."

"Right, Milano."

Ryder didn't pry; the night had been excruciating enough. He took off on his bike—crazy son of a bitch. I'm thankful he was there, though. Tonight, I know he has both of our backs.

Sitting in my driveway, I'm not ready to face Josh … or maybe I'm just not ready to let go of Quinn.

I think maybe, at the very least, I helped her get through the vortex she was getting sucked into tonight. Other than that, I feel like a helpless bastard hanging onto a cliff from a weak, breaking branch.

My hand floats to the passenger seat of my car and rests where she had sat. I know I must be a lunatic, but she was here, just two feet away from me.

My phone bleeps with a text message.

> Get the fuck outta the car. I have a 4:30 am run!

Josh.

I roll my eyes and reluctantly pull myself away from her warmth and scent.

Walking into the house, Bailey comes to greet me. Josh is sitting with his feet up on my kitchen table, drinking my beer.

"Some watchdog you make," I scold, scratching behind Bailey's ears.

"Oh, yeah, there is nothing like being slobbered on and furred—sort of akin to being tarred and feathered only much more—"

I'm tired. "What are you doing here? And you better have saved me a beer."

"Of course, I didn't drink all of your beer, and you already know why I'm here." He tips the bottle straight up.

I go to the fridge and grab one. "Which one called you?" I pop the bottle cap.

"Yeah."

Of course. "All of them."

"How is she?" he asks.

"She's wrecked over her mother's death." I sit down at the table across from him. "But I can't say I understand why. The woman was a frigging monster."

"Yeah, that's not what I meant." He's giving me a look like I *should* know what the fuck he meant.

"Then what?" I grumble.

"I mean, how is *she*? What's she been doing with herself?"

I don't say anything.

"Did you bother to ask her?"

My vision focuses on a spot on the wall. "No, man, I didn't fucking ask her."

"Ah. How did I know?" Josh quips.

"Asking would have meant I wanted to know," I tell him. "And honestly, I don't want to know … alright!?"

I shove my chair back, stand and begin pacing the floor.

"Do you think I want to know if she's happy?" I snap at him. "Hey, Quinn, haven't heard a fucking word from you for ten years, so how's life? Did you get to graduate? Bet you're married. Bet you have two cute little kids and a house out in the country!"

I kick the chair with my boot so it takes a noisy tumble across the floor. "Bet you're fucking happy without me! Is that what I was supposed to ask her, Josh?"

I want a fucking cigarette, and I don't even fucking smoke anymore!

Not wanting to hear Josh's answer, I force the front door open and stalk out onto the porch.

Don't know what good it does me. I stare up at the night sky and only see her anyway.

I lean a shoulder against the porch column and take a pull off my bottle. Bailey comes out to the porch and flops his body down behind me.

"It's obvious she's moved on, and I haven't. Do I really need to hear her say it?" I mutter into the night when I see that Josh has followed me out.

He sits on the step.

"Man, you have no idea where she is in her life."

"I know that what finally brought her back here *wasn't* me."

"I can understand how you feel that way."

"It's not the way I *feel*; it's a cold, hard fact," I retort. "And today it was like, *poof!* She's right there, as if I've been sleeping for the last ten years and suddenly woke up, and it's just like any day where no time has passed." This conversation sucks.

"You still feel connected." Josh nails it.

"Completely," I admit. "When Cade made me take her to her mom's house … and I was near her … I knew her thoughts, I could still read her signals, and it was like I could still feel what she's feeling ..."

"So what's your plan?"

"I got nothing."

"Want to get shit-faced?" He sounds excited at the prospect.

I laugh a little. "No. You know I have a fight with Milano coming up."

"You want to go open up the gym and spar?" he asks. "I mean, it's only one in the morning."

"Shut up, Josh." I shake my head.

"Fine. What's on your schedule tomorrow?"

"I'm tattooing a full sleeve all morning," I tell him. "And I have training in the afternoon."

"I have a thought …"

"Of course you do."

"I'll get a call in to Quinn, and if she's up to it, I'll take the two of you out to that new Japanese restaurant. They make some amazing yakitori, and I can be a buffer between the two of you. She'd probably appreciate the distraction with everything going on."

"Yeah, 'cause you and *buffer* go together synony-mously," I quip sarcastically. "Maybe you should take her to lunch with Ryder. He seems excited to be with her."

"He was just overcompensating," Josh says, excusing him.

How should I answer? Dinner at North House with everyone isn't the same as going out with just her and Josh.

"Dude, forgiveness is tough but not impossible," Josh says.

I want to bite back and say, *Easy for you to say*, but it's not easy for Josh. I know him and pain and forgiveness had a very fragile relationship not too many years back. But still, I don't know if I can do it.

"She didn't leave because she wanted to," he reminds me. "She was dying."

I close my eyes against the agony of memories that threaten to overwhelm me. "Okay. I'll do lunch if she does. Happy? I'm going to bed."

Bailey follows me upstairs and lies on the floor beside my bed. I lay with my hands folded behind my head, staring wide-eyed at the ceiling.

Another hour passes, and sleep is a thousand miles away.

I can't take any more! *I've got to get her out of my head!*

Jumping up, I trip over Bailey on my way to the

bathroom and get dressed in layers for an ice-cold February Minnesota run.

I check my watch. Three a.m.

I sneak out quietly so I don't wake Josh, who's crashing on my couch. Outside, I put in my earbuds and put my iPod on shuffle, hoping to drown out every thought till my head is clear. Theory of a Deadman's "Hurricane" pulses through the buds, and I run. Whether it's away from her or toward myself, I can't tell.

The late night-early morning air circulates through my lungs, and the freezing ache is comforting.

And as hard as I try to hold onto my pain and anger toward Quinn, Josh's words about Quinn dying before she left hit me square between the eyes. If I had been fully honest with her, would I have spared us both a decade of misery? Would it have made a difference?

Could it have helped her?

The guilt and shame I feel is saturating my psyche. Isn't that why I put all the blame on Quinn?

I'm still not sure if it would have brought us to the other side if I'd told her.

And what about now, douchebag? I ask myself.

I don't know about now. All I know is that I feel everything so sharply. It's all-encompassing, like arrows of each emotion being driven through my body. Anger, fear, hate, shame, guilt, pain ... and love.

So much love.

Love that has never faded or died.

I do once around the lake and decide to drive to The Core. Maybe throwing punches, like Josh suggested earlier, would be better than running.

I let myself in the back door and into the private therapy room, which has equipment and a kitchen area. Sometimes, we come in here when a kid is really troubled—one-on-one—work it out, cool down, make a protein shake and talk. These walls have heard a lot of stories.

Might as well add my own.

I blast Nine Inch Nails on the docking station and pound the living shit out of the bag.

"This is what I do, right?" I say to myself. "I fight. I fight for what I want, what I can't have, what I don't have."

I fight my past, and I fight against my future. A future without Quinn.

Time will get you over her, they said.

You'll fall in love again when you're ready, they said.

They were all wrong.

Only Cade gave me advice that kept me going: *Focus on yourself and make yourself healthy.*

I've done that. For years. Now what?

Now this!

She's all around me now. No more imagination

buffer, no more saving grace, just send in the tsunami and break the levee because I'm going down!

She's so painfully beautiful.

Sweat drips from my head down my nose and chin as I pound the bag, trying to relieve the building combustion inside of me. I feel the sweat roll down the center of my back, soaking my shirt. But I can't … hit … the bag … hard enough to satisfy the anger!

The rage fills me, encompasses me, but it won't come out, won't release me, won't let me go. *It will never let me go.*

Fuck this! I use my teeth to rip at the Velcro straps that tether the gloves to my hands, protecting them. I don't want protection! I want the pain.

I spit the gloves to the floor and hammer the leather until I feel the familiar swell and break of the skin around my knuckles. I'm so fucking grateful for the crimson climbing my forearm.

I blame Talon. *It's a sign.*

Dreams suck! They're not premonitions or a picture of something better yet to come. They're psychological tortures that come when you're sleeping and defenseless! *You've somehow managed to shut me up and put me down throughout the day while you did all the shit you could to distract yourself, but now you're all mine, asshole. Oh, how I'm gonna fuck with you!!*

"Liam …"

What the fuck?! I whip around. The air rolls tumultuously through my lungs, making my chest heave. *Quinn??*

"What the hell are you doing here? It's fucking four thirty in the morning!" I bark at her.

Her eyes travel down to her boots—like she's scared … or ashamed, maybe. Maybe I'm reading into it.

Stop looking at her! I shout at myself and turn my attention back to the bag.

You're my everything, Liam.

Lie!

"I was hoping I'd find you here." Her voice is small and quiet against the buzzing fury in my ears.

"Yeah, well, here I am," I snarl.

I'm nothing without you, Quinn.

True!

"I thought … maybe … we could talk," she says.

"I've got nothing to fucking say." It's official, I'm an asshole.

Left, right, left, right …

"Yeah. I kinda figured that."

God, her voice sounds the same as it used to; the tones curl around and make love to the words like a melody.

Focus!

"I can't … um …" she starts, stumbling through her thoughts.

"I don't have time for this, Quinn." I'm furious with myself! *Why didn't I tell her?!*

"Yeah, okay." She goes quiet, and I think maybe she turned and took off.

My body panics at the thought, and without my conscious permission, I wrench my head around.

She's still here.

FOCUS!

But I can't, can I?

This is my life without you, Quinn! Take a good look at the broken, annihilated man you've created!

"It's been a long time," she says innocently.

But it pisses me off to the stratosphere. "A long time," I echo vehemently. "How did you get in here, anyway?"

"Debra let me borrow her car, and I saw yours parked out back." She shrugs. "Cade gave me a key."

Of course, he did.

Quinn continues, "I … um … practiced this moment so many times in my head. What I'd do and say and now … well, now, it's just not coming out." She's obviously fumbling.

I've practiced it, too, I think. And the things I imagined had nothing to do with words or talking.

Her brow creases as she looks at my bloody fingers. "You're bleeding."

"I don't give a shit."

Her eyes stay on my hands. "Of course, you

don't. I should've called you before I came to town and warned you," she tells me.

An angry, sarcastic laugh rips from my mouth as I reach for a towel and wipe my hands. "Yeah, Quinn, that would've been gracious, anyway. Instead, you decide to surprise me and show up ten years later at my work."

"Well, I came here to see Cade!" she says, sounding defensive as her body stiffens.

"Yeah? Then what the fuck are you doing *here* now?"

"I don't know! I don't know what the fuck I'm doing here now!" Her voice grows louder. "I guess with what happened at my mom's, and I thought maybe we were friends once …"

"We were a hell of a lot more than friends, Quinn."

She waves me off. "This wasn't a good idea."

"Really? What gave you the first hint?"

"You're so … stubborn and headstrong! I came to talk!" Her face turns red with anger as she wheels around to leave.

Before I can stop myself, I reach out and grab her arm.

"Spit it out, Quinn. You came all this way to say something, for Christ's sake!"

"I've got nothing to say to you!" She's lying. The color of her topaz blue eyes, her temper, her inability to ever back down … God help me.

I rush at her until she's backed up to the cabinets. Without a word, I lift her to sit on the counter, and her legs fall open for me. I fit myself between them. Her eyes widen as her soft mouth opens in shock.

"Sometimes words aren't fucking enough," I say as I crush my body and mouth against hers.

I want my hands in her hair, but she's got it twisted up and pinned with Oriental hair sticks. I pull them out and release her hair, which falls in golden waves around her shoulders.

It's a rush—a rush of arms, as we throw them around each other; a rush of hands, lifting her skirt and pressing us closer because we can't seem to get close enough; a rush of powerful, contradictory feelings; a rush of our tongues finally tasting each other after so long; and a rush of blood coursing into my dick as it pushes against the growing warmth between her legs.

I kiss her until we're both breathless, then sink my hands into her thick mane and pull her head back, gaining access to her slender throat where I bite and suck, lick and kiss—I'm fucking starving to death—famished for her feel, for her taste.

She crushes her soft tits into my hard, bare chest, and the sensation is fucking delicious!

I keep one hand gripped in her hair and slide the other to the small of her back so I can keep her taut against me, both of us consumed with the friction.

That's when the main lights switch on over our heads.

Startled, I automatically help her off the countertop and quickly move backward. We hear somebody coming down the steps. She straightens her clothes and hair and turns away from me, as if nothing happened.

The door opens. It's Rhonda, the woman in charge of The Core's housekeeping department. "I'm so sorry, Mr. Knight," she gasps, looking extremely embarrassed.

"It's my fault. I came in off-schedule. I hope we didn't startle you too much."

She shakes her head and steps out of the room.

I look back at Quinn but can't meet her eyes now. "I'm ..." *I'm not sorry.*

Man, I am so fucked!

"Josh is going to try and take us out for lunch later today. I'll understand if you don't want to go. Excuse me, I have a client this morning and have to get some ice on these." I indicate my fingers. What a fucking idiot I am.

I don't even know what to say, so I just walk out, leaving her standing there, with her lipstick still smeared over my mouth and the taste of her on my tongue.

THE PURR OF THE MACHINE IS SO SOOTHING. AND the guy I'm working on doesn't talk much. Right now, I'm grateful for the quiet. I've been able to clear my mind and stop thinking. That's one of the reasons I love tattooing. It's an escape from my tumultuous thoughts. I'm always fully present. Most of the time, after I've finished with a client, I come away from the experience with new revelations; shit I've been stressing over falls into place, and solutions to problems I've been mulling through come to me. It's spiritual. Some people like yoga. Tattooing is my yoga.

My client has good skin, and the ink is blending beautifully. I layer each section as I get lost in the fine detail.

I pull back to wipe the excess ink and blood that's beginning to pool in the area before I take a moment to sit back and view the tattoo as a whole. It's a stunning black and white tiger curling up and around his arm, starting at his wrist and culminating at his shoulder. The background consists of a full-color Samurai wielding his sword, along with koi fish and other symbols he wanted incorporated.

The piece is close to being finished. I've been working on it in increments since last week. I can't help but check the clock. The past four hours have been like a fucking vacation, but now, time seems to be hurdling toward me.

Lunch with Josh and Quinn—if I could think of a way to back out, I would. I thought after what happened this morning, she'd cancel.

She didn't.

One more hour before Josh shows up.

Maybe he'll get distracted with Sophie and Charlie, his beautiful new family. Then he can call and apologize for missing it, and I can say, *Better luck next time.*

Damn, I hope that happens.

I shade with snow-white opaque, platinum and charcoal and finish off the edges.

I'm actually thankful to Quinn for walking in on me this morning. I could've fucked up my hands and would've had to cancel this session—and doing this is the best therapy I could give myself.

"I think you're done. Why don't you go take a look?" I tell him.

He slides off the chair and moves over to the full mirrored wall. "Holy Fuck! It's incredible!"

"Happy you like it." I begin cleaning my area.

"Man, it's a fucking masterpiece."

"Thanks."

"Don't get me wrong, I like watching you fight, but aren't you afraid that if you continue fighting in the MMA, you could hurt your hands so bad you wouldn't be able to tat anymore?" he asks.

Wow! That statement hits too close to home.

"I don't mean nothing by it. You're a hell of a fighter and could become a world titleholder," he continues. "But you've got an amazing talent right here."

"Thanks." It's just another subject and another question I don't have an answer for.

After he leaves and my station is all cleaned up, I walk out into the waiting room.

"He was a happy customer," Adrienne chirps.

Adrienne has been working for me since I opened the place. She and her longtime girlfriend live in the apartment above the shop.

"Josh just called. He's on his way," she says.

"Great," I mutter and then look around at what I've built: black walls with red trim and black and red checkered flooring with a Persian area rug welcoming clients to sit on the black leather sofas. My artwork hangs on the walls. They're good, but these pieces aren't parts of my soul. Those are colors I've only ever let one person see. After her, I pulled the dark shades down over those windows.

"Want to talk about it?" Ade shakes me from my daze.

"No, thanks. I definitely do *not* want to talk about it."

"Are you going to talk to *her* about it?"

When I look over at her, she has her arms folded across her chest defiantly. Her spaghetti strapped dress shows off her colorful, flowered arm sleeves.

"You're going to get on my case too?" I accuse.

"You know there are no secrets here." When she tilts her head to challenge me, the light reflects off her silver chin post. "I think fate is giving you a lucky draw from the deck, and you need to play your cards right. You've been pining after her for as long as I've known you."

"Ade—" I begin.

"I'm not finished. This is do or die, Jack, where you find out if she still has a thing for you or not. Maybe then you can get on or move on."

"Jesus Christ, I hate all of this free advice." I sweep my fingers through my hair.

"Free advice just means you have a family that cares about you," she quips.

At that moment, the buzzer rings, announcing someone has opened the door behind me.

I turn. *Shit.*

"Welcome to The House of Ink and Steel," Josh announces.

"Hi there!" Adrienne coos with the biggest smile. "You must be Quinn. I'm so excited to meet you."

"Thanks." She sounds unsure and distrustful.

"This is Adrienne, she's been working here for forever," Josh says.

"Oh yeah! Since Liam opened the place."

"It's impressive, Liam."

When Quinn says my name, I lose track of every other fucking thing in the world.

"Would you like the tour?" Josh asks her when I don't answer fast enough.

"I'd love it," Quinn says. "You know, I've watched you on *Ink Master*."

She's still talking to me.

"You watch that show?" I finally manage to find my voice.

"Well, only when you've been a guest judge. Guess I'm partial to your work as an artist." She bites her lip, and her gaze drops to the floor.

Her admission and the way she takes her bottom lip between her teeth makes my adrenaline rush.

"Come on, I'll show you the alcoves." Josh takes her arm in his. "Talon and Ryder do quite a lot more work around here than he does."

As he leads her through the place, Adrienne comes close and whispers in my ear, "It's going to be alright, Liam. The universe has a way of working things through when it's the right time."

"At least one of us believes that."

"Don't be so cynical," she scolds. "You just got handed a second chance."

Before I can shoot her a dirty look, Josh and Quinn come back through the lobby. "Let's get some lunch," Josh says. "I'm famished."

I give Adrienne a kiss on her cheek. Even though she's just frustrated the living hell out of me, I know she cares.

We step out into the parking lot.

"I like the family SUV look you've got going on here," I razz Josh, who used to drive a sleek Gillette Vertigo around. He still has it, but now he also owns a souped-up (with all the safety features) Chevy Tahoe. It has a pink flowered car seat in the back, which I'm sitting next to, along with the toys I had to push over to make room for my ass. A purple sippy cup sits in the drink holder next to Josh.

"Wouldn't have it any other way," he admits with a shit-eating grin.

"I'd love to meet your family." Quinn smiles over at him from the passenger seat.

"I can make that happen," he tells her.

Soon, though, Josh drives the scenic route around Lake Calhoun.

"Look!" He points to the colorful snow kites gliding over the frozen lake. Before anyone protests, he pulls into the recreation area's parking lot.

"It's been a long time since I've seen those," Quinn says. "It looks like a kaleidoscope."

"Good thing we're all dressed warmly. Let's get a closer look." Josh turns off the engine. "I could use the fresh air, too."

This is turning into more than lunch. Before I lose my

cool, I try to get back into the state of mind I had when I was tatting the guy's arm.

"Sounds good," Quinn says, and that solidifies it.

We all walk out to the lake's edge. There's so much going on here, even in the middle of February, and it reminds me why I love this city. Vendors are serving hot cocoa and warm, freshly baked pretzels; kids are running around in full snow gear, and of course, there are the snow kites. A snow kite looks a lot like a windsurfer, only it's built to stand and sail on ice. The colors remind me of a hot air balloon festival when hundreds take to the skies.

"There must be close to fifty of them," I say.

"Have you ever tried it?" Quinn asks, and I realize she's talking directly to me.

"No. I'd fall flat on my ass."

"Yeah, and break it, then I'd be the one carrying him home." Josh laughs.

"Asshole." I shove him lightly. "You know, Connor's into it. Has his own kite and everything. He's good at it."

Josh asks Quinn, "So, where are you living these days?"

"Georgia. I've been there the past few years."

"Do you like it?" he prods.

"It's hot and humid in the summertime, but the

winters aren't so bad." She shrugs. "I sort of like the storms that blow through."

She hasn't really answered his question.

"It's really cool you two became such close friends." She stares off dreamily at the kites.

"Yeah, I put up with him," Josh quips and shoves my shoulder. "You two entertain each other for a second, I need to use the loo."

I'm going to kill the fucker. I have no idea what to say! And obviously, neither does she. We both just stand there, painfully uncomfortable.

"Adrienne seems sweet," Quinn finally says.

"Yeah, she's cool."

"How long have the two of you known each other?"

"Since I opened shop six years ago." I watch a novice kiter fall on his ass. *I know how you feel, buddy,* I think.

"Six years is a long time," she says.

"I guess." I shrug my shoulders. *I'm now plotting the ways I'm going to kill Josh.* "You never did finish telling Josh if you liked living in Georgia."

"The people are really nice. I love the Southern hospitality and big smiles. The people make you feel really welcome." She pauses before she continues, "I've made some great friends."

"But?" I say while I crane my neck toward the bathrooms.

"But …?"

"It's an easy question. *Do you like* living in Georgia?" It comes out more rough-edged than I intended it to.

"Yes, I do," she snaps back at me.

Perfect, I've made her angry.

Trying to save this conversation, which is already a train wreck, I try, "I'd miss the winter too much to live down south, I think."

"I miss the winter, the smell in the air and the prickly feel of the cold on your face," she says, then slowly states, "For a while now, I've been thinking about … maybe … moving back up into this area."

It's a big city, but not big enough. "Would your boyfriend go for that?" *FUCK. I don't even want her to answer that!* "You know, Josh is taking a long fucking time. I'm going to walk by the bathroom and see what's taking him so long."

I walk away fast, hoping she'll forget that I asked her anything. Now I'm getting pissed off because I'm acting like a fucking teenager!

"Wait, I'll go with you," she says, catching up.

Without paying her much mind, I throw open the door of the men's bathroom and walk inside, calling Josh's name. When I get no answer, I come back out.

"Did you see him?" I ask.

"No." She looks at me like I'm nuts. "Maybe he had to go to the car to get something."

We walk out into the parking lot together, until

we're standing in the empty space where Josh's SUV *had been* parked in.

"Okay … that's weird. You know, I'll just call him." She fumbles through her coat pockets. "He may have gotten a call from Sophie. My phone isn't here. Oh, shit! I just remembered that Josh asked if he could borrow my cell phone when his battery died. He must not have given it back to me."

"I've got mine." I feel my jacket's inner lining and find only a piece of paper.

Sorry, Liam. Josh made me do it. Adrienne

I close my eyes as the reality of what Josh just pulled off becomes completely clear.

"That asshole." I look around the lot, hoping it isn't what I think.

"What is it?"

"He drove us out here, left us on purpose and stranded us further by confiscating our fucking phones!" I'm fuming.

How the fuck could he do that to me? What the fuck would make him think this was a good idea?

I hear a soft giggle beside me. I peer over to see Quinn trying to stifle her laughter behind her mitten-covered hand.

"It isn't funny!" I state. "It's a five-mile hike back to my place."

That doesn't stop her. Her response grows from a giggle to an all-out laughing fit.

"He didn't even fucking feed us." I growl.

But her eyes still sparkle when she laughs, and it sounds so good and beautiful that I can't help but get sucked into it.

"You think it's funny?" I reluctantly smile at her.

She nods with tears in her eyes.

I have to hand it to him; this is definitely one way to force us together.

"Well, I'm starving, so I guess it's pretzels and hot cocoa." I pat my back pocket. "At least I still have my wallet. Come on." We stop at a vendor, and I order for us. "Do you still eat your pretzels with mustard?"

She lands a solid look at me, takes a deep breath and lets it out in a heartfelt sigh. "Yeah, I still eat them with mustard."

"Triple the mustard," I tell the guy.

We sit on a bench overlooking the frozen lake and eat the pretzels silently. I don't know what to say. I was lucky to finish Josh's conversation, and that didn't even go well. I can't help but look over at her every few *seconds*. It's like my mind is trying to come to terms with the reality that she's here.

I need to stop being a pussy.

"I don't think he's going to come back," she says finally.

"I think you're right," I agree, scanning the area

one more time. "Let's get a couple of hot cocoas and start our long trek back."

If we were in the heart of downtown or uptown, we'd be able to hail a cab or hop on the bus, but that ain't gonna happen way the hell out here.

She wraps her mittened hands around the warm cup as we take the greenway around the lake; it's a shortcut, anyway.

"Every time I smell or drink hot chocolate, I always remember the night we snuck out on the rooftop of North House on my sixteenth birthday," she says.

My body jolts. *Every time?* I've always imagined she didn't remember me at all.

"I remember." A hint of a smile appears on my face. "I lifted a bottle of Bailey's Irish Cream—your favorite—from Johnson's liquor store."

"Yes! And we waited until Cade and Debra and everybody else was sound asleep—"

"And I somehow smuggled out a bunch of stuff and balanced two mugs, a thermos of hot chocolate and the Baileys—"

"While climbing the lattice up to the roof." She nods, and the sunlight catches in the hair that's peeking out of her winter hat. "And don't forget the fistful of lily of the valleys—my birth flower—you brought up, too."

"You remember all of that?" The words spill out before I have a chance to pull them back.

"Of course." She sips at her drink. "I remember everything."

That's a revelation I wasn't expecting. The way she says it makes me wonder if, when she does think about it, she longs for those moments again, like I do.

"It was a miracle we didn't get caught that night or die!" She laughs.

"Yeah, especially with all the noise we made——"

"When we almost fell off the roof," she says, finishing my sentence.

I can still recall the feel of her soft body under mine and the sensations ripping through my body as the two of us were making out, hot and heavy. I remember my fingers traveling up through her jacket to get a handful of her breast. Oh, I remember, it had been getting harder and harder *not* to go all the way.

**LIAM
MAY
(PAST)**

"Touch me," she whispers with a warm breath against my ear. She smells like Bailey's Irish Cream, strawberry shampoo and fresh May air.

"I am touching you." To prove it, I caress my thumb over her nipple. She moans, and it makes me press my hard-on between her legs, which are spread apart beneath me. The denim barrier of our Levi's is becoming more and more frustrating.

"I mean, touch me more."

I smile, move my hand from her chest and sink it down into the heat of her panties.

"Oh, Liam," she breathes while I massage her.

This is going to require a serious solo session when we're finished.

I've had plenty of sex with other girls. I started when I was twelve, but I haven't had sex since that night I followed Quinn through the cemetery. Quinn and I have done a lot of heavy petting, but she's so perfect and innocent and lovely ... she's a little scared, and so am I. I don't want to fuck up what we have. I don't want to break her. And I feel like the secret I'm keeping from her will shatter her and what she thinks of me. It makes me feel ... I don't fucking know ... all wrong.

But lately, she's been asking me to do it, to go all the way with her.

"I want to make love with you," she pleads.

"We will soon," I promise.

"You always say that, and we never do," she whines.

"Let me watch you come like this." I work two fingertips into her opening, but I won't go deeper.

She grates her hips up to meet my fingers, and I rub the heel of my hand over her swelled little button.

She pants, then manages between the heavy breaths to say, "I know it's... going to hurt... but it'll be worth it."

She gets her hands beneath my waistband and pulls on my shaft. Her soft fingers will get me there fast.

"I'm sixteen now," Quinn says as she strokes.

"Yeah, you are," I purr.

"Then make love to me." She bites at my neck.

She's killing me.

"Quinn Kelley, it'll happen soon enough. Don't rush it. Just enjoy this. You do like this, right?"

She's past fighting with me about it. She doesn't understand what stops me with her, and she's been mad and jealous about the other girls I've had and has been very vocal about it.

"Will you at least finish in my hand?" she asks a bit sheepishly.

Just the idea nearly throws me over the edge. "Do you want me to?"

She nods.

"Alright then, birthday girl." I balance on one elbow, open her coat and pinch her nipple between wanting fingers while my other hand works her below.

Soon, she's moaning and close to her release. So am I as I buck my hips against her sweet hand.

"Come with me," I breathe as I lick my tongue over her lips.

She opens her mouth to accept me in, and we both climb over the edge together, each of us overwhelmed with the sensations we give each other.

We lay together like this, satisfied, neither of us wanting to move. That's when my boot, which has been anchoring both of us to the sloped roof, slips.

"Fuck!" My hands search for purchase against the roof.

Quinn screams as we slide. The thermos, mugs and Bailey's bottle go tumbling ahead of us. As I hear them hit the ground and shatter, I wrap my arm around Quinn's waist. If we go over, at least I can position us so that I can break her fall with my body.

At the last moment, I feel the toe of my boot catch the gutter. It halts our fall.

When I realize we're not going to die by going off the roof, I ask her, "Are you okay?"

Quinn's eyes are wild and huge with fear. I figure she's going to start yelling at me; instead, she throws her head back and laughs.

She laughs so hard, and it makes me laugh with her.

"Shit! I hope Cade didn't hear me scream!"

"If he didn't, he must have heard the bottle break." We always chance serious punishment by climbing up here, especially since the lattice is outside of Cade and Debra's bedroom window.

"Should we wait up here?" Quinn asks, laughing. "Or should we get our half-drunken asses back into our beds?"

I take her perfect face between my hands. "I don't know … and I don't care." I kiss her. "I love you, Quinn Kelley. Would you marry me? If I asked you to?"

Her blue eyes gaze into mine thoughtfully. "Yeah, I'd marry you."

"I know we're young; I'm not saying I want to run off and get married this second. But I can start saving money now, and in a year and a half, when I'm eighteen, I can get an apartment ready for us," I say.

"Two years … it's not really that long to wait. You're worth it." She kisses me this time, and I want it to last forever.

CHAPTER NINE

QUINN
PRESENT

It's cold out here, but I don't care; it feels so much like old times as if I went through some amazing time portal and hurdled back in time. World War III could be raging around me, and I wouldn't care. Liam's warmth is bringing me back to life once again, his stormy eyes are drinking me in like they used to, and his deep, resonating voice makes me remember him telling me stories, reminding me of everything good in the world, everything I miss with a heartache that never stops.

"So, did you go to college like you wanted to?" he asks me.

"Yeah, I'm in my last year."

He stares at me, waiting for more. "Well?" He

jumps ahead of me and walks backward while he examines my expression. "What did you end up majoring in?"

He knows it was my biggest dream to go to school. "Interdisciplinary studies," I confess. "I couldn't make up my mind once I got there, so I've studied a little of everything."

"Hmm …" He cocks his eyebrow at me.

I slap his shoulder. "Don't judge me!"

He laughs and pretends to be wounded, grabbing his arm.

"What about you, Mr. MMA fighter and tattoo-creating badass? Couldn't choose just one thing to be amazing at?" I tease.

"Don't forget, I still work for Cade," he says as he falls back in next to me.

"I didn't forget."

Liam's a man with incredible talents. I'm fortunate he's been in the spotlight. His celebrity has let me watch him secretly, from a distance.

"Which is your favorite thing to do?" I ask.

"That question's been thrown at me a lot lately."

I shrug. "It seems like you can't make up your mind like I can't."

"Who says I can't do all of it?"

"No one," I answer him. The next thought pops out of my mouth before I can stop it as if some part of me wants him to know what another part of me wants to keep a secret. "I catch your fights, you know, every once in a while."

"You watch my fights?" He doesn't believe me.

"Yeah …" Hell with it, I've already leaped. "I went to the convention center in College Park when you fought Palomino last year and Fuentes the year before that. He dealt you a cheap shot."

"*What?!* Wait a minute!" He leaps ahead of me and grasps my shoulders. "You … YOU went to my matches? Live?"

I lift my chin to keep myself strong after letting my defenses down. "Yes, why wouldn't I?"

He opens his mouth to answer me, but no sound comes out.

"I'm proud of you. You've really made an incredible name for yourself. You deserve all your success. Plus, I got to show you off to my friend Chelly and brag that I knew you." All of a sudden, I feel like I'm digging myself into a hole. A deep, wide hole I may not be able to get out of.

"Why didn't you come backstage to see me?" he croaks.

I didn't think he would ask me that. "I don't know, I didn't want to mess up your mojo." God, that sounded stupid.

He looks off to the side, visibly shocked.

"I've also watched each time you were on *Ink Master*," I say, and he makes a noise beside me. "I'm really happy you continued with your art. You've always had an amazing gift, and I've loved watching you show it off to the world."

"I had no idea you even knew," he says in a low tone.

"You're a celebrity, Liam," I say, trying to lighten up the conversation.

"You hate fighting," he accuses.

"Yeah, so?" I laugh. "At least the MMA is sanctioned with rules and not fighting to the death."

He doesn't say anything, and we walk a little in silence. I desperately wish that I knew what he was thinking. Then I wonder if maybe he's thinking I'm a crazy stalker.

"I think my favorite subject in my interdisciplinary studies program is art history— and the humanities. Definitely. I've contemplated becoming a museum curator after I graduate," I say out of nowhere, trying to turn the silence around.

"What period are you most into?"

I'm relieved he picks up the conversation.

"I don't really have one favorite time period. Actually, I'm more intrigued by the people who created the art and what was happening to them, the world and their society at the time. For example, Chinese art made by women from the Hunan province. They were so oppressed by the men in their society that they formed a secret language to communicate with each other called Nushu. They embroidered the words into ornate fans, cloth books and other things that could be passed to each other as gifts without being detected …"

He smiles at me like he already knew that.

"Are you teasing me?" I ask.

"No. No, not at all. I'm just remembering your passion and your fire. The sound of your voice. I could listen to it all night," he says.

Of course, what he confesses takes my breath away, and I can't form a word.

When the pause gets too long for Liam, he says, "I assume you attend the University of Georgia?"

"I was offered a scholarship at Georgia State."

"What do you do for fun?"

I laugh. "Fun? Well in my free time, I volunteer at the city's homeless shelters. Especially the halfway house for teenagers."

"Of course, you do."

"Don't make fun."

"I promise, I'm not. It all just sounds very much like you."

"I have a few good friends that I stay close to, but really, school and my volunteer activities take up a lot of my time." I gather my thoughts. "What about you? Did you … go to college?"

"Minneapolis College of Art and Design."

"Liam, really? They're so prestigious!"

"Cade and Debra put me through. I kept living at the home while I studied and worked for Cade at the gym, training with the kids who came through.

After I graduated, I never stopped. That's my most rewarding job.

"Cade recently paired me up with a thirteen-year-old boy. His name is Jonah. He's bright, but he's autistic, so he's quiet, and it's obvious that he's frightened and lonely. My entire purpose since he came into my life a few weeks ago is to break through the shell he's built around himself. He doesn't talk, but he can."

I look up at him as he formulates his next thought. Good God, he's so amazing and so gorgeous. He hasn't changed at all.

"My art gives me a way to express the deepest part of who I am. Tattooing also allows me to draw out someone else's essence. When you create a tattoo on someone's body, it's art for life. You help them express themselves, and a piece of you becomes immortal."

I pull on a string unraveling from my mitten, and I find it ironic. Liam is unraveling me.

"Thank God," he says as we round Lake Nokomis. "My house is right around the corner."

"You have a place near the lake?"

"I bought it a couple years ago. I've got a big dog that needed some extra space."

He said "I" both times. *Maybe he doesn't live with his girlfriend. Maybe it's horrible of me to think that way.*

I assume that he and Adrienne are together, considering the fact that he felt the need to kiss her goodbye when he left the shop. At least he only kissed her on the cheek—probably in an attempt to make me feel less uncomfortable. *Uncomfortable* doesn't really describe the feelings I had at that moment. I've always been intensely jealous of other girls around Liam, more than I'd like to admit. All of these years, keeping tabs on his life the way I have, I've relished every article that called him a playboy; it allowed me to imagine that maybe a part of his heart still belonged to me. I know I don't deserve the claim. I just wish …

He kissed me at The Core, but he hasn't mentioned it since. With Adrienne in the picture, he could have chalked the ravaging, soul-reaching kiss up to a mistake.

"And there it is."

"That's your house?"

"Don't you believe me?"

"I believe you, it's just huge," I observe. Too huge for a single man.

Could he actually be married? I think I'd have seen something about it if he was, but the press has pretty much stayed away from his private life for some reason. Josh has been in the tabloids a lot, but Liam really hasn't. I wonder how he's managed that. Could Cade's influence have anything to do with it?

I notice him staring at me.

"It's stunning," I finally say.

The house is constructed mainly of glass. Massive windows are set in rough-hewn wood and slate.

He hasn't mentioned children, but a ball of ill energy forms in the pit of my stomach. "Do you … have… a boat?" *Kids?*

"Yeah, a rowboat. It helps me keep in shape." He pats his abs.

I'd like to see his abs.

He opens the front door and holds it open for me. I hold my breath against what I'm going to discover—all the things he hasn't talked about—when a mammoth bear-dog comes running up to me.

"Oh my God!" The biggest black Newfoundland I've ever seen greets me before he greets Liam.

Happily, he jumps up, getting his paws onto my shoulders and subsequently pushes me against Liam. I have no choice but to fall backward and let Liam catch me, while the dog licks my face. I'm thankful he's licking me because he's big enough to consume me in one bite!

"Get down," Liam commands.

The dog doesn't listen, and Liam takes him by the collar and sets him straight with a firm tug.

"Sit. Now."

The pooch does.

"He's a big baby. He's not even a year old yet." Liam is stroking his soft, dark fur.

"What's his name?" I kneel next to them and pet the side of his neck.

"Bailey." Liam's eyes pierce mine.

Bailey, like *Bailey's Irish Cream*?? No, he couldn't mean that. *Could he?*

"You must be starved," he says finally. "Why don't you take your coat and wet boots off and relax. I'm going to change and then grab a couple of takeout menus. Or do you need to be some-place? I could give you a ride. Or you're welcome to stay and have dinner with me … since lunch is long gone."

"Dinner would be good. I've got nowhere I have to be," I answer.

"Okay, I'll be right back."

"Oh, um … bathroom?" I can't even imagine how terrible I look after a five-mile jaunt.

"Sure, right down the hall." He points.

"Thanks."

He leaves me to myself. After I slip off my boots and socks, I set them by the door and soft-foot down the hallway and into the bathroom.

It's plain, with next to nothing for décor. Rustic wood beams and paneling and simple fixtures. I open the medicine cabinet, and it's bare. No medications or women's pads. I dig around the drawers. No sign of femininity.

I feel somewhat relieved, but a house this size could easily have multiple bathrooms—his and hers.

I get a glimpse of myself in the mirror. "Oh my God!" My hair is a hat-head disaster and my eyeliner and mascara is in streaks down my face. *Perfect.* Great impression.

I wash my face clean with the pump soap that smells like man. I almost start to cry. I can't even say it smells like Liam. I don't know what Liam smells like anymore.

I dry my face with the towel and can't help but smile. *It* smells like Liam. My Liam.

"Oh, Quinn, what are you doing here?" I ask my reflection in the mirror. My voice quivers, and I can't even think of how much trouble I'm in.

I should have stayed away from him. I should have come here and dealt with everything surrounding my mom and what her death means. I shouldn't have added Liam to it all.

"Dear God. I still love him," I whisper. *My heart still aches and burns and hurts so bad I can't think straight. He's never stopped being everything to me.* I swipe the tears from my eyes.

I run my fingers through my tangles until my hair takes a better shape.

Grabbing my winter hat in my left fist, I turn and grip the doorknob with my right, but I don't want to go out there. I don't want a tour through his home, don't want to see how he's moved on.

Fuck! I don't even have my phone to call Chelly. She'd talk me through this.

Back straight. Breathe.

I open the door and find Bailey blocking my path.

"Can I go by you, boy?" I ask.

He sits immediately and licks my hand.

"Thanks." I scratch his head, and he follows me into the main living space.

It's full of Liam Knight. Photos line the walls of his tattoo work, of him and the celebrities he's worked with, and the teens he's trained with.

A photograph of the boys from Cade's, from before I left, hangs in the room's most prominent spot. He called them the brothers of ink and steel. I smile at the thought that he named his shop after them. I recall what he did with them—what they did *for* him, for *me*—that night.

I swallow hard and put the memory back in the vault. It's just a memory that can't hurt me anymore unless I let it.

I rewind further to when those same boys couldn't eat breakfast without fighting over something … or nothing. It makes me smile. They were the roughest, sweetest, most injured boys I'd ever known, and yet, they spilled their blood for me and for each other. Who would have thought? Then they became the closest of friends.

Of all the people who've gone in and out of Liam's life, I'm the one who caused the damage I promised I never would. Irreversible, crushing damage. My hand lifts to the photograph, and I let my fingertips trail over the fragile glass.

I think what I need to do is say I'm sorry, but I don't know how. Or maybe it hurts too much to think he might not say he forgives me.

"Would you like a drink?" Liam's voice floats in from the kitchen.

Would I ever! "Please."

"I've got whiskey or beer. Pick your poison."

"Whiskey." I could use the hard stuff.

Walking through the living room and into the gourmet foodie's dream of a kitchen, Bailey continues to follow me.

"There you are," he says, and I see he's talking to the dog. Liam hands me a glass with ice and a dark, fizzy liquid. I take a sip. Coke and whiskey. Just the way I like to drink it. "Traitor," he whispers at Bailey.

He doesn't really look angry, and it invokes a smile out of me.

I—we—follow Liam out onto a warm sun porch, where the outside light spills in. The fluffy chairs are overstuffed and comfortable.

Admittedly, it's a relief to find the surroundings and his décor are masculine. I almost expected to find him and Adrienne married with kids. It doesn't look like she lives here, and there are certainly no signs of kids. But that thought shoots another dagger through my heart. Liam has so much love to give. He'd be an amazing father.

"I love the view of the lake," I tell him. "I bet this room is incredible at night with the stars."

"It is." He drinks, and his ice slides and chimes against the side of the glass. "Here are a few menus for places that deliver if you'd like to eat in. I still have the landline phone I could order from. Or we could go out if you'd be more comfortable." Liam looks very *un*comfortable as he puts the menus into my hand.

"You don't have to feed me," I reassure him. "I can call a cab from here."

"No …" he says, stopping me. "I'd like to have dinner with you."

"Okay." I nod shakily. "I think staying in would be good." *Because I want you all to myself.*

Oh God! I just thought that!

I down the drink in three gulps. I hope it quickly works its magic on my frazzled nerves. Then I remember what I look like. "The hike took my makeup and hair, and … now I'm a hot mess."

"You are hot, Quinn, but you're not a mess. You've never looked more beautiful."

My breath catches.

Liam stands up, empties his glass and takes mine from my hand. "Another?"

I nod, not trusting my voice.

"How about Moroccan fried chicken from The

World Kitchen and a six-pack of Corona?" He doesn't wait for my answer; instead, I watch as he stalks back toward the kitchen and mumbles, "I really can't be trusted drinking whisky tonight."

Drink the whiskey! I think.

I don't want him to be trustworthy; I want him to finish what he started earlier this morning. Of course, that sends a pang of guilt through me. He's taken, and he's trying to be on his best behavior. I should be applauding him for that—that's the kind of guy Liam is.

I hear him use his phone to call in the food order.

Of course, my resolve falters. Maybe I should just call that cab, after all, and get my ridiculous ass back to North House. But Liam did say he wanted me to stay for dinner.

As I'm contemplating my dilemma, Bailey comes over and sets his muzzle on my leg, demanding my attention.

Fidgeting with my knitted winter hat that I'm still holding, I lean into his sweet, furry face. "Why did he name you Bailey? Is it because it's my favorite drink, or is it simply a coincidence?"

"Hey, Quinn, I'm just going to run down to the store. The restaurant's out of Corona, and I need a couple of things anyway."

"Oh, okay. Do you want me to—?"

"No, it's all good. Make yourself at home." His

moodiness wavers as the side of his mouth tugs upward. "I see Bailey already has."

"Yeah, guess he has."

"Is there anything you'd like me to grab for you?" he offers.

"No, thanks. Could I use your phone, though? It's long distance, but I don't want people to start worrying." I stand up.

"Of course. Stupid Josh. Wait until I see him tomorrow." He grabs his coat and heads toward the door before he pauses.

"Did you forget something?" I ask.

He turns back to me. "I …" He hesitates, then walks straight over to me and buries his strong hand under my hair so he can hold the back of my neck. The action steals my breath. "I may not act like it, but I'm … grateful you're here … in my house. I've missed you like hell, Quinn." Liam places his warm lips on the top of my head and holds them there.

I close my eyes, and shivers dance over my skin from the feel of his mouth, hands and hot breath in my hair.

A moment later, he turns and strides out the door, leaving me breathless.

I rush to the phone.

"I don't recognize the caller ID, so you better talk quick before I hang up."

"Chelly!"

"Quinn? Why haven't you answered your

fucking phone all day?! I've been just about out of my mind!"

"It's sort of hard to explain."

"Try me."

"I don't have time. Suffice it to say the boys—especially Josh—"

"Josh the Jackhammer?" Chelly purrs.

"Yes. He's trying to get me and Liam talking."

"Is it working?"

"Yes. No." I grasp for an answer, barely stopping to breathe between thoughts. "Oh, I don't know what to do! He's just so … perfect … and *him*, after all these years, and I don't see signs of a live-in relationship, but he did kiss this girl goodbye at his shop and … oh God, I don't know … he's calling me beautiful, and he named the dog Bailey, and—"

"Stop! For Christ's sake, woman, calm down! You're not making any sense."

I whimper, "I knew I missed him, but seeing him again, I'm a freaking mess!"

"Honey, it's going to be alright."

"I think he's been seeing this girl for the past few years, and I feel like shit … like I'm luring him into some kind of infidelity."

She laughs. "Luring him into infidelity? Listen to yourself. He ain't married, right?"

"No, he isn't," I answer. "But I still … I want …"

"Of course, you fucking *want*. He's Liam-fucking-Knight, and if he looks half as hot as he does on TV … Mmm! Not to mention, he was your first."

"What am I doing here, Chell?"

"Looking for the pieces of your life that got left behind."

I consider that. "I don't want to go back to where I'm staying tonight. I want to stay here. If he wants to sleep with me …"

"DO IT!"

"Stop it! *Do it.* I don't want him to think I'm a … I don't know, that I'm …"

She busts up laughing. "Easy?"

Chelly is laughing hard, and I lean against the counter with my tongue in my cheek.

"Oh, yeah!" She pants, out of breath. "That's great. That's absolutely rich coming out of your mouth! You've been on what? Two dates since Liam … two! And you didn't even do anything with either of those guys. '*Easy*'."

Now, I'm laughing. "Shut up!"

"Honey, you and Liam have had this connection since you were what, fifteen? It's never diminished; if anything, it's become stronger. At least, I know for you it has. And if your old friends are trying to force you to talk to each other, that's a really good indication that they know something we don't. It could be that he still feels the exact same way. And, Quinn, even if you threw yourself at him—or any man for that matter—they're going to be too busy trying to prove their manhood to think anything about you except that you must be an angel sent from sex-heaven."

Sex-heaven. Leave it to my dirty-minded friend.

I get serious. "Chelly, I'm—"

"Don't say scared. Don't you dare say you're scared! Listen." She pauses, probably for dramatic effect. "Whatever happens, whatever you two do or don't do, whatever you find out, you'll be able to move on and go forward, whatever that means. You know that, as much as you needed to go there for your own closure with your mom, you needed to do this and have this time with Liam so much more.

"But what about—?"

"There is no what about nothing or nobody," she interrupts. "You can't keep living with one foot in the past and the other in the future 'cause, baby, you ain't going in either direction. So go on now and figure it out."

We hang up, and I sit back on the couch. Anxiously, I pull at the woven strands of yarn from my hat as my gaze wanders around Liam's home, trying to reconcile this man with the boy who still exists within my heart and head.

It's all decorated in simple, woodsy colors. Very manly.

In a heartbeat, Bailey snatches my hat in his

drooly jowls and races up the stairs in an impromptu game of chase.

"Bailey, no!" I tiptoe up the stairs in pursuit. Reaching the top, I realize Bailey is hiding. "Come on, good boy. Bring back my hat," I whine.

No Bailey in sight. Suddenly, he lets out a loud, deep bark that echoes over the hardwood floors and bounces off the walls. It comes from down the hall.

"Please, Bailey," I try, realizing I'm trespassing into Liam's personal domain. I hear Bailey panting from one of the rooms with an open door. When I peek in, he's standing proudly on the other side of a bedroom. My hat is sitting on the floor in front of his large paws.

"Good boy, now leave it," I command, hoping he knows it and won't make me play tug.

I approach him slowly. "You're such a good dog," I say in my best baby voice. "Do you like belly rubs? I bet you do." Instead of going for the hat first, I scratch his soft belly until he drops to the floor and rolls happily over onto his back.

"You're such a good boy, Bailey," I coo as I pet him with one hand and scoop up my forgotten hat in the other, tucking it into my back pocket for safe-keeping.

I lift my eyes to look at my surroundings. More of Liam's artwork decorates the walls. Through the open closet door, I can see the expensive tailored suits and jackets. For a moment, I think about how far he's come from the boy who had nothing except a backpack.

There is a desk with a few books and magazines. An industrial style lamp sits on the one bedside stand with a half drunken glass of water and an old alarm clock radio that's flipped upside down.

Then it dawns on me, I'm in *his bedroom.*

Oh, I've got to get out of here. My thoughts race as I make a beeline toward the door, but then something catches my eye.

The bed is barely made. Six plump pillows with black and white silk cases are tossed around messily while a steel gray, expensive-looking bedspread lays haphazardly over the bed. And there, in the center of it, sits a metal keepsake box with an open lid. Spread out on the bed is a plastic sandwich bag of crumbled autumn leaves, a sealed letter with my name on it but no address and an instant color Polaroid photo strip of the two of us. There are three tiny picture squares. In the first, we smiled like a couple of goofballs, the second, we were both laughing as he pulled me up onto his lap, and the third, my favorite, I'm smiling as he kisses my cheek.

Tears blur my vision. I remember when we took this. It was in a booth at the Mall of America where we liked to hang out. It was after we'd been at North House for a few months. We were happy. For the first time in so long, we'd both felt safe. We were fed and warm. You can see the peace in Liam's eyes.

QUINN
FEBRUARY
(PAST)

"Quinn! Are you here?" I hear Liam shout. His voice echoes through the cemetery.

"LIAM!" I bolt as fast as I can.

I haven't seen him for three weeks, not since he was stabbed by Vince's thugs.

I run up the hill as he runs down it. We meet in the middle and come crashing together.

"I thought you might have died!" Tears are streaming down my face. "I thought they killed you!" My hands search and paw all over him.

"I'm sorry it took me so long to get back to you, but I promise I'm never leaving you again." He holds me so tightly I can hardly breathe. "Are you okay?"

I nod, but I can't talk, I hang onto his neck for all I'm worth, afraid this will just be another one of the million dreams I've had since he's been gone.

"Come on, let me look at you." He pulls his face

back. "Please don't cry, baby. I'm here now." He strokes his thumb under my eyes.

I gaze into his face. "You are here. You're real. I don't know if I can believe it!"

"I'm real." Liam softly kisses me on one cheek, then the other one. He presses his lips against my forehead. "And this is real." His mouth comes over mine. I close my eyes as I sink into the kiss and his arms.

"What happened to you?" I ask when we finally pull apart.

"Cops came and took me to the hospital. After about a hundred fucking stitches ..." He pulls back and picks up his shirt to show me the scars.

"Oh, Liam!" My fingers trace the lines.

"I don't mind. It shows people not to mess with us," he says. "Once the doctors fixed me up, the cops threw me in juvie for a couple weeks, where I got into a shit ton more fights, then they brought in Cade North. You remember him, right? From North House. Social Services transferred me there about a week ago. I ran to get back to you, but Cade caught me. We had this big talk. He's different, Quinn. I think we can trust him."

I search his face, trying to figure out what he means.

"It's a safe place for us."

"No place in the system is safe." I shake my head.

"Yeah, that's what I thought, too. But he's like us. He's lived like us; he thinks like us."

"What are you saying?" I ask nervously.

"I'm saying I think we should go back and stay there—at least give him a shot."

"I don't know."

"I'm here alone because he let me go. He told me he understood and told me about him and his older brother going through the system when their parents died. When he caught me busting out, he told me he wouldn't stop me from going, and he wouldn't call the cops for twenty-four hours," Liam explains. "He asked me why I wanted to leave. I told him I had to get back to you. He invited us to come and stay there to give it a try. If we don't like it, he'll let us leave."

"That sounds like a trap."

"It's not. He's for fucking real." He's trying to convince me, but it seems way too good to be true.

"What about St. Anne's?"

"He told me he can pull a few strings and say that you're under his supervision."

I want to believe him.

"I've been there for a week, watching how he interacts, trying to catch him being two-faced. I came up with nothing," Liam says. "He's got no locks to keep anybody in. If you want to go, you can."

I try to grasp the fact that not only is Liam back in my arms, but he's suggesting this crazy idea.

"It's his policy. He works to keep kids together. It's what he does."

He weaves his fingers through my hair. "You've gotten so thin. When's the last time you got a hot meal?"

I drop my eyes and shake my head. "Don't ask me that."

"Please, let's give it a try. If he turns out to be a douchebag, I swear, we'll hitch to Florida like we talked about," he pleads. "And look." Liam pulls out a twenty-dollar bill. "Cade gave me the money to buy you something to eat and take the bus back to the house."

I look at Liam and know I can trust him.

"I'll follow you wherever you think we should go," I say.

CHAPTER TEN

LIAM
PRESENT

I come back into the house, and everything is quiet. No sign of Bailey or Quinn. I think maybe they went out for a walk, but her coat and boots are still where she left them.

Where she left them … Where *Quinn* left her coat and boots.

Oh, I am so fucked.

After I hang my coat and put my boots on the rug next to hers, I walk through the house and set the food bags on the kitchen table. I check the bathroom.

Where could they be?

I don't know what possesses me to climb up the stairs to my bedroom, but I do.

Bailey sleeps, sprawled on the floor next to the bed.

And there's Quinn, curled on her side in my bed, asleep. In her fingers is the photo of us that I keep.

I can't stop the smile that spreads across my face. I'm not even upset she's up here and found it. It's so fitting, so perfect.

So us.

And in that instant, it's like she was never gone.

I'm overwhelmingly lost in her, on my bed, next to my dog, holding our picture.

In the next moment, I risk everything—the crumbling of every angry wall I've erected, my foolish pride and dignity, and the possibility of receiving her right hook—as I walk to the opposite side of my bed, move the metal box and items, and crawl in beside her.

I dare to get as near to her as I can without waking her, that is, until I hear her soft breaths and breathe in her sweet scent.

Her warmth is so close … so *fucking* close … but not close enough.

I last less than five seconds before I pull my body up flush to hers. I bury my face in her golden hair and wrap my arm around her waist.

Oh, God … I'm dying! But at the same time, I'm impossibly alive again for the first time in ten long, lifeless, loveless years.

My fear of waking her is replaced by hunger … a hunger that's been suppressed for all that time.

With the smell and feel of her comes the overpowering need to taste her, to kiss her, to prove she's really here and I'm not just dreaming.

"I've missed you, Quinn," I whisper the words against her ear and hope they reach her soul.

A moment passes before I hear her softly say, "I've missed you, too."

I have to get closer. I work my fingers through her beautiful hair and pull it up onto the pillow so I can taste the back of her neck.

The first kiss feels like I'm waking up. It's just my lips against her skin, but really it's so much more than that. I do it again. Quinn tilts her head down to offer me more. And I take it feverishly.

This time, my mouth opens to taste her flesh. It's beyond waking up; I'm being resurrected.

She's warm and soft and sweet. She moans and presses her back against my front, and my blood races.

My restraint fails. My tongue darts out against her, my teeth nip and scrape at her skin, and my nose traces the curve of her neck.

I've been walking dead without you, Quinn.

"I have to see your eyes," I tell her, even though I'm so fucking afraid she's going to stop me now. Tell me she can't and run away, and I will have fucked up again.

She begins to turn, and I tangle my arms around her, one moving with her head and the other over the length of her back in an attempt to keep her from running.

"Nothing has been right since you left." It's the truth. *You make me whole.*

I kiss her neck and over the shirt at her shoulders as she turns. She doesn't get all the way around before I cover her mouth with mine and bring her closer.

I taste the salt of her tears as they reach her lips, and it makes me kiss her harder, makes me trace her lips with my tongue to catch them.

When she moans, it comes from deep within her throat.

I feel her breasts press into my chest, and her nipples harden as she crushes her body against mine.

I can't help but think this is how it's always supposed to have been.

"Oh, God," I groan.

"The photograph," she says.

Without opening my eyes, I continue to land kisses against her skin and feel my way up over her arm to her hand to take the picture from her so it won't be crumpled between us. I extend my arm behind me to drop it on the bedside table, but instead, it falls to the carpeted floor. The action makes me laugh.

"Why are you laughing?" She's breathless.

I open my eyes to look at her. "I couldn't help thinking of those fucking Pop-Tart wrappers I threw to the floor when we were on the bed together that first time."

She says nothing; instead, flames ignite in her eyes. She plunges her hands up under my shirt and begins to tug it up.

God yes! I twist and lift my torso so she can get it off.

Quinn's fingertips tickle down my shoulders and chest.

"*Even the stars cannot compare.*" She traces the script that's written over my breastbone.

I wait. This is when she snaps out of it when she realizes her head doesn't want what her body does when she gets back out of my bed and walks out of my life ... again ... forever.

"That night ... what you did, Liam ... it was the greatest gift you could have ever given me," she says.

My brow presses down. *What is she saying?* I need to know exactly what she means.

I watch her eyes searching me, gazing at the tat.

"That night you gave me became my true first time. I learned that when I thought of the other, I could overshadow that image with your love for me."

Her admission squeezes my heart like a fist.

"And even though I left … you wrote this on your chest for forever." She begins to kiss each letter of the ink as she talks. "I've seen pictures of it when you've posed for ads and articles and magazines. You still loved me, even though I hurt you."

"I've never loved another, Quinn." I stroke her hair as the sensation of her mouth on my chest drives me into a frenzy. "It didn't matter that you were gone; you'd always be the best part of me."

She lifts her gorgeous topaz blue eyes to mine. "I've always loved you, Liam. I never stopped."

Suddenly, the decade of torment without her evaporates, as if the separation had never existed—like we've always been together, and no time has passed.

LIAM
OCTOBER
(PAST)

I carry Quinn through the field of tall grass out behind North House as she cries against my shoulder.

I promised I would protect her, and I failed.

"It was supposed to be ours. I saved it for you.

He stole that from me, and I can never have it back!"

I press her into me, tighter. I have no words, and I bite the inside of my cheek to keep my emotions in check.

"We can't do this," she protests. "I mean, I want to—more than anything, but—"

"We can do this," I say firmly. "I should have done this a long time ago. I made you wait. I'm the asshole."

"No, you're not, Liam. Take it back!" scolds Quinn.

I can't, I fucked up in too many ways. If only I had been there.

Why did I let her go alone? Because that's how the social worker set it up. But that's just an excuse. *A lame fucking reason.* I should have just gone on my own and sat outside of her fucking mother's house! I knew it then, and now she's scarred forever, and I'll always be reminded of the grave mistake I made. This kind of pain can never be erased. It can never go away.

"I should have been there, Quinn. If I had just gone and waited outside of the house, it wouldn't have happened."

"That's not fair. How could you have ever anticipated that?" she says. "You couldn't have. And there were so many of them. They could've killed you."

The words tear out of my throat with a sob. "I blame myself."

"Blaming yourself is just as foolish as me blaming myself." She ends it there as if that absolves me.

But what she says next is crippling.

"I still see them, you know. Every time I close my eyes. Every time I hear a noise in the house or outside … I *feel* the fear. When you're with me, it's better, but when you leave to go to The Core or to the fucking bathroom, and I'm all alone … I feel like he's waiting for me, watching through the windows and stalking me, waiting for another chance … and that maybe this time he'll kill me." Her voice is laced with panic, and then she adds outraged and defeated, "I'll never have my first time back. He stole my first time."

And we've circled back to where we began.

I set her down so her feet connect to the earth underneath us. The huge sky envelopes us in shadows while guiding us with the light of a million stars tossed and scattered in endless midnight.

"*That* … was not your first time." My voice shakes with anger, pain, and so much regret. "*That* will *never* be your first time." I make her look at me. "Your first time will be about love and want-ing. Your first time will be about sweetness and gentleness … and tenderness, with me holding you all through the night as you sleep in my arms, content and satisfied. That will be your first time, Quinn."

She's crying as I lay the blanket that I carried over my shoulders onto the ground.

It's the middle of October, and the grasses have turned to gold, but tonight's air is unseasonably warm.

"*This* ... this is your first time. *This* moment, *this* memory that *we* create tonight, will be the one you remember." I lay my hand over her beating heart. "The one nobody can taint or steal or tarnish." My own tears start to burn my eyes. "*This* is your first time because it's about you and me and our love."

Quinn sobs, and I wipe her tears as they fall. "It's about me loving you and you loving me back. Do you understand?"

She nods but only slightly.

"Quinn, do you understand me?" I want to shout. I want to erase all my fucking choices. I want to turn back the clock and save her.

"I'm ... damaged, Liam," she whispers.

I swallow hard. "I know you feel that way." *Dear Christ, please help us.*

"You don't know how I feel," she whispers again as if the volume of the words themselves could shatter her.

Actually, I know exactly how she feels.

"I know you feel scared. I know you feel violated and like you can't let another person come close and touch you. *But you're not damaged!*" I wipe my eyes and face against my arm. "Not to me ... *never* to me."

"What if ... what if they ... gave me something, Liam? Something the doctors haven't seen yet, something that could kill me ... and could kill you?"

I know what she's saying. She's worried about passing an STD on to me.

"I don't care." I shake my head. "People die every day. My fate is tied to yours, Quinn."

She takes a deep, shuddering breath as I bring my hands to her face.

"This is us, becoming one. No matter what happens in our lives—if it's great or if it's a fucking tragedy, we'll hold on together, no matter what," I say.

She nods her head yes and squeezes more sadness from her eyes. I kiss each cheek to absorb the tears.

"If, at any point, you need me to stop, tell me. I don't care what the reason is. If it hurts, if you're scared ... anything, you tell me, okay?"

She nods again.

As gently as I can, I lift her back into my arms and cradle her against my chest for a moment before I lower her onto the blanket.

"I love you so much, Quinn ... so fucking much." I lay over her and kiss her.

I carefully remove her clothes, then mine. The stars above us are breathtaking.

"Look up," I tell her.

She does and smiles. "They're beautiful."

"You're beautiful."

She smiles that sweet, shy smile she has that possesses me. I tilt my head to peer up into the sky, but not so much that I can't still see her.

When I look back at her fully and take her eyes with mine, I say, "Even the stars cannot compare."

Together, we make love—under the canopy of a million pinpoints of light, blanketed in a meadow of sweet-smelling autumn grass, and for a time, no one else exists apart from her and I—as we become forever one.

CHAPTER ELEVEN

QUINN
PRESENT

He begins to treat me too carefully, like precious and breakable china that is kept on the shelf.

"Liam, I'm not the fragile creature I once was. I've been wishing and waiting for you, and for *this*, for a very long time. Please don't be worried you're going to break me."

I think about what I want to say and how to say it. I want him to know … need him to know what I feel.

I peer into his stormy, ocean-colored eyes. "I've been without you for so long, and I've *hated* to think of other women with you. But I believe there's a part of you that you saved just for me … that you didn't give to anyone else. And I want it."

I can't stop the tears that begin to fall, but for the first time in a long time, they're loving and healing tears. "I know you have so much passion and emotion inside of you … and I want it all. All of your love, all of your rage, all of your fear, all of your courage. I want every part of you, from what people see to what's hidden deepest within you." I reach up and lay my hand over his heart. I feel it beating wildly. "Don't you dare hold anything back from me."

I wrap my legs around his waist and grind into him as I whisper with heated breath in his ear, "Every last drop."

That breaks the dam, and I'll be lucky if I can hold on.

"I've been burning for you for ten of the longest fucking years of my life," he says.

All ceremony ends, and he can't get my clothes off fast enough. Off goes my shirt, and down comes my jeans.

"Oh dear-fucking-Lord, I don't know where to start." He examines me as I lie before him in nothing but a bra and undies. My blood heats under the intensity of his gaze.

A second later, Liam brings the inside of my right hand to his lips. Sensually, he kisses each finger, down my palm and to my wrist, sending little goosebumps thrilling up my arm.

He looks over at me, and a smile fills his face. "I swear to God, I'm the happiest man alive."

I bite my lip to contain my own joy.

His mouth trails from my wrist to the ticklish bend of my elbow, where he stays to dart and swirl his tongue. Up my bicep to my collarbone, where he lifts my chin up and licks and sucks over my neck to my ear, making me crazy.

I turn my head to catch his lips with mine.

We kiss, caught up in each other. His lips are so soft and warm and hungry. I can't get enough. When we both open our eyes at the same time and see each other, we laugh, and it feels fantastic.

While he laughs, he kisses a line from my chin, down the center of my throat and straight to my breast. He loops his fingers around the bottom of my bra straps, close to the cups, and uses both fists to pull the bra down and around, freeing my tits for his pleasure.

"Oh fucking Christ, Quinn," he growls.

The sound of his deep need makes my pulse race wildly, and he sucks my left nipple into his hot, wet mouth. He teases it with his teeth, gently scraping up and turning it hard before he tortures it with his tongue.

A ragged moan escapes my mouth as he presses his hard-on against the softness between my legs.

The denim of his jeans rubs against the thin, flimsy silk of my panties.

"I need to feel your heat," I pant. "Take off your jeans."

Liam quickly moves to my other breast, lavishing it as he brings his right hand down to undo his button. Next, I hear his zipper, and he tries to shove his pants off, but he only gets them to his thighs before they get stuck there, and it becomes obvious he doesn't want to relinquish my breast.

He mumbles something gruffly against my nipple, and the vibrations drive me crazy. Keeping his gaze looked on mine like a burning torch, he gets to his knees. His absence causes the cool air of the room to chill my hot skin, and I miss his presence immediately.

Mesmerized, I watch the muscles of his arms and torso ripple, and his tattoos come alive as he does it.

As soon as the pants are gone, he returns to me, and I raise my hips to rub myself against the enormous bulge behind the blue fabric of his designer briefs.

Liam's eyes are hazy and dark with desire as he groans and grinds back into my needy wetness. "Oh fuck, Quinn."

"I've dreamed about this moment so many times," I confess.

"So have I," he rasps.

Quickly, like a man on the edge, he slides his torso down over me. His rock-hard abs create a delicious friction over my center.

We both moan gutturally.

"Your wetness is all over me," he croons.

Liam pauses when his mouth reaches my waist and takes a mouthful of my flesh, biting and sucking it.

I cry out as he traces my curves with his tongue, leaving a moist path to my burning clit. He breathes over my silk panties, and the heat ravages me, making me scream for more.

In a second, my panties are gone, replaced by his mouth.

"Oh God, Liam!" The feeling is glorious. Fireworks ricochet from my core throughout my entire body. I've never felt anything like it.

"Fuck!" I slide my eyes closed while my back arches, offering him all of me.

He dives his hot tongue deep into me and works it in and out before he licks me, lapping and stroking until I'm a crazed mess.

I feel so alive, so free, being naked like this with him.

When I look at him again, his eyes are searing me as he watches my body quivering under his workmanship. All of my nervousness fades away.

His tongue lashes across my clit as his fingers roll my nipple.

"Your fucking taste is heaven, Quinn."

"Oh my God!" I grab his head with my hands and crush him against me.

His gorgeous eyes lock on mine. I'm lost in the emotions and sensations overtaking both my mind and my body.

His beard scruff scrapes my most tender area, and I start to careen over the edge.

He slides his big, strong hand down to my ass to hold me in place and hums into my insanely aroused flesh.

My reason is torn apart as he thrusts two fingers inside of me.

"I'm going to come!" I cry, close to delirium.

"Mmm … yes, you are, all over my face," he says, and then he tells me, "Taste what I taste."

Liam presses his fingers between my lips and over my tongue.

"Lick," he commands me, and I do. I imagine his fingers are his cock in my mouth.

My body buckles from the intense, animal pleasure. Liam's other hand and fingers grip my hip, forcing me steady, keeping me positioned on his tongue as I rise as high as I can get.

My legs shake as my entire being seizes with my orgasm.

He keeps rubbing his entire face and nose over the swollen, hypersensitive area as I come.

"Fucking mouthwatering," Liam rumbles.

"I've got to feel you inside my body, Liam." I'm out of breath, covered in a sheen of sweat and desperate to feel his hard body against me, making love to me. "I want to be one with you."

He slides up until his face hovers close to mine and breathes over my lips. "You are my only fantasy, Quinn." He glides the tip of his cock over my clit, making my body shudder and shake with aftershocks.

My head spins. My pulse throbs. My body burns with desire and need.

I want him to consume me until every moment; all the pain of our separation is overtaken by the power we still feel.

He wedges his hand between the pillow and the back of my head, sweeps his tongue across my lips, and presses it into my needy mouth as he begins to drive himself inside me.

I gasp, scream and moan at the pleasure and pain of his body stretching mine. It has been so long that I forgot how it felt.

"Oh fuck, you're so tight," Liam groans and presses his forehead to mine. "Jesus, Quinn."

I moan from the pure sensuality of his words, his proximity and the sensations his body is rocketing through mine.

My heart beats roughly, and I can't steady my breath.

"It's okay, baby," he soothes as he presses down on my thigh and massages it to relax me.

His cock is huge, and I'm grateful as he gradually pushes himself slowly deeper until he's fully buried and wrapped up in me.

I'm a fucking mess, panting and moaning as he finds a slow, pulsing rhythm.

I grab his hard ass and squeeze the muscles there.

He curses and moans, and it sounds so fucking hot it makes my pussy squeeze him intensely.

Our sounds join and mix, reverberating off the bedroom wall, and both of our breaths are becoming ragged.

I'm beyond gone as he keeps up this rhythm.

Sparks light across my skin, and a new heat builds and grows in my belly, threatening to take me over.

I grip the bulging muscles of his arms and hold on tight.

He watches my face as he pulls out achingly slowly to his tip and then thrusts hard and deep back inside me.

I cry out in ecstasy.

A smile lifts the corners of his mouth, and he does it again.

I scream in pleasure.

"Do you have any fucking idea how hot you are?" His voice is rough and rugged.

I can't think straight. I feel fucking delirious with his body on top of mine like this, the length of his shaft rubbing my inner walls, and his muscular arms covered in ink walling me in to him.

An emotional storm fills his eyes as he continues to gaze at me, his forehead still against mine. "You're so beautiful, Quinn. It makes my chest hurt."

"Oh, Liam." I feel like I'm in a dream.

He moves his forearms underneath my shoulders, grabbing them to hold me there.

"Your body is so fucking perfect." His voice is hoarse and raw as he pumps harder and faster.

Beads of sweat form on his skin and mix with mine, and I fucking love it! His musky, manly scent fills my senses.

We both go over the edge together.

He shouts my name, and his body seizes on top of mine. Goosebumps cover his flesh, and I feel his cock pulsate inside me as I flutter around him, my own orgasm taking me.

He lies on top of me as we catch our breath.

"Did you like that?" he asks.

"I loved it."

He kisses the tip of my nose. "Good. There'll be another round in about five minutes."

I can't help but giggle.

"First, however, I need sustenance."

At that, he hoists me up off the bed and throws me over his shoulder.

"I'm naked!" I protest.

"It's okay. I don't mind."

"Liam! Let me put my clothes on!"

"Nope. No can do, sugar."

"Okay, at least my panties."

He just laughs. "Those are drenched and useless now, baby."

As we get closer to the kitchen, I smell something incredible. My tummy growls, reminding me just how hungry I am.

He pulls a couple of forks from the kitchen drawer, tosses them onto the table, then grabs a couple bottles of Corona from the fridge.

When Liam finally sits, he keeps me flush against his body but lowers me to sit on his lap, facing him.

Immediately, I'm wet for him.

He reaches out and pulls the takeout bag closer, and while he keeps me pinned to him with his right arm, he takes the cartons from the bags and organizes them on the table.

"Um … are you trying to tell me this is the only chair that works?" I ask, looking at the other seven chairs circling the large table.

He grabs a fistful of my hair and pulls my face to his mouth. He drives his tongue deep between my lips while his soft, plump lips send electricity through mine. His right arm crushes my body against his chest as it presses down against my shoulder. My hungrier-than-my-stomach vag tightens at the sensation of his growing shaft between my legs.

When he lets us up for air, he says, "No, you're in the right seat."

I bite my lip happily, feeling a little bit shy.

"Don't do that, or we won't eat," Liam says with a growl.

I clamp both of my lips together. My heart races, and tingles thrill across my skin in anticipation at the feel of his hard-on rubbing against my wetness.

"Too late." He stands up with me as I wrap my legs around his waist, and he shoves me up against the kitchen wall. "I can feel you're wet for me again."

Liam lavishes my throat as he takes his cock in hand, works it over my vagina, then buries himself inside me again.

The action causes both of us to moan as he sinks deep into my core.

"Oh fuck!" His hips piston while he grips my thighs with his strong hands and holds me to him.

I scream as my body stretches to accommodate his length and girth. The feel of his cock buried deep inside me sets my temperature to scorching. Another orgasm blooms in my belly.

He peers up at me. "I want that lip between my teeth," he demands as I feel one of his arms come under my ass and his other hand fists my hair. He bows my head and bites my lips ever so seductively.

Capturing each of my moans with his mouth, he grinds me against the wall.

The muscles of his arms and torso pull taut as he holds me, and I grab his shoulders and watch his facial expressions move from lust and passion to love.

We stare into each other's eyes.

This is really happening, I think. *He wanted me, too.*

He's so perfectly deep; it doesn't take long before we're both shouting and coming again.

He leans into me, pressing me harder against the wall as he takes in ragged, deep breaths.

Liam kisses me gently, then carries me to the kitchen sink and sets me on the counter.

"Now what?" I say, full of wonder like a kid at a carnival.

He laughs. "I just need a few minutes to recover."

Opening the drawer, he reveals nicely folded kitchen towels. He soaks one in warm water.

He lathers the cloth with a bar of soap. "Spread your legs for me."

"Again?" I flirt. "Oh yes," I say and open them very slowly and seductively.

"I can see we'll be shut in here all weekend."

Lovingly and full of tenderness, he wipes me clean then rinses me. While he cleans himself, he lays sweet kisses all over my face.

He drops the cloth in the sink. "I'll deal with that later." Picking me back up, he takes us back to the table, sits—with me on his lap again—and opens the food cartons.

"The food is still warm." I'm surprised.

"Insulated food bag."

Liam opens the first carton, spears a piece of chicken with the fork and holds it to my lips. Who am I to argue? The gorgeous man wants to hand-feed me. I can handle that!

I take a bite. "It's so good," I mumble.

"Best Moroccan chicken in the city."

"I tend to remember your affection for Pop-Tarts and Hot Pockets."

"Yeah, but a boy has to grow up."

"And that you have." I look over him with admiration.

LIAM
PRESENT

Quinn's gentle fingers glide over the tattoo on my left shoulder and bicep. A serious expression paints her face. She closes her eyes tightly, but not before I see the flash of pain, and then leans in and kisses across my shoulder and down my arm.

"It's been so long, I forgot about it," I say, remembering the first tattoo I ever gave myself. *Damned* had been scrawled over my bicep in messy script. She hated it.

She smiles up at me and swipes at her cheek; whether it was sweat or a tear, I don't know. "It's perfect that you covered it with an image that represents your name and true character—the knight on his steed. It's beautiful."

"Thanks. Talon inked it from a drawing I made." I look at the horse rearing up over my arm, its rider covered in plate and chain mail armor. "And what about you?" I ask, even though I'm not sure I want to know.

She spins around to show me the back of her right shoulder. I draw along the outlines with my fingertips. Two small birds flying free from a gilded cage still adorn her body. It was her first tattoo, the first tat I ever did on someone's body other than my own, and it meant so much to the two of us.

I'm stunned it's still there. "I … honestly …"

"Thought I'd covered it?" Her tone is incredulous. "Never."

LIAM
JUNE
(PAST)

"Come on." I shake her awake.

"What time is it?"

"Two, and we only have a couple of hours before Cade wakes up."

We sneak down into the basement.

"I've already got it all set up. And ..." I show her the mini liquor bottles I lifted from the convenience store. "Enough to take the edge off, but not enough to give you a hangover."

She looks them over. "No Baileys?"

"No. You need something more fast-acting. Now swig."

Quinn opens the first little bottle and downs it.

"We still doing what we talked about?" I ask to make sure.

"Of course. Why would you think I'd change it?"

"I don't know. What if you fall out of love with me?"

"That could never happen, Liam."

"It's going to hurt like fuck," I warn.

"I can handle it."

I switch on my homemade tattoo machine. It's noisier than I'd like, which is why we had to hide down here.

I kiss the virgin porcelain of her shoulder. "You're sure?"

"I'm ready. Do it."

"Okay." I set the needle to her skin.

"OH MY GOD!" she cries.

"SHH!!" I warn. "I told you it was going to hurt."

"Yeah, but … oh my God!" She cringes.

"Sit still, we just started."

"What happened to '*You don't have to do it, Quinn, if you change your mind.*'?"

"Have you changed your mind?"

"No! But it stings like a son-of-a-bitch!"

"You got this," I say sincerely. "Take another drink."

"Remember to make them into an outline so that when you get colored ink, you can make them blue."

She loves mountain bluebirds.

"I remember."

After a few minutes, she gets used to the feeling and calms down.

"Why is life always such a fight? Will we always be fighting?"

I hear the sorrow in her tone, and I'd do anything to wash it away, but I don't have the answer she wants. "I don't know, Quinn."

She sighs. "You shouldn't have to fight. People should just leave us alone."

"Maybe someday," I say, but I don't even sound convincing to myself. "Oh. And don't even think for a second that I don't know how you sprained your wrist, Quinn Kelley."

"What's … that … supposed to mean?" She stumbles over her words.

"Josh North is an asshole, and if he ever touches you again—drunk or not—he'll be a dead asshole."

"What?" her voice sounds strangled.

"I know you slugged him over something. He's been looking like a whipped puppy since you hurt yourself. It doesn't take a fucking rocket scientist."

She laughs softly. "Guess I'm thinking more like you, more like a fighter."

"That's a good thing. What Cade is teaching us —how to be strong and to defend ourselves—it's all good fucking stuff."

She's quiet a minute before she asks, "Are you happy here?"

I think about that. "You're safe. We're together."

"That's not exactly what I mean. Do you like Cade and Debra?"

"Yeah, I think I do. So far, they've been the most honest people I've met."

"Me too."

"That is unless they fuck it up and go two-faced." I know that can happen from experience.

"It scared me when Ryder and Connor ganged up on you."

"I could've taken them both," I assure her.

Connor has a medium build and doesn't fight with venom—he's like Reese and Chase, really just letting off steam and killing time.

But Ryder is a different animal. He wants to draw first blood. He's got a lot of anger. He's usually punching walls. I've lost count of how many times he's been in detention because he put a hole in the plaster somewhere in the house after a group session.

"And a few days ago, when Ryder beat Josh to a pulp—it was like he just laid there and let him hit him. He didn't even try to fight back."

"Yeah, that wasn't like Josh. He usually likes a good rumble."

"Are we safe here?" she asks.

"Josh is a good match for Ryder—Josh is the one who laid down and played dead, though I don't know why."

"I don't think Chase or Talon really want to fight."

"No, they fight because they have to, or they think they have to prove themselves to everybody else."

"Yeah, especially when new kids come in," she says. "I hate that. You all turn into idiots."

"Hey, remember who's holding the needle,

Quinn," I say. "It's a guy thing."

"It's a street thing—you all have to prove to each other who's the toughest."

"Yeah, you're probably right. Who the fuck cares? It's just the way it is."

"I do. I care. I just … want to stop trying so hard." She shrugs her shoulders.

"Hold still," I scold.

"I'm sick and tired of the fighting—seeing you black and blue or having to clean up your bloody nose … I'm tired of fighting for food, fighting for a warm, safe place to sleep, fighting for survival …"

"As soon as we turn eighteen, I'll have earned enough money working for Cade to get us to Florida safely on a bus, not fucking hitchhiking. I know it feels like it's still far away, but it's better than running again—living on the streets. And I think Cade'll give me references so I can get a job. Maybe I'll even find a position to train as a real tattoo artist." I think about it. "We'll be free, Quinn."

She sighs deeply.

I pull out two mirrors—which I unhinged from the upstairs and downstairs bathroom medicine cabinets. Putting one in her hand, I hold the other behind her shoulder.

The tat depicts two small bluebirds flying off together, having escaped from their cage. I love the symbolism.

"You and me," she says. "I love it! I also like the drawing of the tree branch."

"Yeah, I thought the cage looked more elegant hanging from the tree. I know it's just an outline; I'll fill it in, along with the leaves and the rest of the tat, when I get some color."

"Liam?"

"Yeah?"

"I love you."

LIAM
PRESENT

"You know, I could fill it in for you now if you'd like me to."

"I don't know. You're a pretty hot, sought-after artist. How much do you charge?"

I tickle up her ribs as she squirms and laughs and tries to break away. "How much do I charge?" I mock.

She turns back around, still naked on my lap, to face me, and we settle down and go back to our dinner, "I really like the other one you have on your rib."

"It's the only other tattoo I have," she says.

I lay her back a little to study it and read it out loud.

> **In the midst of winter, I finally learned that there was in me an invincible summer.**

"It's an Albert Camus quote. He was a philosopher who won the Nobel Peace Prize. He fought during World War II as a writer for a resistance newspaper in Paris," she explains. "I got it a couple of years ago … after a lot of therapy. It reminds me that I'm a survivor. For a while there, I wasn't so sure." Her eyes become clouded, but she covers it quickly. "Camus also wrote that 'no matter how inexplicable existence might be, human life remains sacred.'"

I look at her in fascination at how she puts into words what's so deep in her soul.

Out of nowhere, Bailey comes over, sits down hard beside us and stares.

We both start laughing.

"I'm assuming he likes chicken?"

"Yeah, he likes everything." I roll my eyes and throw him a chunk.

"And you don't spoil him either, right?"

"Maybe I do."

"How did you become the surrogate father?"

"Ha! Perfect way to word it. Cade and Debra

got him for the home—as a sort of therapy dog for the kids—but he was a handful, so he somehow ended up mine. He accompanies me everywhere just about, and the kids at North House love him."

"He seems like a good friend."

"He is." I look up at her.

"Like a wingman,"

"What do you mean?"

"He stole my hat and led me into your bedroom." She explains.

"Ah, good boy, Bailey." I toss him an extra-large piece of chicken.

"So, Bailey…?"

"Yes …" I confess. "After your favorite drink."

She gazes at me; her eyes are full of emotion.

Bailey nudges my leg.

"Don't move," I tell her as I set her on the seat next to us. "I've got to put him out."

"I won't move."

The sides of my mouth tug up into a smile. "Okay."

Bailey goes bounding down the back hallway, and I shout behind me, "And don't get dressed."

"I won't," she giggle-shouts back.

I let Bailey loose in the fenced-in backyard so he can do his thing.

When I get back to the table and see Quinn sitting there, naked and waiting for me, I immediately scoop her up into my arms. "Let's go back to bed."

I start to carry her through the living room, but her warm hand reaches down and slides between us until she has a grip on my cock.

"Why wait so long?" she purrs.

We get as far as the couch.

I lay her down, and she rests her head on the dark red pillows propped against the armrest. I kneel over her so she can keep playing with me.

"You're so thick and long, and I love how you feel like steel in my hands."

She puts her fingers in her mouth to wet them and then dances her fingertips over my most sensitive area, right below my head, around the neck and on the underside of my dick. I close my eyes and tilt my head back, lost in the feel of her hand and the sound of her voice. A moment later, she tickles my balls at the same time. I feel myself quickly swelling toward combustion.

"I've never…" she starts but finishes with, "You are so unbelievably perfect," before I feel my cock slip between her lips and inside her warm, moist mouth.

Her name escapes my throat as a moan, "Quinn… *You're* unbelievably perfect."

Sinking my hands into her hair, I tangle my fingers in her gorgeous blond locks.

"God, you're so huge." Her breath caresses my cock. `

I growl as she grips my dick and sucks me from as low as she can go, then back up to the tip, exploring my ridges, bends and veins with her delicate tongue.

I'm getting a full-body appreciation of her decadent mouth.

I watch her as her sexy but sweet-looking innocent gaze peers up into mine as she licks my tip like it's a lollipop before going back down.

I'm going to fucking melt.

She chokes for a moment as she accepts me into her throat, then comes back up, making the sexiest sound as I pop out from her lips.

My blood roars, and my cock throbs at the sight and feel of her.

"Stop." I nearly shout. "We can't do this."

"Am I doing it wrong?" Confusion paints her expression. "You don't like it?"

"Wrong?" My sex-addled brain doesn't compute. "No, I love it. But I want back inside of your hot, tight pussy."

She blushes.

I close in on her until I can feel her breath across my lips. "Oh, you like it when I talk dirty." It's not a question.

"Maybe." She whispers shyly.

"Spread your legs for me. I want full access to your sweet cunt."

She mewls as I press her thighs apart and softly stroke her drenched folds with my fingertips. I make little circles over her clit, which soon has her writhing her hips in search of more friction.

"Do you like when I touch your clit?"

"Yes." Quinn whimpers, and as her back arches, her breasts jut out toward my mouth. I suck her rosy tips deeply between my lips and flick at them with my tongue. The feel of her flesh pebbling in my mouth, the taste of her skin, and her soft shy whimpers as she presses up beneath me, wanting me to fuck her again, makes my erection jerk.

I lick and lap as she grows more and more needy.

I lift my head to watch her eyes become hungry with desire.

She moves her head toward mine and licks my lips, which I immediately part to kiss her. I plunge my tongue into her mouth, and our tongues tangle as her hips begin to buck faster against my hand.

"You're so close, baby."

She reaches out and tries to grab my aching dick. I pin her wrist. "Not yet. I just want to focus on you as I make you come."

Quinn's expression is pure pleasure as she surrenders to me.

My heart leaps in my chest. "God, you're so fucking beautiful."

What began as soft whimpers escaping her have turned to throaty moans and sexy cries, and all her sounds shoot straight to my throbbing cock. I have her running so hot I could come by just watching and listening to her.

And in this moment, she is mine again. All mine. Only mine.

Taking a moment to peer down, I gaze at my fingers as they tickle through her silken folds. I look at her with an artist's eye. "Your pussy is such a gorgeous palette of colors—hues of soft pink and dusky rose." I bury one finger inside, up to my knuckle.

"Oh, Liam." She groans, and her head drops back.

"There you go." I pump my fingers inside her until her every breath is a sensual sound, then scoop out her moisture and use it to massage her clitoris.

Sucking on her tit again, I make sure my eyes never lose contact with her face—I want to remember this forever.

She moans while I fuck her with my hand, and I have to kiss her again. I have to swallow her moans and sexy noises. I press my body against hers and relish the sensation of her frenzied movements underneath me.

"Come on, baby," I coax.

Her breath is ragged and full of sex.

She is seriously the most exquisite work of art.

Her wetness soaking my hand is making me crave her. I've got to taste her again. I'm holding on by a thread.

She whines my name. "Liam."

Thread snaps.

I move down her body like a shot, squeeze her firm, round ass in my hands and pull her smooth, long legs apart as I bury my face in her sweet-tasting pussy until her decadent juices overwhelm my senses.

"You taste so fucking good. There is no other taste like you, Quinn. Your skin, your sweat, your pussy…" I growl like a wolf.

She shatters on my tongue.

Her orgasm, wild and hot, overtakes her. I lick every drop of her cum as her pussy swells and pulses in my mouth.

Jesus Christ, I'll never get enough.

QUINN
PRESENT

BEFORE I HAVE A CHANCE TO RECOVER, HE COMES up fast to a sitting position with his back against the sofa and lifts my body into the air —like I weigh nothing—positioning me over his amazingly beautiful cock.

I gaze down and watch as it flexes, searching for my opening. He's so huge that I wonder if it's going to hurt in this position.

He holds me, suspended over him. He's so incredibly strong! His lean muscles bulge and flex as he holds me there.

"Oh yeah." Liam situates himself to his liking, with me still in the air, and licks and sucks the pink, aching tips of my breasts.

Our faces meet, and he licks my lips. Full of my taste, his tongue plunges between my lips, sliding across my teeth and the roof of my mouth before tangling around my tongue.

"Oh my God," I whine, heady at his lips and tongue, at his hands pressing me over him, and my taste in his mouth.

He moves his head back and watches my eyes as he spears his long, thick cock into me.

I whimper as my eyes plead for no mercy.

His groan is like thunder as he lifts me up and down over the length of his shaft, penetrating me, body and soul.

I'm so wet and open for him; every nerve in my body sings with pleasure.

Liam's gaze drifts between us to where our

bodies are bonded together. He moans as he watches himself fuck me—hot and slow.

I whimper and can't hold a coherent thought in my head.

He makes an animalistic sound as he hoists me up with him and lays me down, my back presses hard against the couch. He leans on his elbows and weaves his fingers into my hair.

"I missed your hair." He pounds in.

Slowly, he pulls himself back to the tip. "I missed your voice."

He pushes back in, and a cry is ripped from my throat.

"I missed your scent." He's losing his tight control.

"I missed you... the feel of your body, the touch of your hand, your stubborn, sassy mouth," He cries out.

I reach up and hold him as close as I can get him.

His strokes turn frenzied as he pumps inside of me with powerful thrusts.

I love the feel of his hips, which are holding my legs open and apart for him so he can take me completely. It's rugged and rough. I love the sensation of his rock-hard cock as he expands me to fit around him—I'm massaging him, milking him, gripping <u>him</u>, and I love his heart, which is still so open and honest—so one with mine.

Our breathing flows together in gasps and pants, and I'm caught up in the rapture he creates as he fills my every sense with his presence.

Liam moans and hammers harder and faster until he cries out. His cock pulses and pumps inside of me—I absorb every inch, every contour, every last drop as I squeeze my inner muscles loving the way his vibrato whiskey rough voice sounds when he's taking me.

"Ah, Quinn." Liam rests his forehead against mine, his tone raspy and sex-laden.

His eyes close and he rolls onto the couch beside me, pulling the gray knit throw blanket over us.

Then, just like old times, we fall asleep in each other's arms.

CHAPTER TWELVE

QUINN
PRESENT

"If they killed each other, I'm pretty sure you'll be held as an accomplice to murder," I hear a man's voice say.

"Shut the fuck up, Connor. You're not a lawyer … yet."

That was Josh, no doubt.

I try to open my eyes, but I'm so tired, and I wonder if I'm just dreaming.

"They're going to be all curled up together in his bed," Josh says, sounding sure of himself.

"Dead," Connor quips.

"Oh shit!" Josh and Connor blurt out together.

I pry my eyes open and see that they're in the living room.

"What the fuck! Don't you two know how to knock?!" Liam roars and quickly helps to detangle the blanket around us so I'm covered up.

I try not to laugh. "At least they turned away. If it'd been Ryder, he'd be trying to join us."

All three guys burst out laughing.

"Told you they didn't kill each other." Josh shoves Connor.

"Hey, it could have gone either way," he defends himself.

"If anyone was going to be dead, it would've been Josh about sixteen hours ago," Liam states, glaring at Josh as if he's still thinking about following through on the threat.

"Yeah, but I'm fucking brilliant. See what happened?" Josh crows. "I knew it."

I can't help but laugh at him. "I'm going to sneak away upstairs. I'll be back in a few." Quickly, wrapped in the blanket, I leave Liam on the couch with only the pillow to hide his manliness.

"And you guys are here *why*?" Liam asks.

"To bring you these," Josh says, laughing.

"Our cell phones, how gracious of you," Liam says.

Josh lowers his voice, thinking I won't be able to hear him. "Are you glad I did it?"

I listen harder.

"Fucking hell, yes!" Liam laughs. "Stupid, dangerous, fucked-up move, but it was brilliant."

Suddenly, I hear a crash that makes me jump, and Bailey starts barking.

"Hope we're in time for Sunday brunch." It's Reese's voice.

Reese's Peanut Butter Cup, I remember fondly.

"Yeah, and that stunt you pulled had Cade and Debra nervous last night," I hear Talon scold Josh.

Oh God! I hadn't even thought of them once.

Josh says, "Uncle Cade and Aunt Debra were fine last night when I called and explained the situation."

They start talking as I wash my face and quickly get my clothes on. I start hunting for my purse for a brush until I remember Josh stole it, since it was in his car yesterday too. I find Liam's brush and use it.

I'm so excited to see them all—it feels like a homecoming reunion—but before I get ahead of myself, I sit on the top step and listen to them banter.

Someone's annoyed nobody made or brought pancakes. Someone else says we can all go out to breakfast. Then one of the guys complains about money and asks who's going to break out the money bags.

Ryder, Josh and Talon have handled me being back in a really great way. But what about the rest? Will they look at me like they used to? After *that* night?

Has enough time passed for all of that to have been washed away?

If it hasn't, and someone does mess up, will I be strong enough to be okay, or will it cut me open?

All of them are down there—Josh, Reese, Talon, Ryder, Connor and Chase—they're whistling and making loud cat calls to Liam, who is obviously bare-bottoming it to the laundry room for pants.

I cover my mouth to stifle a giggle.

"GET DOWN HERE, WOMAN!" Ryder calls out. "YOU COULDN'T MAKE YOURSELF ANY PRETTIER! WE ALL WANT TO SEE YOU!" He lowers his tone and quips, "And maybe she'll come to her senses and finally dump Liam for me."

That doesn't sound like judgment or pity—that just sounds like pure fun.

"Shoulders back; remember who you are," my inner coach whispers. And I start down the stairs.

"Holy shit! That's Quinn!?" Reese squawks. He always was the comedian.

"Shut up and be respectful!" Josh nudges him with his elbow.

"It's sweet. I'll take it as a compliment," I tell them.

"Wow! Just wow! You're even prettier than you were as a kid." Chase walks over and gives me a hug. "It's so good to see you."

Reese is next, and then, one by one, they all hug

me. And, of course, I can't keep myself from crying.

"You made her cry!" Ryder shoves Connor, and Connor rolls his eyes.

And though they're trying to hide it, their eyes aren't dry either.

"I've really missed you. All of you."

"Yeah, but I'm devastated." Reese shakes his head mournfully. "You obviously missed Liam the most." He turns to Connor. "I told you she always played favorites."

"Yes, she does." Liam comes up behind me and puts his arms around my shoulders. "So, is someone really taking us all out for breakfast?" he asks.

Reese points at Connor, who points at Talon.

"Fine, I'll buy. I didn't need that new car anyway," Talon jokes.

Chase asks, "Where are we going?"

"Hell's Kitchen, of course," Liam says.

"God save the waitresses," I quip.

RYDER AND REESE VIE FOR FIRST PLACE IN THE hostess line. The brunette hostess gets a look at the two of them together, and I'm sure, by the expression on her face, she's already having panty-melting fantasies about taking them both on at once.

Reese's blonde hair tumbles just above his

shoulders and looks like a sexy mess—especially when you pair it with his athletic build and silver brow barbell. Ryder's brawn and predatory demeanor give off a vibe that makes you *want* to be prey—his short brown hair, green eyes and leather attire leave you panting. One is light and fun; the other is dark and brooding; both are all alpha.

Liam is hugging me from behind—his protection and loving possessiveness make me feel safe and wanted. I love him claiming me and showing everyone else around he's mine and I'm his.

Another waitress, wanting to get in on the action, comes over with a huge smile. The boys tell them there are eight in our party, and the girls' mouths drop as they glance back toward the door.

By now, the ruckus that's starting up behind us is hard to ignore, and so are the men making it. Josh, Connor and Chase are playfully going on about idiots who don't know how to properly park a car while quiet Talon walks in and rolls his eyes at them.

Liam and Josh's fame—or notoriety—precedes them, and, of course, all of them look like hot, rugged movie stars with bodies to kill for.

Most of the women are probably thinking they are porn stars. I laugh to myself.

The two waitresses lead us to the back corner of the restaurant, flirting shamelessly the entire way. When they begin to put two tables together, the guys politely tell them they'll do it. We all take a seat while Ryder puts in the order, stacks and stacks of pancakes with all the fixings, enough for seven hungry brothers and their would-be sister.

It feels like home, old times, and family, and I love it! I love them, each of them.

They take turns, each of them telling me what they're doing with their lives: Chase is attending the tribal college on the White Earth Reservation, where his family is from; Reese is at Minnesota State with a football scholarship; Connor is studying law; and of course, Josh is a big time MMA fighter. I heard all about Ryder's bounty hunting business in Liam's car the other day, and Talon is a tattoo artist at The House of Ink and Steel.

I'm in awe that they all turned out to be such incredible men and that they're all so close. I can't help but giggle. Who would've believed it?

QUINN
JULY
(PAST)

"This is absolutely ridiculous! Can't you idiots tell when you've got a good thing going?" I rage.

We've all been incarcerated in the group room, where we're being forced to sit together until Cade comes in here to dole out punishments. The fighting between the boys got ugly this evening after group. Liam and Josh always have it out for each other, but a couple of weeks ago, Josh grabbed my ass in the hallway. I punched him so hard that I sprained my wrist. He was so sorry—genuinely sorry—I couldn't tell Liam, or anyone for that matter, what he'd done. Like everyone else in here, the attitude he carries is just another way to mask the pain. Of course, Liam knew something had made me that angry, so now he's constantly picking fights with Josh—and this time, everybody wanted in on the action.

Group does that to them sometimes. Usually Cade brings everyone straight to the gym afterwards, but tonight they couldn't wait that long.

Cade just set the bone in Liam's nose, and there's blood all over his shirt. Josh is holding an ice bag against his swollen face. Reese is whining on the sofa, still holding the tender area between his legs that somehow got kneed during the melee. Chase has a wet washcloth pressed against the bleeding above his eye. Ryder's brooding dangerously in the corner of the room because his arm got twisted, and Cade said it might require a trip to the hospital. All the while, Talon and Connor are nursing bloody knuckles and busted lips.

"Debra and I spent over an hour making those pancakes. OVER AN HOUR!" I shout. "I don't know about you all, but I've never had anybody care about me enough to cook like that."

They all gaze down at the floor or their shoes in shame.

"I mean, honestly, if you hate each other so much, why don't you just leave?" Furiously, I throw the ice bag I'm holding across the room. "We sit in group together every freaking day; we know just about everything there is to know about each other. We know we've all been dealt a fucked-up hand, and I don't care how tough or hard you are, I know you all want a family and a place to call home. I would think that should bring us closer together!

"Maybe this is our chance!" I look around at the four walls of the room. "The only chance we'll ever get for a home! Or a family!" I shake my head. "And you guys want to waste it?" My voice is trembling, and I feel like I'm about to cry.

"Quinn—" Liam and Josh say at the same time.

"No! No, *Quinn*." Whatever apology they were about to make, I shut down quickly. "I care about you guys. I know each one of you and know you deserve better than the life you've been born into." Here come the tears. "You've come to mean a lot to me. To me … you're like brothers—*my brothers*—I trust you all and know none of you would ever hurt me."

I shake my head. "What makes me think any of this will sink in? You've had a thousand chances." I shrug. "You all want to hate each other? Go ahead. You can throw the blame around for everything else, but this right here …" I stir my finger in the air. "It's all on you. You guys have the chance to be brothers—for some of you, these might be the only brothers you'll ever get—and you're trashing it. Breaks my fucking heart!"

I'm out.

I storm out of the room.

Stupid, hard-headed boys. They'll do what they want, no matter what. I can't force them to see sense and reason!

I need to get out of here. I march out the front door into the summer sun.

I wipe my eyes, wondering why there has to be so much hate. You'd think they, of all people, would understand and try to do it better.

"They obviously don't care. Why should I?"

Once I reach the park on the corner, I sit on a swing and draw in the dirt with my toes.

There are a few families here, moms and dads with little kids having a picnic, some older kids playing Frisbee, a couple making out by the large oak tree, and then there's me, wondering about life. How much of it is random? Maybe simple and not-so-simple events that just *happen*. Without reason.

Like a rock that gets dislodged from its place

because it rains or an animal walked over it. While it rolls down the hill, it smacks into other stones; maybe it chips or breaks in half; maybe a piece of it falls on the road, where a car passes and its tire kicks it up further, so it ends up on the side of a creek. Just random acts that moved it along.

Does destiny or fate *really* exist? Is someone bigger than all of us controlling our lives? Or at least watching over us? It doesn't always seem that way. I know I prayed to the angel, and Liam came into my life. But I also prayed to the angel that my mom would love me, and that didn't happen.

But maybe the watcher isn't always benevolent? And maybe each one of us has our own choices to factor in?

Maybe it's not all God or the Universe or angels … or random selection or chance … maybe we should stop being so concerned with what or who and just try to live like good people and help each other.

And maybe I'm an idiot who just daydreams too much.

BY THE TIME I GET BACK TO NORTH HOUSE, it's completely quiet. Cade is sitting at his desk with his door open.

"Glad you're back," he says to me.

"Where are the guys?"

"Half are in the attic, and the other half are in the garage. By the time evening rolls around, I'm sure they'll have both places clean and organized," he tells me, then looks back at his computer screen.

"Too bad about the water park," I lament, thinking of Cade's promise that if we'd earned enough points today, he'd take us tomorrow.

"I know. Maybe next week," he says, sounding as disappointed as I feel. "At least you'll get the chance to finish the three books you're reading."

I laugh, pleasantly surprised he knows that.

I start to walk away when he says, "Quinn, make sure you go through the kitchen. The boys have something for you in there."

Can't think what that would be. I wonder if it's some code for the fact that I get to do the laundry or something.

I push through the swinging door into the kitchen. The room is gleamingly clean and spotless, and there on the table is a huge bouquet of wild-flowers with a note.

Sorry, Quinn. We're going to try to stop acting like assholes. Even if it's just for you.

They all signed it.

CHAPTER THIRTEEN

LIAM
PRESENT

B reakfast is full of chaos and insanity. I feel like I'm on the outside looking in, watching Quinn, watching my brothers, all of us sitting here together. It's too ethereal, and I can't make it make sense. I keep trying to believe it's reality, but it's fucking with my head.

"Don't like the food?" I ask Quinn, who's raking pieces of cut pancake around her plate with her fork.

"The food's great," she responds thoughtfully.

"JOSHY-DADDY!"

We all hear Charlie's sweet voice sing out through the restaurant as she and Josh's fiancée Sophie walk toward our table.

Josh stands up, and Charlie runs and leaps into his arms. After they hug, Josh grabs a couple extra chairs from nearby.

"I didn't think you two were going to make it!" He taps Charlie on the nose and kisses Sophie.

"I didn't either, but I'm all caught up," Sophie says tiredly.

Sophie is not only Josh's fiancée; she's also his personal masseuse on his MMA training team. She recently implemented a massage program for the kids at North House with two other massage therapists and tries to work with them as much as she can when she's in town.

"UNCLE LIAM!" Charlie falls like she has no bones from Josh's lap to mine, and I scoop her into my arms for a hug.

"Hey, Charlie-bear! What's the word, hummingbird?" I ask.

She giggles. "Pancakes!" she cries, then grabs a piece of pancake from my plate and puts it in her mouth as fast as she can.

"Hey! Where did it go?" I look baffled.

"Disappeared!" she mumbles with the half-chewed pancake in her mouth.

"Sophie, this is Quinn," Josh introduces us. "Quinn, Sophie."

"Hi." Sophie and Quinn shake hands over me and Charlie, smiling at each other.

"Nice to meet you," Sophie says.

"Same here."

Everyone sits and eats and talks as the excitement starts back up.

Josh and Sophie are so obviously in love, and it makes my heart swell to think of Quinn actually sitting beside me, but when I look over at her, I can tell that something's going on behind her beautiful eyes like she's lost in thought.

That's when reality starts to cave in.

There is no guarantee for her and me. We made no promises or commitments. Sex, reminiscing and breakfast doesn't erase the past pain and regret or create a shiny new future. The meal will end. Soon, the plates will be cleared, Talon will pick up the check, and everyone will go home.

Where will we go?

One minute at a time, Liam. I force myself to calm my mind and lace my fingers between hers underneath the table. She leans her head on my shoulder. That's all I need to fill my emotional hot air balloon and go soaring again.

"You sure you want to do this now?" I ask her as I'm fitting the key into the door to The House of Ink and Steel.

"I'm positive. It'll help me get my mind off tomorrow," Quinn says.

Tomorrow. That's something I haven't wanted to think about … *at all.*

She means her mother's funeral.

I mean the future—her future, my future—our future *together*.

She still has school in Georgia, but she's already said she was thinking about moving back. I can't bring it up. I can't speak about it at all. What if she decides against it? What if she decides the memories are too painful here?

I lead her into my alcove, where she takes off her shirt and gets comfortable on her stomach on my table as I begin preparing everything.

She wants me to color the tattoo I made for her so many years ago of the two mountain bluebirds flying free from the cage.

Could I move to Georgia? Realistically?

Leave the brothers and Cade and the kids? Move my shop? That might be like living without my kidney.

She turns her head toward me and looks over her shoulder. "Is it going to hurt as much as it did the first time?" she teases, her eyes shining brightly behind her lashes.

I smile. "No. Are you going to whine like you did the first time?"

"Probably."

Not being with Quinn is like living without my heart. Been there, done that. It hurts like death.

I start up the needle. "Remember not to squirm. Save that for me for later."

The needle touches her skin, and soon, the birds come to life.

"You know, after I saw you kiss Adrienne good-bye, I thought she was your girlfriend?" Quinn doesn't say it like a statement; she asks it like a question, as if she's still not sure what to believe.

"So you think I'd cheat on my girlfriend with you?" I cock an eyebrow playfully.

"Oh my God, is she your girlfriend?" she asks, panicking.

"Would I be a real asshole if I said I wouldn't care?"

"LIAM!"

"QUINN!" I mock her tone.

She goes quiet for a moment, then confesses, "I'd cheat for you."

"Yeah, me too. But to put your mind at ease, no, Adrienne is not my girlfriend. Her girlfriend would be pretty pissed if we ever started dating."

"Her *girlfriend*?" she emphasizes. "Suddenly, I feel much better."

I laugh and then say, "I have no girlfriend. And although I've gone out, nothing could ever be serious. I figured I'd be a bachelor forever."

You took my heart with you. I know this because for the first time in ten years, you came back, and I can feel it beating again.

If I had to choose between my heart and my kidney, my heart would win every time.

I want to ask what her plans are. What's she going to do now? Now that she knows I still love her? Now that she's admitted to still loving me?

"I'm going to freshen up these lines. It's faded some," I tell her.

"Okay."

I wait a moment before asking, "Would you like me to come with you tomorrow?"

"You would do that?"

"Of course, I would."

"Thank you. I might be able to handle it better if you're there with me," she says.

"Quinn?"

"Yeah?"

"Why do you *want* to go?" I ask. "I don't mean to be disrespectful, I just …"

"Don't worry about it. It's a valid question." She explains, "I don't have an answer for that, except that maybe it gives me the chance to say goodbye. Maybe it gives me closure. Maybe watching her being dropped into the earth will be healing. She's dead, so she's not pretending I don't exist anymore. She can't hurt me anymore. It's final. I don't know, maybe it's stupid."

"It's not stupid. Sounds human."

"Speaking of human—MY GOD, THAT HURTS!" she cries.

"Sorry," I say with a laugh. "I'm in the tight spaces of the wings. It's looking beautiful, though."

"I'm sure it is."

I think of what our next step could be as the hum of the needle fills the silence.

"Quinn?"

"Yes?"

"If you want, we could stop by North House and pick up some of your clothes if you'd like to stay the night again … with me?" I hold my breath.

She's quiet for a moment. "I'd like that very much."

Breathing again—with a huge-ass, fucking grin on my face.

"Quinn?"

"Yes, Liam?"

"Seeing your tits crushed against my tattoo table is making me hard."

"Good," she replies. "When you're done, we'll have to do something about that."

I sigh contentedly.

"Quinn?"

"I'm right next to you. Why do you keep saying my name?"

I think about that for only a second. "Because I have ten years of not saying it to make up for."

"Oh, Liam …"

I finish the tat, set the needle on the table and

gently kiss her shoulder above the above the tender area of the tattoo. "Ready to see it?"

She nods, and together, we stand in front of the mirror. I hold up the large portable one so she can see behind her.

"They're perfect, Liam! Absolutely perfect!"

They are too. I shaded the birds with different hues of blue, black, white, pink, orange, and gold to add light and contrast. Their spread wings in flight now catch the light of the sun as they soar.

I think about how long she's had them and how she never had another artist color them.

"Want to feel how hard you make me?"

"Yes." She says a splash of blush colors her cheeks.

I kiss her hand, then slide it down my abs to my dick.

Her eyes become hooded as she moans.

I drop to my knees in front of her, hike her dress up, and shove down her winter leggings and panties.

I slip two fingers through her folds and find them drenched. "Hmm... your pretty pussy is so wet for me already. I knew it would be."

She looks down and watches me with hot curiosity.

My lips curl into a grin, and I lock my eyes with hers as I pull her apart with my thumbs and strike my tongue against her soft, pink nub.

Her legs nearly buckle as she moans, and her clit immediately throbs in my mouth.

"Fuck yes." I watch the clouds of lust form in her eyes. "You like that, baby?" I ask with my lips moving and rubbing against her clit as I speak each word.

"Yes," she whimpers.

"Good." I push her thighs apart. "Because I'm going to worship you."

She gasps as I eat out her gorgeous, soaking-wet cunt. Soon, she is screaming my name and bucking against my face. With her legs quivering and unsteady, she reaches behind her and grabs onto the tattoo table.

My cock is straining against the buttons and zipper of my pants. I quickly undo them along with my belt as I continue to kneel before her, flicking and lapping my tongue at her lush, little clit.

Quinn's moans and rough breaths fill the room. It's never sounded so good in here.

My cock jerks at her breathy cries, "I can't wait to fuck you again."

"Oh God!" she squeals, and I plunge my tongue into her until she swells and comes on my face. Her wetness explodes in my mouth, spills down my chin, and coats my lips and tongue.

I am a man possessed, obsessed, and addicted. No woman had ever been able to satisfy the craving

I've had all this time for Quinn and have had to live without.

I lay quick waste to my pants, and since she can't lean on her shoulder, I spin her around so her elbows rest on the table and her perfectly round ass is like an offering for me to squeeze.

I grip her hips possessively and grind my thick arousal against her opening.

"Oh fuck, Quinn." I thrust my cock all the way to the hilt inside her hot walls from behind. A scream rips through her chest as her cunt squeezes me violently.

My balls tighten as my own orgasm builds at the base of my spine.

"You feel so fucking good." Every hard inch of me is buried deep in her as she quivers around me and swallows me whole.

My cock is slick with her juices.

"Quinn," I shout her name and grip a handful of her hair as I drive forcefully into her perfect pussy.

"You're so deep, Liam!" She's losing all self-control. "Oh God, don't stop!"

"Baby, I'll never fucking stop," I growl possessively and slide a hand up over her tit to play with her nipple from behind.

"I'm … I'm …" She can't finish her sentence.

"Come for me, Quinn."

She does. Like an F7 tornado.

"OH, FUCK!" I cry and explode inside of her with full fury.

I shoot my cum deep in her walls, my dick pulsing hotly with my orgasm.

"Holy fuck, woman." I breathe, landing open-mouth kisses down her spine.

When I regain my breath, I say, "It's like we christened my alcove."

"What do you mean?" She lies spent and sprawled on her tummy on my table.

"First time I've had sex in my tattoo shop."

"Really?" She looks like she's not sure if she believes me.

"The rule for all the brothers is no dates in the shop. The first woman who has ever been in here, not receiving a tattoo, is Sophie, once Josh got serious with her. Now you."

"I'm the only woman you've ever had in your tattoo shop?" Her eyes sparkle.

"You're the only woman who was ever supposed to be here."

WHEN THE EARLY MORNING LIGHT PEEKS THROUGH the windows, I reach over to get closer to Quinn, but she's not in bed.

Bathroom, I think.

But soon, I have to go, and she's not in there.

I throw on a pair of shorts and walk downstairs. Bailey's lying next to the front door.

"Quinn?" I call and make my way to the kitchen.

No answer. No Quinn.

Maybe she went for a walk? She woke once last night from a bad dream and cuddled in next to me.

I check my phone. No messages.

I check the counters and end tables. No notes.

It's only two hours before the funeral. I consciously decide I'm not going to freak out. I jump in the shower and dress in a dark suit.

An hour and a half later—after several calls and texts—I have no idea where she is. I also have no idea which funeral home the service is at.

I'm not sure what to think. Did she decide she didn't want me to go with her? So she just up and left with no goodbye or explanation? Why would she do that?

Did I fuck up and scare her off? Could have to do with that cheesy line about saying her name.

No, we had some pretty great sex after that.

When my phone rings, I snatch it up.

It's Cade.

"Hey," I answer, "I got something going on here."

"Here, too. Do you know where Quinn is?" he asks. "Someone's here trying to find her."

"I woke up, and she wasn't here. I was supposed

to go to the funeral with her, but now I'm just about going out of my mind. You know what? I'll be right there. Maybe she'll show up there." And although it sounds like he's about to say something else, I hang up and rush over.

Who's looking for her?

Friends of her mother? Or other family relations?

Where the hell could she be? The funeral is starting.

I PARK IN FRONT OF THE CORE AND RUSH IN. I TAKE double strides to Cade's office and push open the door.

"Excuse me," I blurt out when I see a guy sitting in the office chair opposite Cade.

"It's fine." Cade stands up. When he does, the other guy stands, too.

I notice he's in a suit—not too many people come to The Core dressed up. This must be the person who's looking for Quinn.

"Liam, this is James. Quinn's fiancé."

CHAPTER FOURTEEN

LIAM
PRESENT

My mouth goes dry, and I feel like I've just blacked out, but I'm still standing.

James reaches his hand out to shake mine. My expression becomes stony, and I fight the most powerful urge to take him to the floor and kill him.

He sees my face, swallows, and drops his hand to his side.

"James wanted to attend the funeral with Quinn but couldn't get out of work in time to get here, but as you can see … he made it after all," Cade explains with an expression of concern—as if he knows I'm going to blow.

"I haven't been able to get ahold of her for the last few days," the fiancé says. "She was supposed to be staying at a motel in the city, but when I called them, they told me she never checked in."

"I explained to James that she was staying with Debra and me," Cade says slowly.

My body gets cold as my blood boils. This can't be right.

"Fiancé?" I reiterate harshly.

"Yes, that's what I said." Cade answers for him.

"I feel terrible for not having been able to make it here for her earlier. I thought I'd surprise her and come, but now I'm worried," Asshole tells us.

"Has anyone tried the funeral home?" I bite out.

I can't look at him, or I'm going to hit him. My fists are already clenching at my side.

"Yeah, I've called over there a few times now," Cade says. "Reardon Funeral Home. The funeral has started, and the director says no one with her name has checked in with him or signed the guest book, and no one that young is even at the service."

"And Debra hasn't heard anything?" I try.

"No," Cade answers.

The fiancé shakes his head mournfully. "I shouldn't have let her come out here alone."

"Really, asshole? What led you to that fucking conclusion?" I'm a volcano ready to erupt.

"Excuse me?" His expression changes from concern to fear, and he takes a step back.

First smart move he's made.

I have to get the hell out of here.

Freaking Quinn! Way to prepare me. Way to tell me!

What happened with all the girlfriend-boyfriend-cheating talk yesterday? Did she *not think* that would've been the best time to tell me that she was *engaged to be married*?

FUCK!

I turn to leave.

"Liam, I need a word with you out in the hall," Cade tells me.

I do NOT want a word with Cade!

But he closes the door behind us, and we walk down the hall.

"Listen to me—" he begins.

"No! No, I won't. Not this time, Cade," I rage. "She lied to me. Bold-faced, right-out fucking lied!"

"She didn't tell you; I understand."

"You don't understand!" I say. "I've just spent all weekend making love to her, and she has a fucking fiancé!"

"Liam—"

"I can't do this again, Cade. I'm going to get shitfaced, or I'm going to kill the guy in your office."

I can't even think of any other guy touching her the way I've touched her.

Cade grabs me firmly by the shoulders. "Son, you need to listen to me."

Son. He has my attention. But it takes everything I've got.

"I know you and Quinn like I know my own name. The two of you belong together—always have. She knows it, too. I don't know who this guy is, and it doesn't matter."

"Doesn't matter? He's her fucking fiancé."

"There is no ring on that woman's finger. Do you understand me, son? She either took it off in hopes of seeing you, or it's not a true commitment."

I shake my head in disbelief.

He nods. "You and Quinn share the rarest kind of love. It was strong enough to save both your lives. If you believe in it, I think it can again."

"What am I supposed to do?" I rub my temples with my fingers.

"Find her."

FIND HER.

Rarest kind of love—strong enough to save both our lives.

I test the engine of my Nissan as I speed across the highway at nearly one hundred miles per hour.

Fucking Talon and his signs. I should have known better. I should have stayed away from her.

I fishtail off the exit.

Beeline to the nearest liquor store.

My cell rings; it's Talon.

Don't need it, don't want it.

I let the call go to voicemail as I take up two parking spaces in front of the liquor store. As I go in, I realize this is Johnson's Liquor Store, the one I stole Baileys from on Quinn's sweet sixteen.

I rip open the door angrily.

I grab a bottle of tequila and slam it on the counter.

"Drinking angry makes for a bitter hangover," old man Johnson says.

"It's agony just to be alive, so the hangover will be a relief." I throw a twenty on the counter and start to walk out. "Here." I turn around and toss another twenty-dollar bill down. "This is for her Baileys. Now we're even."

"What?" Mr. Johnson calls after me.

I get back into the car and see my phone on the seat.

Looks like Josh called while I was in the store.

Not a chance. Been there, done that.

Where the fuck am I going to consume this? I can't go home; she's all over my house now.

I can't go to my own fucking shop because she's there too!

Fuck!

Fiancé. *Asshole fiancé!* He wasn't even here for her when she needed him.

Oh God, I want to crack this bottle open. I

want to smash it over his fucking head. "Where the fuck can I go?!" I shout against the dashboard.

Then I hear my mouth say, "Where the fuck are you anyway, Quinn? You came here for a funeral, and now you're not even at the fucking funeral??"

Goddamnit! I hop on the highway and drive to Reardon's Funeral Home. Can't I just leave the woman alone? She's the one who left my bed this morning.

Obviously not, I think as I park across the street from the home and run over.

Opening the door, I walk into the solemn service and stand in the back, checking heads for Quinn, but I don't see her.

On the other side of the aisle, there is someone who appears to be an usher or the director.

I approach him. "Excuse me. I'm looking for the daughter of the deceased, Ms. Quinn Kelley …"

"I'm sorry. No one by that name has checked in or called."

"Thank you."

My attention is diverted. At the podium, one of her mother's friends is talking about what a wonderful woman she was and how she'll always be remembered as a friend and caring volunteer in the community.

Bunch of fucking bullshit. The woman was a cruel monster.

I remember the first time I met her. It was after she nearly killed Quinn by not letting her use a fucking phone. I went to her home to accuse her. Cade dragged me away. If she had been a man, I would have beat the fuck out of her.

And Quinn came back for her, not you, I remind myself.

I turn away and leave. I can't take it.

Back in the car, I check for a message from Quinn. When there isn't any, I text Cade.

> Any word?

He comes back.

> None.

> Is the douchebag still with you?

> Yeah, can't get rid of him. Now I have his sister here too.

Better Cade than me. His life expectancy would drop dramatically.

I put the key in the ignition.

"Where are you, Quinn Kelley?"

I've never stopped loving you, she said.

She didn't leave you, Josh said. *She was dying.*

Dying.

Dying.

I tear away from the curb and race to the other side of town.

LIAM
JULY
(PAST)

"Where the hell is she, Cade?" I shout as I move past the police flooding Cade's office at North House.

"It's none of your concern, boy," one of the cops says.

"It's all my concern," I spit vehemently and go to grab the cop, but then stall dead in my tracks when I see Cade covered in blood.

"Liam."

I've never seen the man broken. Not once. And I can't even fathom or describe the terror, agony and fury that he's wearing on his face, along with the splattered blood. I shake my head against anything he could possibly say as if I could stop whatever it is or make it not real.

"She's in the hospital, son," Cade almost whispers.

"Why?" I grit out between my teeth.

Cade loses his calm, always-at-the-ready demeanor and breaks down crying.

"TELL ME WHAT THE FUCK HAPPENED!" I scream, banging my fist on his desk.

"You're going to have to leave!" A cop grabs my arm and starts pulling me away.

I yank my arm back. The cop is about to have a busted nose.

"No, wait." Cade stops him. "I'll talk to him. He needs to know. The girl is his fiancée."

He stands up and walks around his desk. "Follow me."

We go into the family counseling room. It's empty and dark. The only thing to hear is the sound of our breath. He clicks on the table lamp.

Now that he's standing in the light, I can see the blood all over his hands, shirt and pants. The perfect outline of a slender, bloody handprint is set over the shoulder of his white t-shirt.

"Is the blood …?" I'm shaking now.

"Hers." He swallows. "She was jumped by Vince and some of his thugs."

"Jesus Christ." *Hospital, he said hospital,* I remind myself. "Is she …?"

He shakes his head and pushes out with a sob, "Son, I'm so sorry … they're not sure if she's going to make it."

It's a nightmare. I'm sleeping, and it's a fucking nightmare. WAKE UP, LIAM!

I step forward and take hold of Cade's hands. I smear the blood with my fingers. "This is *all* her blood?"

He nods.

"Is any of it Vince's?" I ask, not looking up.

"No. I found her behind the gas station …" he chokes out. "It was all I could do to keep her alive."

Someone knocks hard on the door. "Come in," Cade calls out.

"Mr. North, we just got a call from the doctors," one of the cops says as he and his partner walk toward us.

Debra bolts into the room and grabs Cade, sobbing.

The cop says, "They've taken Ms. Kelley into surgery—her ribs are fractured, one of which has punctured her right lung, her nose and jaw are broken, her arms are dislocated, and she has internal bleeding. They're not sure what else."

This isn't happening—it isn't real. I'll wake up, and she'll be in the kitchen with Debra, making breakfast, and then we'll go to the Mall of America to the amusement park. I'll win her a stuffed animal, and later we'll ride the Ferris wheel, and when the car stops at the top we'll kiss and not be able to keep our hands off each other.

Debra reaches over and takes one of my hands from Cade's.

The cop takes a moment to pause. "The tests show that she was sexually assaulted. A DNA test is being done to determine the number of assailants."

DNA test? Number of assailants.

"I need to see her." I rub the pads of my finger-tips into her blood, which now paints the palms of my hand.

"The doctor said family tomorrow … if she makes it through the night. They'll have her in the ICU."

"We are her family," Debra cries.

"Of course, ma'am," he says. "I'm so terribly sorry. They're doing everything they can to save her."

If.

If she makes it.

Quinn … could die.

Is dying.

That's when the gravity of the situation crushes me. The angel was supposed to protect her. I was supposed to protect her.

If she dies, I die.

What's happening inside of me is indescribable —I've never felt it before. It's as if one switch inside of me has been turned off while another is switched on.

Cade and Debra are both crying. I will not cry.

Not yet.

Quietly, I move toward the door.

"Liam …" Cade and Debra say at the same time.

I don't answer. I leave the room and walk past all of the cops talking in the hallway.

What I mistake for the deepest numbness settling over me is really a white-hot rage that devours every other emotion in its path until I am consumed by it, and nothing else remains.

I climb the stairs to my room and begin getting dressed.

"Where are you going?" Josh, who is sitting on the edge of his bed, wide awake, asks me.

"None of your fucking business."

He nods. "Okay, I get that."

I pull my blue jeans on over my shorts and throw on the first t-shirt my hand gets hold of—my bloody hand.

Quinn's blood.

I grab my leather jacket.

Talon is shoving on his sneakers. "Where are we going, Liam?"

"You're not going anywhere. Now, butt the fuck out," I warn him.

Ryder comes crashing into the small space of a room Josh and I share. "I heard 'em talking after you left. She's in the ICU on oxygen and has a fucking tube in her chest for her fucked up lung!"

He slams his fist against the wall, leaving indentations of his knuckles. "Did you fucking know that?!"

I lace up my heavy steel-toed work boots then go for my pack that I still keep ready in the closet. For a moment, my eyes land on Quinn's pack, which is right next to mine.

Reese leans his head against the doorway. "Connor, they're talking about a forensic exam that might end up showing multiple strains of DNA. What does that mean?"

Somehow Connor is in the room too and answers, "It means that she was …" He goes quiet, then finishes with, "probably assaulted … by more than one guy."

I hear a sound rip through my throat. My breath comes out like fire. I ignore it and unzip my pack. I grab two rolls of quarters I've hidden in the lining, making a mental note to take the metal baseball bat that's in the garage as well as any other makeshift weapons I can find.

Leaving my open pack on the bed, I turn and walk out of the room. I won't need it again, not where I'm going.

"If you're going for Vince, we're coming," Josh says.

"I'm going to take Vince to hell," I reply coldly.

Connor gets in front of me. "You can't get out through the front or back door; it's swarming with cops."

"I don't give a fuck about cops." I walk around him into the bathroom, where I lift the window and climb out.

"It's two stories up. What's your plan?" I hear Talon's voice behind me.

"My plan is to get into the garage." With that, I disappear out the window and climb down the vined lattice Quinn and I used to sneak to the roof.

Quinn ... dying.

Doing everything they can to save her.

Save her.

Stay focused.

The sky is pitch black with no stars. I open the garage side door and rummage through it for the steel bat. When I find it, the smooth, cool metal feels perfect in my palm. Perfect for the vengeance I'm about to exact.

I take off down the sidewalk.

Josh runs over. "Connor wired a car a few streets over. You didn't plan on walking all the way to Westhill, did you?"

It hadn't even crossed my mind.

We quickly make our way through the neighborhood. The car is there with all of them in it. I shake my head. "You guys are not coming."

"The hell we aren't," Reese barks from the back seat.

"Do you understand that I'm going to kill Vince?" I ask, feeling eerily levelheaded.

"Goddamnit, just get in!" Connor snaps from behind the wheel. "It won't be long before the cops pick Vince up or figure out we're not at the house anymore."

"You're not coming," I repeat. "And you're wasting my time."

"You need us," Ryder argues. "They know you. They know your face. You used to fight in the city's underground clubs. You've got history here. You're not going to just walk the fuck up and in."

"What? You assholes are going to fight *with* me?"

"*With* you. *For* Quinn," Ryder's expression is deadly serious as he opens the door for me. "Let's go."

I sit by the window, squeezing the handle of the bat. Looking beside me at Ryder then through the rearview mirror into the back seat at Josh, Reese, Chase and Talon; they're all readying their weapons. I don't know where they got their hands on this kind of arsenal—chains, metal dumbbell bars, a couple hammers, and other improvised arms —but they did.

Josh leans toward me. "We've got your back, man."

And for the first time, I believe him.

CHAPTER FIFTEEN

QUINN
PRESENT

"I TRUSTED YOU! I BELIEVED IN YOU!" My voice sounds raw as it echoes across the expanse of space and time as I shout at the angel. The angel in the graveyard where I had met Liam a lifetime ago. "I loved you! Couldn't you have loved me back?" I sob and scoop a stone from the pile of rocks I've made on the ground at my feet.

"Instead of helping me, it's like you conspired with my mom to kill me!" The rock I throw sails through the air and nicks the statue's torso.

"And now I've suffered without Liam, and I made him suffer, and I've had to put myself back together piece by piece—*with no help from you*!" I propel another stone, and it hits her wing. "I thought all those years you put us together … but you let *it* happen and ripped us apart!"

"AND I BLAME YOU! AND MY MOTHER!" Screaming, I hurl more rocks against the stone I once believed guarded us.

"Now she's dead. My battle with her should finally be over. But I can't even grieve right—because when someone dies, you're supposed to feel sad and sorry and brokenhearted—and I don't feel any of that! I feel forgotten, and unloved, and thrown away! I FEEL HATE!" I grind my teeth together and throw with all my power.

Another.

Another.

Another.

"She's dead, and she never has to say she's sorry! She never would've anyway." Dropping to my knees in a wilted, soggy patch of grass, I bend over and press my hand against my stomach to try and offset the agony of too many emotions all at once. "How does it still hurt like hell? How can you miss something you never had? Like a mother? How can you miss an idea?"

"I would have done it, you know, Angel—gone to the hospital or her bedside before she left this world. I would've forgiven her." I pull as many rocks as I can into both my hands and squeeze. "It doesn't matter now, does it? It's just always going to hurt. It will always feel unresolved because I loved her, and she didn't love me back."

I shake my head as I fill with fury. "Every part of me has been violated—because of her! My mind, my heart, my soul, my body! Just a fucking phone call, that's all it would have taken to protect me."

The violent wave builds again as I scream, "I'M NOT SORRY SHE'S DEAD! MY LIFE HAD *FINALLY* FELT LIKE IT HAD COME TOGETHER! *AND THEN YOU LET THEM SHRED ME!*" The flurry of stones catapults from my hands, slamming across her feet.

QUINN
JULY
(PAST)

I HOLD ON DESPERATELY TO THE PLASTIC, LIFELESS phone receiver before it's yanked cruelly from my hand as the men pull me away and begin dragging me down the alley behind the dark, abandoned gas station. I kick and scream as I press my Chucks into the dirt and gravel to get purchase.

Vince spits, "Secure the bitch."

The four men who are with him each grab one of my limbs. They half carry me, and half drag me, with my back scraping against the dirt and stones.

I can't let them get me back there! I have to get away from them! I flail my arms and legs, trying to get even one of them free, but I'm no match for the four of them together, they're too strong.

"Bitch ain't stoppin'," the big guy holding onto my wrist says.

Vince stoops down so he's in my face and, with cruel glee, says, "Pull her apart and break her like a wishbone."

His command creates a sickening dread in my belly. *They don't intend on leaving me alive.*

"Cade North is on his way! He knows you're here!" I scream.

"I figure that gives me about ten minutes." Vince grabs my cheeks hard in his hand and squeezes. "I can do a lot of damage in ten minutes."

Please, Angel, please!!

My vision blurs as hot tears gather and burn in my eyes.

They break me apart, piece by piece. The pain is too much.

The situation is more horrific than my mind can take. The reality of what's happening shatters me into a million tiny pieces. My mind refuses to believe it. Refuses to understand and pleads against it.

Vince gets on top of me as the other men hold down my broken body.

ANGEL!!

But I can't fight. There is no rescuer. I'm abandoned and at their mercy.

I'm flickering in and out of reality.

All I can think about is that I'll never see Liam again.

I close my eyes against the pain and the fear and focus on Liam's face—his blue-green eyes and dark hair and the way it falls across his forehead. I think about how his strong arms feel around me, and I'm safe.

Safe.

Loved.

A thought drifts by. I wonder if I live, will he ever be able to love me after this.

The edges of my vision start to go black, and I can't hold onto his image.

I think I hear a car door slam and then a gun firing. Maybe they shot me. But it doesn't matter anymore. I've lost Liam's face.

"Quinn?? QUINN!!"

Cade?

I can't breathe.

It's so fucking dark.

I LISTEN AS DEBRA READS MY BOOK OUT LOUD TO me. She cries as she tells me she loves me and that I'm the daughter she never had.

I hear Cade begging me to stay and begging me to forgive him.

I feel Liam's warm hand on mine. I know it's him; I can just tell. He doesn't talk for a long time.

After what seems an eternity, he starts telling me that when I get better Cade's going to give us enough money to go to Florida and get an apartment. He tells me stories about what it will be like, walking on the white sands and listening to the ocean waves hitting the shore.

He tells me he loves me, and I feel his mouth right next to my ear, as he pleads with me to wake up, says that he doesn't want to live without me, and his tears fall against my cheek.

I would do anything for him, but it's still so dark, and no matter how badly I want to, I can't open my eyes.

THERE'S A SHARP PRICK IN MY ARM, AND THE BLACK starts to recede. But with the light comes enormous pain. I can't move at all.

"It's okay." Liam's voice reaches me. "I'm right here. Don't try to talk. Just rest."

And although I hear him, I'm not sure if he's real or if I'm hallucinating.

Not being able to move makes me feel like I'm back under Vince or one of his men. I can see their faces. I try to thrash and get free, but they're still holding me down.

Liam cries out, and I try to yell back so he'll hear me … so he can help me, but before I can, the blackness swallows me again.

Beep … beep … beep … beep …

I wish I could make that infernal sound stop! Over and over again. It's not loud, but it's annoying, like a snooze alarm you can't turn off.

"Liam," I whisper. *How I wish I could see his face.*

"Quinn?" Liam says next to me. "I think she's waking up!"

I try to talk, but something's wrong.

"Come on, Quinn, wake up for me, please. I want to see your pretty, blue eyes." He's begging.

By sheer willpower, I pry them open.

It's all blurry at first, but Liam comes into focus. He's holding my hand, smiling and crying at the same time.

The room we're in is dim. I'm about to ask why

when I see the heart monitor machine that's making the annoying beeping racket. There is a needle in my hand with tape over it and a thin tube disappearing above my head. There are machines all around me and like a marionette, and I'm wired to them.

Then I remember.

CHAPTER SIXTEEN

LIAM
JULY
(PAST)

C onnor drives across town to the other side of the city and parks the car a couple blocks over from Vince's favorite hangout, The DuBois, a rundown hotel that serves as the Westhill Cartel's home base.

The place is infamous in this part of the city. It's four stories of dirty, grey chipping paint with sections of red brick and a concrete exterior. The dilapidated HOTEL sign is covered with rust, and the neon lights don't work, or no one has turned it on. Single pane windows are either broken, smashed out entirely, or boarded up with cheap plywood. The shithole could've been condemned years ago, but it operates as the headquarters for Vince's operation of drug running and prostitution. He must have paid others off to keep it open.

Having formulated a plan, we step out of the car and split into groups.

We watch from our hiding places, as Talon and Chase walk over to the guard at the front entrance and start talking to him about buying some merchandise. I can't hear them, and my entire body is shaking with adrenaline. I will get into that building and at Vince's throat.

I'm out for blood. I will spill his like he did Quinn's.

Steadying myself, I watch as Talon and Chase play it cool. The guy gets annoyed, but more than that, as we planned, he's distracted.

Ryder comes up stealthily from behind him with a thick metal chain already pulled taut between his fists, throws it around his throat, and pulls back hard. Ryder's expression is stone as he turns his rage onto the guy, twisting and tightening the chain as the guard flails. There is no hesitation about what we're doing.

None of hesitate.

Reese shoves a rag into the guard's mouth and duct tapes it in place as Josh quickly works to zip tie his hands and feet together. His cries are muffled and broken from the cloth and chain.

After Ryder drags the guy into the alley, Connor relieves him of his automatic rifle.

Talon and Chase stand guard for us.

The guy loses consciousness as Josh pats him down and finds a holstered Glock, an FN 5.7 on his thigh, and machete strapped to his hip.

"That's everything he's got on him," Josh says.

The metal links shift and groan against themselves as Ryder wraps the chain tighter until the guy's pulse is undetectable.

"Welcome to the grave, asshole," Ryder seethes is a soft voice next to the guy's ear.

We all share a knowing look, no words needed.

After leaving his body in the darkest part of the alley behind a couple of rusted dumpsters, we head back to the front and push through the main entrance.

The smell of piss and sweat permeates the lobby. A grimy sofa, a few chairs, and a folding table sit to the side. The ceiling and walls have exposed wiring, and the dry wall is falling apart. It's empty except for the seedy guy sitting behind a partitioned front desk. He looks like the person who takes money from check ins.

"What do you want?" He hardly bothers to look up.

Chase crawls across the filthy rug under his desk, gets behind the partition, and puts the end of a steel bar bell against his temple.

"No noise or I shoot," Chase whispers menacingly.

"Where is Vince?" I demand.

He looks up at the stairs. "Room fourteen." He swallows, fear spreading over his expression.

I get right in his face, grab his throat and squeeze. "How many guys are up there?"

"I don't fucking know. Maybe ten, maybe more." Tears of pain and fear fill his eyes as he gasps for air.

Good. I think. *He's one of them.*

I pull back my arm in rage and bring down my fist like a hammer against his jaw. The blow propels his body out of the seat and onto the floor.

I don't need to know anything else. Chase kneels over him lifting the metal bar bell in the air above his head. His lips pull into a thin, unflinching line as his expression becomes brutal, and he brings the thick steel bar down against the man's skull.

I run up the steps two at a time as rats squeal and scurry away from my boots.

Standing at the top of the stairwell, I resist the urge to kick in the door and listen instead. Music is playing, and I hear the muffled sound of guys talking and girls laughing.

After a moment, Josh, Ryder, Talon and Connor are standing beside me, waiting expectantly for my next move. Reese must be with Chase.

I step over and try the knob, but it's locked.

We conceal ourselves in the stairwell as Talon stays at the door. His eyes meet mine before he nods, knowing his next move, then wraps his knuckles against the door.

A big guy wearing a semi-automatic slung over his torso opens the door. Talon grins widely, his body swaying and his speech slurred as if he's drunk as he speaks to him in Spanish. Talon is supposed to be telling him he can't find room number eight and asking if he could show him.

They start conversing in Spanish, and I don't have a fucking clue what he's saying but the guy laughs, and Talon looks like he starts to stumble away, but the moment the guy turns, Talon puts the Glock we confiscated to the base of his skull and holds the collar of his shirt tight so he can't pitch himself forward.

Talon whispers in his ear, and the guys takes a slow, careful step toward the doorway. From our plan, I know Talon threatened our "organization" would kill his beloved family if he tipped off anyone in the room, and he took the bait.

Reese and Connor quickly darken the yellowed, flickering lights on the wall and ceiling in the hallway with black spray paint so they don't see our silhouettes, buying us a couple extra seconds.

Talon and the guard take two more steps through the threshold together. Following close behind, I move into the shadows with Ryder on my right and Josh at my back. Sizing up the room and situation, I realize they are having a party.

While my Quinn lies in a hospital bed.

Vince and his thugs are reclining lazily on chairs and couches throughout the large room. There are several girls—some sitting on their laps, others are on their knees giving blow jobs, while a few are having sex.

Rage consumes me.

There are nine or ten guys. Any of them could've been there. She was held down. No one helped her. They're testing her for multiple strains of DNA.

As far as I'm concerned, they're all guilty.

Ryder aims the FN 5.7 semi-automatic he lifted from the first guard we took out and immediately shoots the guy closest to the group's munitions stockpile on the other side of the room right between the eyes. He drops.

"What the fuck?" some guy shouts.

But they're too late. In my peripheral, I see the boys attacking Vince's men with their weapons and hear the sharp popping sounds of bullets being fired.

I don't care if I die tonight—in fact, I'd prefer it. Quinn is dying; I have no reason to live. The only thing that matters now is that my target is right in front of me.

Quickly, I close the space between me and Vince.

The girls scream and run.

Vince reaches for the pistol hilt tucked into the front of his pants.

My muscles bunch and coil, and with a burst of speed, I pounce. Stepping up and over one of the chairs, I come down hard, violently slamming my boot against his face.

I will break him like he broke Quinn.

As he stumbles, the gun he was fumbling for slides across the floor, and I swing the steel bat with all my power, striking Vince's spine, then turn to send a shot against his ribs. The cracks are audible, and Vince howls in pain.

A second later, some asshole's fist jams into my kidney from behind.

I roundhouse kick the guy in the gut, and he falls over a couch. Another comes at me with a switchblade in hand. Before I do anything, Josh and Connor grab him from behind and throw him against the nearest wall before pummeling him.

People are shouting, and there are bodies on the floor, but none of it matters.

I will avenge her.

I turn my attention back to Vince, who's barely standing, his hands on his knees. Fury makes me see red around the edges of my vision.

"You hurt the wrong girl," I seethe.

Using my steel-toe boot, I kick him in the ribs I already hit, which propels him onto his side. I grab him, throw him on his back and pin him down. Gripping my rolls of quarters to strengthen my blows, I slam my fists against him over and over.

"You're going to wish you never laid eyes on her."

He gets some punches in, but they do nothing to hurt me. There is nothing anybody can do now to hurt me. One of his lieutenants could shoot out my brains, and I wouldn't feel it.

Nothing matters. I wasn't there when she needed me the most.

Dying …

I punch him in the liver, the ribs, the jaw, the throat—again and again and again. He spits out a curse with blood and teeth. His blood is all over my hands and shirt, covering his mangled face and streaming down his neck. My mind flashes back to Cade covered in Quinn's blood. My sweet, beautiful Quinn,

Vince pants, "She was squealing like a little—"

He doesn't get to finish his thought. I jump to my feet and catch hold of his arm twist it up and around behind his back until it dislocates then kick him over to his belly. With a tight grip on his arm, I jerk it up harder as I drop and shove my knee against his now fucked up spine. Vince screams.

"Shoot this motherfucker!" he cries.

"No one's going to save you … and I'm going to rip you apart," I grit out. "How does it feel to know you're about to die?"

He howls in agony.

I reach around and get ahold of his jaw, twisting it hard to the side. He shrieks, and I know it's broken.

"LIAM!" I hear Talon shout behind me.

Turning fast, I see a guy coming at me. Bouncing to my feet, I'm ready. He's got a pistol trained on me.

"Big streetfighter Liam Knight," he sneers. His face is bruised, and above his left eye, the skin is split and blood trickles down his face.

I recognize him but don't remember his name. I'd fought him before in one of the illegal fight clubs, and I beat the shit out of him too.

"Is all this because of the pretty blonde you like?"

The blood in my veins flows even hotter. "Are you one of the motherfuckers who touched her?"

"She was real sweet." For a heartbeat, Vince's movement catches his attention.

That's all I need. I step in close, grab the gun with my right hand and yank his arm down. The gun goes off before I wrench it from him.

Getting a strong grip on the barrel end of the slide, I strike him hard with the sight across the side of his mouth.

The impact forces his mouth open as pieces of his crumbling teeth and bone, and a good chunk of his tongue he must've bit off, tumbles out of his mouth as he falls to the floor.

His head is painfully tilted to the side, and I realize the blow snapped his neck.

He won't be getting up again.

As I turn back to Vince, I quickly register the scene around me.

Most of Vince's men are down. Josh and Ryder are fighting with a couple guys to the side. Connor is wielding a broken bottle against a guy with a blade.

Reese is standing in the doorway with an automatic rifle. Nobody in, nobody out.

I don't see Chase.

Talon is directly behind me, grappling with a guy, and I realize he's been my rear guard. When I get my eyes on Vince again, he's crawling across the floor—like a half-smashed cockroach. Kicking him over onto his back, I stand over him and position my boot over his Adam's apple and press. I've beaten him so badly, he's barely recognizable and gurgling in his own blood.

He starts to choke and sputter and flail his good limbs as his eyes grow wide with fear.

My thoughts snap to a vision of Quinn, being overpowered, terror burning in her eyes. Helpless. Defenseless. His body on top of hers.

Raw, indescribable fury rises through me like mercury, boiling my blood and pulsing through my veins and muscles until it consumes every part of me.

"Rot in hell, you son of a bitch." I press harder and listen as his airway is cut off and then crushed under my boot as he gasps for his last breaths.

"For Quinn," I say.

THE SUN IS STARTING TO RISE AS WE CLIMB THE lattice back into the house.

I go straight to my room to clean up. About ten minutes later, the guys are standing outside my door.

"What do you want?" I bark.

Talon stands tall in the doorway. His face is badly swollen and his shoulder is bandaged. "Quinn wanted us to be brothers."

"Yeah?" I shake my head. "What of it?"

"Tonight, we were," Josh states, walking past Talon and into the room. He's wrapping his hands with gauze, but the blood is seeping through.

I nod my head. "Tonight, we were."

"We should stay brothers," Ryder says. His t-shirt is ripped and blood is smeared across the front of it. He's pressing a wet washcloth over a knife slash on his right cheek bone.

"We spilled blood tonight for each other and for Quinn," Connor adds in a low voice. "That makes us family now." His ear is twice it's normal size and has blood dripping from it. His left arm hangs in a makeshift sling.

"Hell yeah, we did," Reece groans as Chase wraps his ribcage with Cade's sticky, kinesthetic sports tape.

Chase who had gotten shivved in the leg stops what he's doing to watch my reaction. "Tattoo it, Liam," Talon says. "On each of us as a sign of our brotherhood."

Quinn wanted us to be brothers.

Without a word, I rise and go to the drawer where I keep my homemade tattoo machine and the bottle of black ink.

As I set it up, I remember a photo I came across in *Ink Magazine* of soldiers who scribed matching tats on their biceps. I had always longed for that band-of-brothers closeness.

"*I am my brother's keeper,*" My voice is hoarse. "Quinn would like that." *Would've liked that …*

"That's perfect," Chase says, and everyone agrees.

Josh picks up his dirty, bloody shirt, holding it in his clenched fist. "It should go on our left upper rib —closest to the heart."

I try to say okay, but I can't; the emotions I've

been holding at bay seem to be rising. I choke them down and say gruffly, "Lay down."

When I turn on the needle, the sound soothes me and makes me think of Quinn. The last time I used it was to etch the birds on her shoulder. A peace comes over me that I can't explain. At that moment, I think of her and the angel.

Josh is first, then Talon, then Ryder.

Hours later, I'm sinking the needle into Connor's skin as Cade steps through the door and quietly studies us.

He doesn't say a word and doesn't look as surprised as I thought he would about us being all fucked up like we were and all seven of us in the same room, not killing each other. I also expect him to be pissed off when he realizes I'm giving out tattoos, but he isn't.

Immediately, I think he's going to tell me Quinn didn't make it through the night. Or that the police figured out what happened, and I'd be going to prison.

Instead, he comes in for a closer look.

"I am my brother's keeper," he reads out loud from Josh's torso then takes a deep breath. "I thought you'd all like to know, the police went to the Dubois to apprehend Vince and his men…" Cade pauses and looks directly at me. "But they found him dead. Along with the other members of his group that were there. The police believe it's the work of a rival cartel."

I keep my breath steady because I don't know what's about to come out of his mouth next. He can totally see we're bloody and beaten up. I don't care what happens to me; I'm only worried about Quinn.

"And?" I ask gruffly.

"And when the police questioned me, I told them all of you had been home sleeping."

We're all quiet.

Cade continues, "I'm going to need to fix that lattice out the upstairs window. Make sure it's secure to the wall. I think it became loose with last season's snow." He sets his warm hand softly on my shoulder. "Looks like you're now the brothers of ink and steel."

After he walks out, no one says a word.

Ink and steel. I think of the steel baseball bat I used to beat Vince and of the bars some of the *brothers* carried. I think about the steel we regularly lift at The Core and how it's made us strong—both physically and emotionally. I think of the black ink going beneath our skin to our souls.

It's the perfect title for what we've become.

LIAM
PRESENT

MY BOOTS LEAVE THICK TRACKS IN THE MUD AND slush of the path into the graveyard as I run past the headstone I leaned against when I first saw her …

And there's Quinn, where I knew she'd be, by the angel.

I glide to a stop, slipping in the wet mud and snow.

My brow presses down, and my jaw clenches. She's yelling and sobbing. Her agony-filled voice reverberates across the open space.

Immediately, I'm consumed with her pain.

Taking a deep breath, my anger disappears.

She didn't tell me about her fiancé. So what? I would've done the same thing.

She didn't come back for me, but for her mom—why she came back doesn't really matter. What matters is that she *did* come back.

And for a little while, all the planets aligned, and she was once again the most beautiful star in my universe. I wouldn't give that time up for anything.

We'd burned brighter than a fucking supernova, even if we weren't meant to last.

All of a sudden, Quinn shouts and spins

around, sees me and freezes. I straighten my shoulders, not sure what to expect.

She squints her eyes as if she doesn't believe what she's seeing, then buries her face in her hands and drops to the ground.

She starts rocking back and forth.

I move to stand next to her and suppress the urge to hold her. I don't know what she needs.

"Ten years ago," she begins in a strained tone, "I never said goodbye to you because … I didn't want it to be final. I was *going* to come back. I *wanted* to come back, but it was just too much." Tears stream down her face.

I think back to when she came home from the hospital. She wasn't the same, even after she'd physically healed. She had terrible nightmares nearly every night; her bloodcurdling screams would wake everyone in the house. After a while, she began trying to stay up all night so she'd exhaust herself in hopes of sleeping without dreams. She'd startle and jump at the smallest noises and cry at random times.

She blamed herself, she blamed her mother, she blamed the angel and the social worker who dropped her off with no one home and no cell phone … but she never blamed me.

But I did—and still do.

"When I came home, I was like a cripple. Everyone stared at me with this mix of pity and pain. Especially you," she cries. "I knew you were thinking you could've stopped it or made it right if you had somehow been there. You weren't there. And you couldn't have been there. And it doesn't even matter because what happened, happened, and it couldn't be taken back, and it couldn't be undone or fixed! It just was. Just like now! The circumstances we're in, it just is."

She takes a second to wipe her eyes.

"The silence at the dinner table became torture. Playing Frisbee or volleyball outside, no one would touch me. Everyone was afraid they'd hurt me. Group became unbearable. They all wanted me to open up about it. How the hell could I? Vince and my mother stole *everything* from me, including you and the only home I'd ever known." She stares at the ground. "I couldn't stay."

Dear God, her admission kills me, and my heart crumbles in my chest.

Quinn sniffs back more tears. "We were only kids. And how does anyone heal from that? You actually did so well loving me again, holding me, touching me as if I wasn't soiled." She cringes at the word.

You were never soiled. I try to say it aloud, but my mouth won't form the words.

"But no one knew how I felt!" Quinn almost shouts the words in exasperation. "Every time I closed my eyes, they were there, and every time I heard a noise, I felt like it was going to happen all over again."

"I knew how you felt." It spills out of me like the beginning of a reluctant but long overdue confession.

She shakes her head. "You only think you know."

"I know more than you think." And isn't this where I blame myself the most? "After years of Cade's help, I came to terms with the idea that what happened wasn't my fault. And that I couldn't have stopped it. But what *was* my fault, and still *is*, is that I never told you."

She looks tired, and I've got a hunch she didn't sleep last night. "I don't understand what you're saying, Liam."

"Of course, you don't." I swallow the fear down as I face the monster I've never told anyone about. It tastes like bitter regret. "If I had shared with you that I did, in fact, know how you felt, you may have found the peace or strength you needed to stay. I know it would've made a difference. But I was scared, Quinn, and selfish."

"You've never been selfish," she corrects me.

I lift my hand to stop her. "Please, I *was* selfish. I may have been able to help you heal, and heal myself, but I didn't. At first, I could blame myself. But then, when you never came back, I hid behind the blackest part of my heart, justifying my feelings and turning the blame on you for leaving. I'm sorry for that."

"Please don't be sorry. I had to go. I always thought I'd come back, but then time just kept passing, and all too soon, it had completely gotten away from me." She presses the backs of her hands against her tear-filled eyes. "You lived in my heart, Liam. I would pretend or think back to what it was like when we were together. Sometimes, I would trick myself into thinking that I could actually feel you there. When I finally got the courage to call or write to you, I couldn't bear to know that you were with someone else. Or that you had fallen in love again. I couldn't face that. So, I avoided you entirely."

Hearing her finally talk about this—what she felt like and what she went through—is shattering me. "I was never *with* someone else. Not seriously." I take off my outer coat and lay it on the cold, wet ground. "Move over and sit on this." She does, and I slide next to her. "I've never loved anyone except for you."

She lays her head on my shoulder and sobs. "I'm sorry I took so long. And as more time passed, I figured you didn't even want me back."

I don't even try to stop them when my own tears spill from my eyes. "You live in my heart, Quinn. Always have, always will, no matter what."

I pull her over onto my lap so she's wrapped around me while she cries against my shoulder.

"The funeral finally gave me an excuse, a reason that was viable ..." she gets out.

"I understand," I promise.

"I fucked up everything by running away."

"Please, let me finish what I was going to say before. It has to be said," I tell her.

I try to live in this second, this moment. I concentrate on her love and on her fear so that this can be all about her, and I can keep myself separate from what I'm about to tell her. "Remember when I told you that I didn't know my father?"

"Yes."

"I knew my dad, Quinn," I say point-blank. "He is ... was my grandfather. My step-grandfather."

She falls silent.

"He regularly raped my mother when she was young. When she got pregnant with me at fifteen, my grandparents kept her hidden until I was born. After she had me, she ran away and left me with them." I take a deep, shuddering breath. "Do you remember the drawing of the boy in my sketch-book? The one with the monster crushing his skull?"

She whispers, "Yes."

"When I was about six, he began coming into my room in the middle of the night, telling me he wanted to play a game with me and how good it would feel. He'd bring me a candy bar during the day and explain how I had to keep the game a secret, and if I didn't, something very bad would happen to my grandmother and me." I push through the vivid, full-color memories. "After the preliminary touches, he'd hold me down with my face in the mattress to muffle my cries, smothering me with his huge, heavy body as he… raped me. It was almost nightly for years until he died when I was eight."

A sob racks through my chest as I get the last words out, and for the first time, it feels as if I've unlocked the cage and let the beast go.

But I realize it wasn't my father in the cage at all; it was a little boy who looked a lot like me.

"If I had told you then, told you that I could share in some of your pain, it could have changed everything. Maybe it could've kept us together. You wouldn't have felt so alone. I'm sorry, Quinn. I failed you in so many ways."

She doesn't say anything but turns to face me as she wraps her body around mine. We hold onto each other as we both cry.

"I never told anyone about that."

"Thank you for trusting me with it," she reaches into her bag for Kleenex. "I remember the drawing, too. Liam, saying that I'm sorry doesn't express what I feel … it's not enough.

What he did—*what they did*—was reprehensible. Your own father … and your mother and grand-mother knew. They could have saved you." She squeezes her eyes shut, and fresh tears streak down her face. "Oh God, I hate them all right now."

FOR A LITTLE WHILE, WE SIMPLY AND QUIETLY HOLD onto one another. The warmth of her soaks through me like the rays of a spring sun.

I'm so grateful for this chance to be with her one more time, to finally confess what has eaten away at my soul for decades, and to have been able to love her again even though I know it isn't our forever.

Inevitably, it needs to be said, and when I gather the strength, I tell her, "Losing you nearly killed me. I missed you so fucking much. I still do." My fingers are tangled in the back of her hair as I hold her against me. "You were my world, Quinn. You were the first person to believe in me, the first person to love me … you were my best friend, and even though I love my brothers, no one could ever fill the void you created when you left and while you were gone.

"And … I know you've moved on with your life, and I understand that. But I can't let this moment

—or you—go without telling you how I feel." I choke back the emotions I'm drowning in.

I hadn't meant to get like this; I meant to stay hard and focused like the fighter I am, but I can't fight Quinn, or the storm, or the calm after the storm she's created. It's the kind of calm that comes after a violent storm has passed. The sun breaks through the darkened sky, the clouds recede and make way for the vibrant expanse of blue you thought you'd never see again, and the light it brings infuses everything with hope. I'm filled with that calm again.

Gently, I untangle us and move her to where I can see her beautiful face.

Talon would say to take the moment as a gift.

I reach my hands up and wipe her tears. "Please don't cry anymore. We've both done too much of that."

I'll let this moment heal me, as I hope it heals her, with no expectation of a future. Because this weekend with her has resurrected me, and I'm so fucking grateful to her—to the universe—for bringing us together.

At least this time, we'll get to say goodbye.

"I want to read something to you." I reach into my inner suit coat pocket and take out the envelope she must have seen on my bed with the metal box where she found our photograph.

I can't help but smile. "I don't know how far you

peeked at my stuff, but I …" I shrug and pull up my suit cuff to reveal the bracelet she gave me for my sixteenth birthday.

"Oh, Liam, you still have it." Her soft fingers grip the band and my wrist. "I would've never dreamed you kept it … after what I did."

"Baby, you didn't do anything wrong. I understand everything—you needed to go—I don't blame you anymore. And I can tell you I forgive you if it makes you feel better, but you really have nothing to be forgiven for. You were in a pain most people can't fathom and you did what you had to do … I'm just so fucking happy you came back, even if it's not forever, even if it's just right now—baby, I'll take it."

She smiles through fresh tears.

"You know, this was the first birthday gift I ever received." I acknowledge the wristband, the wood and silver beads faded with use and age.

"How can that—?

"They didn't celebrate my birthday. I was an abomination to them." I think back. "I remember the night you put it on me and lit a candle on that cupcake. It was one of the best moments of my life. In fact, *all* the best moments in my life include you."

Her fingers comb through my hair and down my jaw.

Lifting the envelope again, I explain, "I wrote it a few years back, in autumn, when all I could think about was how much I missed you and would always love you, even if you never came back."

Carefully, I tear the corner of the sealed envelope, rip it down the crease and remove the crisp, folded paper inside.

"I had been going dark-side, and a worried Cade gave me a few books of poetry. I especially got into Frost and Hemingway. Reading their works was therapeutic and helped me—clumsily—express some of what I was feeling by writing. I wasn't any good, and I never showed it to anyone, but it helped me cope." I shrug. "I wrote this, thinking about you, and stashed it away. I told myself that someday I'd find a way to give it to you."

More tears gather and spill from her eyes.

"'We are entrusted with the most precious gift one human being can give to another. Love. And even after we've been given that gift, we don't understand how to hold it and how not to damage it—which we seem to have a very high propensity for doing. In fact, it seems that, more often than not, we do just that. We squeeze it too tight or get hurt when we doubt it's really ours; we fumble and drop it because it moves and changes and alters and redesigns. Love is a real, living being. A tangible matter that we stomp on, ignore, violate, misuse, mistreat and offend.

"'I just want to hold your love quietly, feel it pulse in my palm like a delicate and thriving heartbeat. I want to keep it close so I don't lose it or damage it. But I'm human and fuck up.

"'And obviously, we don't learn from our mistakes, or the whole human race would be damn close to perfect by now.

"'But here we are, holding out that gift, willing to take the good with the bad, the pleasure with the pain and the joy with the sorrow. Why? Because love is a two-player game. It's meant to be shared, given, received and reciprocated.

"'And even though love can hurt like hell, the good is so damn good you'd do anything to experience it again.'

"I'm always going to love you, Quinn." I gently stroke away her tears with my thumb.

Soft whimpers color the edges of her voice, "I've always loved you, Liam."

I squeeze my eyes closed, absorbing her words and the feel of her wrapped in my arms.

"Liam, could a love like ours get a second a chance?" Her voice is so broken it rips me apart.

"I believe it could …" I say in a raw, rough whisper.

I think about what we've been through in our past, seeing her again for the first time after so long, when I found her sleeping in my bed, her birds finally colorful and free, the feel of her skin, the touch of her hand…

Then my thoughts trip back to the encounter in

Cade's office this morning. I laugh a little manically before I have to pull away and hold back the painful howl that quakes through my chest.

"Quinn, I want you so bad, but—"

"But?" She stops me, her eyes red with emotion search mine; her dark lashes soaked with tears.

I confess, "Quinn, I met James."

"What?"

"James. He was at The Core this morning looking for you."

"I'm confused," she looks like she's trying to figure out what I'm saying, as if I'm speaking another language

"Jesus, Quinn, you're going to make me say it?" My voice breaks. "*Your fiancé.*"

"I'm not en—" Slowly, realization paints over her countenance.

A second later, she's smiling. *I'm dying, and she's smiling.*

"Blond hair, kinda short?" She's still smiling.

"Yeah, the son-of-a-bitch looked like that." I growl.

"Liam, I'm not engaged." She looks sympathetic.

"What?" I'm only half listening as I think about where I would hide his body.

"That was James Marshall, my best friend Chellie's *brother,*" Quinn says with a burst of giggles. "They were both going to come and support me, but Chellie had final exams, and James had a client emergency. But he'd promised me that if he was able to come, he would tell everyone he was my fiancé so I could save face and deflect some of the hurt if I found out you were in a serious relationship with someone. I didn't think they were coming at all, and I got so wrapped up in you ... well, I never let him know the plan was off. And I told Chellie that I thought you were with Adrienne, so she probably thought—"

She stops and gives me the funniest look, humorous and apologetic at the same time.

"So ... you're *not* engaged?" I ask slowly, not sure if I understand what I think she's saying.

"No, Liam, I am not engaged. I don't even have a boyfriend."

I let go of the breath I've been holding in relief. "You do now!"

The tension and pain are fully released as her sweet laughter echoes through my ears, my heart and my soul.

In a moment, I'm laughing, too.

"Confession, I've never had a boyfriend except for you." She explains.

"Never?" I ask in shocked disbelief.

"I went on a couple dates, but they weren't you." She says slowly. "I went away to heal and get stronger. I didn't want anyone else..."

"No?"

"No." She shakes her pretty little head, and a strand of blonde falls over her eyes.

"But you were so sexy and passionate when we... and you're telling me you've not had...?"

She shrugs. "That's why I wondered and asked you if I had done it wrong."

"Oh, Quinn."

Everything comes together in this moment.

"You are my home, Liam."

I hold her beautiful, happy face in my hands, gaze into her beautiful blue eyes and quote Frost.

"'Was there ever a cause too lost? Ever a cause that was lost too long?' Not ours, Quinn ... we're immortal."

EPILOGUE

LIAM

I've been waiting ten years for this moment.

Standing on the polished wood deck at Summit Chalet, I feel like I'm looking out from the top of the earth. Dense, green forest stretch as far as my eyes can see with mountain peaks still frosted with snow. The Lutsen Mountains are magnificent in spring.

The music begins, and I feel myself trembling.

Out of the corner of my eye, I see Talon's smile —as if he knew all along.

He was right

Jonah comes down the aisle first, looking brilliant in his coal-black tuxedo and yellow cummerbund. I couldn't be prouder. His hands shake a little as he tries to keep the white silk pillow steady. And although I can't see the two gleaming gold circular eternity bands Quinn and I picked out together, I know that they're there and that they represent our forever.

Next comes Charlie, walking *very* slowly after Jonah. Everyone smiles at her and coos at how adorable she looks in her yellow frilly gown. Her little fist is wrapped around the stems of half a dozen daffodils. Sophie, who's sitting up in the front row, kneels down on the side of the aisle to lure Charlie the rest of the way. And as soon as she gets up front to the podium and takes Josh's hand, the music changes …

But I can't hear it anymore. Everything in my field of vision tunnels, and every sense that I possess is fully consumed with Quinn as she reveals herself, steeping out from behind the standing white cloth partitions that are set up on the other side of the massive deck.

Nothing else in the world matters except for her.

When her eyes find mine, she blushes, and I know I have never seen anything so incredibly beautiful in all of my life—not a colorfully hued sunset or sunrise, not a towering mountain peak, or the turquoise blue and white of the surf as it crashes to the shores—nothing could even begin to compare to Quinn's beauty and power. And she is about to give herself to me for the rest of our lives.

Her strapless satin white gown hugs her breasts

and hips and flatters her hourglass shape, accentuating her every delicious curve. She holds a bouquet of lilies of the valleys—her birth flower—the same kind I picked for her that birthday night on top of Cade's roof. She's classic, timeless elegance …

And she's mine—this is not a dream—*forever and always mine.*

She kept her hair down and flowing in full waves, just the way I like it, except for a comb in the back that keeps in place a sheer white veil that frames her.

I feel the heel of my foot start tapping up and down—I want to run down there and carry her away—and my patience is ebbing.

As if he senses my adrenaline, Cade smiles up at me as he escorts Quinn down the aisle.

I step down from the podium and wait for my dad to bring me the greatest gift I've ever known.

"Who gives this woman to this man?" the Justice asks.

"Her mother and I do," Cade says with a look toward Debra, who stands from her seat in the front row, crying.

Cade puts Quinn's hand in mine and squeezes my opposite shoulder with so much love in his eyes for the two of us.

Then all that exists is the touch of her soft hand and her radiant smile, the everlasting sky in her eyes, and the eternal possibilities of our lives together.

QUINN

IMMENSE LOVE AND HAPPINESS FILL ME LIKE HELIUM in a balloon, and I swear I'm floating.

Liam takes my hand, and as we look into one another's eyes, I think back to his MMA match over a month ago, and what he announced after his win. "Family, friends, and fans, this has been my last fight—I'm retiring to become a full-time artist—and marry my best friend."

I fall more deeply in love with him every day, and I didn't think I could ever love him more than I already had.

I was so scared to come home, and now look where we are—Liam and I are getting married on top of a mountain, surrounded by a family that loves us. This is anything but a typical, traditional style wedding, and why would it be? We've had anything but a typical, traditional romance—and we're anything but a typical, traditional family.

Liam and I share the same incredible mother and father who love us with the intensity many natural parents never know or forfeit.

And then there's our wedding party, dressed in their designer charcoal tuxes with a yellow rose over each one of their hearts. There are no bridesmaids —only brothers. Behind Liam stands Talon, Josh and Reese; behind me are Ryder, Chase and Connor. They flank us on both sides, and I've never felt more protected. I know that they would give their lives for one another or for me in a heartbeat.

And I'm thoughtful that after *everything* my family has been through, and even though life dealt each one of us an unhappy, violent hand, a powerful force much stronger brought us all together and infused our lives with real love.

Oh, my amazing Liam, who never gave up on me. He loved me through the seemingly ever-widening gap of time and distance. I have no doubt that it was his love that kept me going, that kept me alive, that helped me heal. The flame of hope that the two of us would eventually come back together never truly went out for either of us.

Some might say our love was or is impossible, or improbable, that it couldn't have survived all that it has suffered—the overwhelming pain and grief and the years of separation. And I can't speak for anyone else's experiences, all I know is that this amazing moment feels like salvation and tastes like the sweetest redemption.

And it's mine to hold for eternity.

As the Justice talks about commitment, family

and marriage, I am lost in the clear waters of Liam's eyes, the strong angles of his face, and the way his jaw clenches as he stares emotionally back at me. I remember that our story began ten years ago, beneath a concrete angel, in a place where life seemingly ends.

It was there that we were joined together and where we each brought the other to life.

I remember having been sixteen and coming to my first real understanding about love.

Real love always burns. And how it's used is dependent upon the hands that wield it.

When it comes to Liam Knight, our love burns bright and brilliant, shining the way home like a white-hot star. It warms my soul, guards me and keeps me safe, feeds me and gives me light.

And I'm so very grateful.

"I do," Liam says, his voice husky and deep.

I breathe deeply of the life-giving oxygen he is to me. And when I blink, I feel tears fall from my eyes—tears that are made of pure happiness.

I'm finally home.

THE END

A FINAL NOTE FROM THE AUTHOR

Dear Reader,

If you enjoyed BURN, please consider leaving a review.

Even just a few words mean a lot <3

Now that you've finished reading BURN, check out Ryder's story in …

DEFY (Brothers of Ink and Steel Book Three)
https://amzn.to/4evnE19

ABOUT THE AUTHOR

Aurora Wilding is a USA Today and Top 100 Amazon bestselling author.

From gritty angst and dark romance to suspense, romantic comedy, and everything in between, Aurora crafts heart-racing stories with intense chemistry,

steamy passion, irresistible swoon, and always a Happily-Ever-After.

She can often be found traveling and adventuring in her van, whether on the beach or in the mountains, daydreaming and weaving tales about

heroic alpha males and strong-willed heroines, all while plotting the perfect ways to make them fall in love!

FOLLOW ME
Website:
aurorawilding.com

Goodreads:
goodreads.com/author/show/49928567.
Aurora_Wilding

facebook.com/aurorawildingromance

instagram.com/aurora_wilding_romance

tiktok.com/@aurora.wilding.romance

bookbub.com/authors/aurora-wilding

amazon.com/author/aurorawilding

youtube.com/@AuroraWildingRomance

ALSO BY AURORA WILDING

True North and Brothers of Ink and Steel are an Interconnected Series. DARE is the "bridge book" to both.

All books in each series can be read as standalones.

TRUE NORTH SERIES

Finding Home (True North Book 1):

A Second Chance, Military, Brother's Best Friend Romance

https://amzn.to/3VMFLJ6

Finding Us (True North Book 2):

A Small Town, Friends to Lovers, Boss's Daughter Romance

https://amzn.to/3xk1ChU

Finding Now (True North Book 3):

A Reverse Age Gap, Professor/Student, Rockstar Romance

https://amzn.to/3yYDVMn

BROTHERS OF INK AND STEEL SERIES

Dare (Brothers of Ink and Steel Book 1)

https://amzn.to/3UMTm2G

Burn (Brothers of Ink and Steel Book 2)

https://amzn.to/44vucc2

Dare You Forever (Brothers of Ink and Steel Novella 2.5)

https://amzn.to/4ag7DcK

Defy (Brothers of Ink and Steel Book 3)

https://amzn.to/3WxM44e

Risk (Brothers of Ink and Steel Book 4)

https://amzn.to/4bs2D5J

STANDALONE NOVELS

Stripped (A Romantic Comedy)

My Book

amazon.com/dp/B01DKVAE2Y

Orion (A Constellations Novel) A Military Thriller Romance

My Book

amazon.com/dp/B0777MKM9T

Made in the USA
Columbia, SC
23 November 2024